The Wind In The Grass

The Wind In The Grass

A Memoir in Prose and Verse

James C. McGuire

iUniverse LLC
Bloomington

THE WIND IN THE GRASS

iUniverse books may be ordered through booksellers or by contacting:

iUniverse LLC
1663 Liberty Drive
Bloomington, IN 47403
www.iuniverse.com
1-800-Authors (1-800-288-4677)

ISBN: 978-1-4917-0487-5 (sc)
ISBN: 978-1-4917-0488-2 (ebk)

Library of Congress Control Number: 2013915435

Printed in the United States of America

iUniverse rev. date: 09/20/2013

Contents

Credits

Also by James C. McGuire:

Is The Beer Cold Yet?

Poetry, Articles and Short Stories:

Navy Times
The Poet—Peu'a Peu
The Mudville Diaries
Fan Magazine
Lyric Magazine
Bardic Echoes
New Earth Review
College Quarterlies, Newspapers

Dedication

Whether one is a world-famous author, a very good writer who puts a good book out every few years, or a minor American writer, a hack, if you will, like me, all of us need help in the construction and completion of a book or manuscript. When it comes to Dedications, writers usually pick their children, an old military chum or their wife. In my case I'll pick the latter.

My darling Barbara has been instrumental, intrinsically so, in the creation of this book. Without her dedication, it would never have reached a page past the title. However, that's not the reason or reasons I have.

In spite of my obnoxious lifestyle, my explosive Westmeathian temper, my know-it all nature, my raucous and ill-mannered demeanor and especially having more faults than the California coastline, she loves me as much as she did from the beginning. I dedicate this book to her. I only wish this little book were the world because it's what she really deserves.

J.C. McGuire
Danbury, Connecticut
17OCT12

Introduction

I refer to sea oats and sea grass, preferably crowning the dunes down at the Cape. Always, always at the end of the afternoon, the beaches are just about emptied. The people have gone back to their houses to shower, smear some sort of white gook on their sunburn and get ready for dinner, planning to overload on food.

What I always do at that time of day, is go out on the dunes and sit down and nurse my scotch, looking out over the beach with the sea oats brushing together from the wind. It's always quiet at that time of day. The stillness of any sound except for the waves, magnifies the grass sounds all around me. One has to listen close. You may not hear it right away. It may take a few minutes, maybe longer. But the grass will "speak".

It speaks of all it has seen and all the grasses before them. Long before there were expensive houses lining the shore, long before the Nags Headers and the Wright Brothers and the donkey with the lantern on his neck there were other things . . . .

Amerigo Vespucci, sailing past, with Verrazano right behind him. The old destroyers *Jacob Jones* and *Ruben James*, both too old for sonar, searching for the German interloper. The Union soldiers aboard the USS *Oriental*, foundering 100 yards from shore. Blackbeard, Edward Teach by name, swinging his cutlass in the lee of Ocracoke. Story after story, related by the grasses brushing against each other. The absence of sound, save for the waves and the grass . . . .

I will be buried there, at sea. Barbara too. It's in our Will. History moves and I intend to move with it. And, at the beginning of the evening, forever, the stalks of grass will swing in the wind and the wind will supply the words, as each day goes down.

jcm
22MAR12

The Saga of Teymor the Younger

The wind was a cutting wind, as it came around Balin Head in what is now Donegal, on the west coast of Ireland. The wind, some say, started far above the Arctic Circle in the grey pack ice, far above Spitzbergen and what is now Novaya Zemlya. It came down the Norwegian coast, shaving tern and puffin from their nesting places on the cliffs. On bad days the helpless birds could only face the relentless, biting wind and close their eyes. It was a shrieking wind. It was a Viking wind.

The little group of Irish monks pulled their cloaks tighter against their bodies, straining their eyes, trying to see through the offshore mist. They were the first alarm, the ones who would see the dreaded men from the north, if some of them happened to venture near their shore. It was late in the Year of our Lord, 797 and the monks were tired and wet. They had been on watch from their tent high above the surf, three hundred yards from their abbey at St. Katharina behind them. All year, up and down the coast, Viking ships had been plundering and murdering their way inland, escaping with whatever goods the poor Celts had. There was barely any defense against them, save for the stone towers.

Each abbey had their own stone tower, the entrance high above the ground. The monks would climb the tower with whatever they could take with them, pull their ladders in with them and close the small wooden door. Eventually the raiders would leave, or try and knock the tower down. Some of the towers were 40 feet tall, with the doorway 20 feet up. On this raw, November morning, the monks were about ready to go back to the abbey to partake in their meager early meal when a dark form appeared in the center of the offshore gloom.

'Look!', cried Brother Niall, pointing out to sea. The other monks looked and sure enough, there it was! A long and slender Viking ship, moving slowly toward the small beach below. Their sweeping oars were silent as the 90-foot dragonship came toward them, faster and faster. Before the monks could collect themselves, a giant figure leaped from the bow of the ship, landing knee-deep in the surf. Others followed as the ship grounded on the shale and stones of the beach.

'I see you!', screamed the big man, looking up at the monks. They turned and started running back and away from the cliff.

'Run, you dogs! Run away!', the big Viking bellowed. His silver helmet and red beard dripped sea water as he waded onto the dry beach. The other men followed, carrying their shields and weapons. When the big man stopped, they stopped. He drove the tip of his broadsword deep into the sandy pebbles. His name was Teymor the Younger, Grandson of King Thorvald of Kugshallat.

Teymor the Younger was a fierce fighter, a feared leader. He treated his men well and they rewarded him with their loyalty. He was known throughout Kugshallat as a man to be reckoned with. On this day, the Irish monks were no match for him. Teymor knew they wouldn't be on the land side too long. They began to make their way up the paths to the top of the cliffs.

Meanwhile, the monks had clambered up and into the tower. They already had their gold plate and silver coin in sacks inside the stone haven. It wasn't long before they saw the 60 to 70 Viking raiders coming through the deep grass toward the tower. They were dragging a good-sized oak which had fallen during the summer before. Some of them were hacking the branches from the tree as it was being pulled along. As Brother Niall watched, he knew they were going to use it as a battering ram against the tower!

'Come down now! Come down or die in the tower!', bellowed Teymor the Younger. The monks started praying.

'BOOM!', and the monks felt the jarring as the tower shook slightly. Niall looked out of the door and saw the Vikings 20 feet below. Off to the side stood Teymor, feet spread wide, hands on hips, his great sword stuck firmly in the ground beside him. The tree was being held by almost 30 men as they ran at the tower again.

'BOOM!' it sounded again and this time two stones fell from the structure!

'Climb down, yo dogs, and bring your treasure with you. If you do, we won't hurt you!', cried Teymor. The monks looked at each other.

'BOOM!', and another stone fell out of the tower's base. The tower was constructed of grey granite, but around the base were boulders of dolomite quartz. The dolomite stones went up three feet, then the rest was granite. It was as if the original builders wanted to use the dolomite but then changed their minds. It didn't matter. It would just be a matter of time before the Vikings knocked the stone tower down, with the monks inside!

Niall slowly opened the wooden door again. He came eye to eye with the fierce Teymor.

'Come down, holy man.', Teymor said in a normal voice. Niall had no choice. He noticed almost a dozen quartz boulders on the ground. Out came the ladder and out came the monks. Down the rickety ladder they came, the last two monks carrying the cloth bags with their earthly possessions.

Once on the ground, the monks were stripped of their goods, tied hand and foot then thrown onto the grass. One of the Vikings stepped forward, swinging his sword back and forth. Hs name was Njal Arnfinn.

'Step aside!', he said to his friends, Grinda and Egil, who were dealing with the monks. 'Get out of the way! It's time to teach these dogs a lesson!' He advanced on the helpless monks with his sword.

'Stop!', came the voice of Teymor the Younger. Njal turned, his eyes meeting the glare of his chieftain.

'They die!', snarled Njal. Another Viking, Smula Goddadson, a good friend of Njal, came forward holding a long spear.

'I say, kill them!', growled Smula. He was bigger than Njal. Even bigger than the great Teymor.

'They live. Step back.', Teymor said to them in a low and even voice.

'No!', yelled Njal at the top of his lungs. Teymor pulled his sword from the ground and held it at his side.

Smula Goddadson, with a scream, lunged around Njal toward Teymor, bringing his spear up. In a flash, Teymor swung his broadsword and cut Smula's spear shaft in half! He turned in time to meet the lunging Njal and brought his weapon down onto Njal's sword hand, cutting his right thumb off! In one second, it was over. Teymor the Younger, true to his word, kept the legend going . . .

Today, on the peninsula, standing where the ancient monks had their lookout tent, is the small town of Burtonport. Three miles to the east is the hamlet of Dungloe. Not even on the map but in between the two towns is an area called Teymoora. For centuries, the villagers around that area have referred to it as such. The only thing there is the abbey of St. Katharine's. It's a 210 year-old grey building, 32 clerics in attendance. It replaced the old abbey which was built in 1565. Some say the old abbey was built on the ruins of an even older abbey or convent. No one knows for sure. On the grounds of the abbey, up a small hill to the west there is a round stone structure. Some say it was a defensive tower back in the days of the Viking raids. Others say it was the beginning of a grain silo. No one knows. The two-foot high base is all that's left. When the sun is shining down, one can still see the quartz glinting in the dolomite stones.

Teymoora lives today, as a wooded landscape with St. Katharine's nestled in against the trees. As for 'Teymoora', no one knows where the name came from. When the breeze comes in from the ocean on those hot, summer days, the quartz still glistens and the tall grass sighs.

jcm
5/24/11

Man Of Gold

There was a night which seemed so long ago
but was only yesterday
when the flapping numbers of the clock woke me.
Creaking from the creaking bed I left the room,
feeling with my toes the pathway to the hall.
  Movement in the big mirror made me start;
  a form in winter-pink, shadowy and hunched.

It was me.

  I stopped to stare, the apparition
  staring back; scraggle-faced and sad.

. . . Once, a long time ago, I was a man of gold
and a sailor in white. I was fleet of foot, limb and tongue.
  But you were a pudgy child.
  I didn't know where you were.
You'd have seen a promising contender with a comb
in his back pocket,
instead of what the mirror mirrored back . . .

  I turned to look at you in the blue
  of the streetlight, your arm suspended out,
  your face slack and blonde.
  No more the pudgy child and no more
  the flippant bride.

What love you must hold in your body for me!
What vision you must have, to look past the broken tiredness
to the nimble youth I was.
You don't see me as the mirror does
nor I hope, will you ever.

jcm
2/6/84

'Can You Help Me With These Bags?'

Mikey,

Remember the movie, 'Young Frankenstein', in 1974? It was a Mel Brooks movie, starring Gene Wilder and a number of other people. It was a typical Mel Brooks movie if you recall, but there was one scene that I remember to this day. It was hilarious and I always wanted to use it.

Gene Wilder showed up at Frankenstein's castle in a driving rainstorm with Madeline Kahn, Teri Garr and their luggage. They knocked on the giant door and Igor, played by Marty Feldman, opened it. Wilder said they had an appointment with Dr. Frankenstein. Igor told them to come in. Gene Wilder asked him:

'Can you help me with these bags?'

Feldman answered: 'Okay'. You take the blonde and I'll take the brunette!'

It was a great line and I never had the chance to use it. Every time the movie was on TV, I waited for that line. It was pure Mel Brooks.

Last year, 38 years after the movie, I had probably forgotten about Wilder and the two girls showing up at the castle door in the rainstorm. I was standing in the store where I work, a long stairwell leading to the second floor. I was talking with two girls from the bakery, Nancy, a blonde, and Lorraine, a brunette. Down the aisle came my boss, Alex. He was carrying two huge plastic bags, heading for the stairs.

'What do you have there, Alex?', I asked.

'The Secret Service is coming tomorrow morning to teach the cashiers how to spot phony bills. These are all goodie bags for everyone who comes to the meeting, upstairs in the conference room.', he said. Then, with a straight face and looking at the stairs, Alex said to me:

'Can you help me with these bags?'

. . . From 38 years ago, I could hear Mel Brooks yelling: 'Now! Now . . . !'

(I don't have to finish the story, do I?)

jcm
10/10/12

In Flanders Fields . . .

'In Flanders Fields the poppies blow
between the crosses row on row . . .'

Another Memorial Day is gone. I watched the Yankee game yesterday afternoon with each team wearing red caps. The Mets had a flyover with Marine Ospreys and small town after small town had their mini-parades. It was Fleet Week in the city and all the sailors with their shapeless new white hats were all congregated in a freshly-scrubbed Times Square, snapping away with their phone-cameras. There were the usual clips on the news of the pretty girls with face-painted American flags on their cheeks, not really sure why the flags were painted on. There was the President laying wreaths at Arlington, at the Tomb of the Unknown Soldier. All the usual scenes so familiar to me now.

I tried to remember when I was a youngster, growing up in Peekskill; watching the parade and the sight of a waving Jack Buhs, a paratrooper who was crippled on D-Day when he landed wrong in a field outside Ste. Mer Eglise. up at Depew Park pond, the veterans always launched a metal boat filled with flowers. Each year the boat was pushed out onto the pond, promptly turned and stopped. I always thought that strange. The moment of silence. It was a somber day once, a day of actual national pride. I don't remember the military-hating Leftist people then. I don't think they were born yet. The day wore on with the Yanks pulling away from the Texas Rangers, when Barbara walked in. She started to ramble on about her day then said to me:

'I stopped up to see my Dad today, to say 'thank you'. Then she started to tell me about a woman she met at the same cemetery who had lost her husband two months ago, another World War II vet, but I wasn't listening.

Barbara's Dad was a combat medic staff sergeant in the 44th Division, 'The Backward Fours'. He landed at Cherbourg, France and walked all the way to Germany. I was thinking about the story he told me once when he cut a Ghurka soldier's orange and got in trouble because he used the Ghurka's knife. Wendel lies beneath the lilacs now, on a hill overlooking a beautiful creek which empties into Diverting Reservoir.

I thought of what the writer, Barrie Pitt said when he tried to explain the appearance of the 'men of action' in times of trouble.

'It is good for us, good for this nation of ours that in between wars when things grow quiet, this spirit does not die. It only sleeps.'

And so ended another Memorial Day. 'Thanks' from me too, Wendel.

> 'In Flanders Field the poppies blow
> between the crosses row by row,
> that mark our place and in the sky
> the larks, still bravely singing, fly . . .'

jcm
5/31/11

Stone Pony

I'm afraid to go out again.
The sun streaming through the kitchen window
tells me it's a beautiful day
but I know the damn thing is still out there.

I move to the window and see him,
tethered to the mailbox.
My great, raw-boned, ugly horse named Jealousy—
saddled with Frustration.
He looks at me with those dull black eyes.
I look back, staring him down.
How we hate each other!

I think I can get a good price for the saddle,
but no one will take the horse off my hands
much less, make me forget that I own him.

jcm
2/7/84

The Four Horsemen Of The Apocalypse

Today, September 11, 2011, there will be speeches, commemorations and many a somber moment throughout this great land, honoring those of us who died ten years ago at the hands of the terrorists. As usual, the ones who decided to kill some of us, attacked those who couldn't fight back and didn't really care who it was they destroyed. Terrorists have been cowards for a long time. The last time one of them fought someone face to face was back in the Crusades. Subterfuge and deviant action courses through their veins like blood. But enough about the Evil of the World.

There was an overabundance of heroes on that day ten years ago, too numerous to list. Each of us has someone or some thing to point at; an incident or a person which makes us feel good about ourselves or about them. I have four such individuals who come to mind, every time I think of that day ten years ago.

Their names are Mark Bingham, Tom Burnett, Jeremy Glick and Todd Beamer. They're gone now but their actions, to me at least, was the start of the Retaliation.

They were some of the men, ordinary American men who kept Flight Ninety-three from continuing on it's destructive path toward our Capitol Building in Washington, D.C. We all know the story of Flight Ninety-Three, how a handful of passengers fought their way into the cockpit and prevented the terrorists from using the airliner as a bomb. They brought the plane down, in a vacant field in Pennsylvania, 200 miles from Washington.

Up to that moment, we, as a nation, had been taking punches it seemed, from every direction. That was the turnaround. That action was the Beginning. We don't know exactly what happened but we do know some things. We do know it was a planned, concerted effort. We do know they used the 300-pound coffee cart to ram their way into the cockpit. We do know there was a tremendous fight. We do know the flight came to an end because of them.

Yesterday, I hung my American flag out. Today, I'll think of my next door neighbor's sister who died in the World Trade Center. I'll think of the 343 brave lads of the FDNY who didn't come back. I'll think of Father Mychal Judge, the New York City Fire Chaplain who said once:

'Do you want to make God laugh? Tell him what you have planned for tomorrow!' Father Judge didn't make it. He was victim 0001.

All four of those men, Burnett, Glick, Beamer and Bingham were athletes; ex-quarterbacks, judo experts, etc. I'll think of them today, in my most pensive of moments. I'll also remember that I'm an American by chance, but I'm a New Yorker by choice. A.E Housman wrote:

> 'The day you won your town the race
> we cheered you through the market place.
> Man and boy stood cheering by
> as home we took you, shoulder-high.
>
> Today, the road, all runners come
> as shoulder-high we take you home
> and lay you at your threshold down.
> Townsman, of a stiller town.'

God Bless America
jcm
9/11/11

Thirty Miles

Thirty miles apart.
It seems a watchword, a slogan,
a caption under a photograph of us.
    We pass on the highway
    never seeing each other,
    trading places and thirty miles apart.
I see your tracks in the new snow on the sidewalk,
your lone coffee cup in the sink,
your note on the counter.
I walk through the house through imaginary dust-clouds
stirred up by your bustling an hour before.
I hear the shower run,
the damp smell of steam,
the whisper of your atomizer.
I see the towel hanging limply
knowing without feeling, its wetness.
    I can see your face in the jumbled animals
    on the pillow, bunched together like cartoon characters,
    but you're thirty miles away.

It's dark when I finally see you
but it gets darker while we argue.
Arguments like thunderclaps,
icy stares that trigger the thermostat.
    Why do we argue in the little time we have?
    What do we gain in a no-win situation?
The silence in the room sounds like a landslide.
The icy stares have gunned us down.
We've lost another day.

Now it's my turn to leave,
hurried apologies,
hurried embraces and promises to talk.
You in the window, waving.
My car knifes through the darkness,
headlights cutting the highway in half.
Sorrow and tiredness share my mind
until the car stops.
Thirty miles away.

jcm
2/8/84

'. . . and the Cross of St. George shall lead us!'

Dear Anna,

Just like a new baby, a new book is special. I'm up to my knees in 'The Little Ships of Dunkirk', the 50th Anniversary Edition. I found out about the *Medway Queen*, my own personal 'fave'. She's tied up in Bristol, being worked on after receiving a 1.8 million pound grant from the government for renovation. She's an old side-wheeler who saved 7,000 men from Dunkirk and shot down three German planes during her trips. Great, great book. The wait was well worth it.

There were 700 ships and boats that performed the evacuation. Around 125 are left. They're all Landmark boats, protected by the government. They all fly the flag the Queen gave the Association, the white ensign (Cross of St. George on a white field) with the Dunkirk City crest in the middle. One of them, the *Defender*, a cockle bawley, is laid up in regular in St. Aubin, Jersey. She's waiting for restoration but there isn't any money. A beautiful old boat. Maybe after the tapestry is done, you ladies can take up the saving of the *Defender*? There's group after group looking for money for these old boats. It costs a fortune to fix them back up again.

Do you remember John Masefield's 'Sea Fever'? . . .

> 'I must go down to the sea again,
> to the lonely sea and sky.
> And all I need is a tall ship
> and a star to steer her by . . .'

He rode along on one of the boats back in 1940 and helped with the evacuation. When it was all over, he wrote a poem for the boatmen. It reads in part:

> '. . . . Through the long time the story will be told;
> Long centuries of praise on English lips,
> of courage God-like and of hearts of gold
> off Dunquerque beaches in the little ships . . . .'

Vice Admiral Ramsey took control of the 700 boats at Ramsgate. After 9 days, they managed to bring back 385,000 men, including 100,000 French. They enabled the war to continue. It would have ended had the B.E.F. ceased to exist.

There were two quotes among many which I remember from that short period. Ramsey told the Royal Navy; 'We will bring the army back. Nothing will deter us. The Cross of St. George shall lead us!'

Churchill, who had been PM for three days uttered the first of many quotes: 'There was Agincourt, then Waterloo and now, Dunkirk.'

I feel a story coming on, except there have been hundreds of stories about Dunkirk. I wish you could see this book! It came with a copy of the London Daily Express of May 31, 1940 and a current edition describing the state of new-found Dunkirk boats and a cardboard casing for the whole thing.

Newsflash! Emil and Wendy were down last night and they want to go and rent a villa in Tuscany next year. Austria may be put off again. I'm continuing my plotting of the trip anyway. I'm almost to the German border. I'll get there someday.

Chuck
(jcm 9/19/11)

'In this corner, Tommy Butler . . . !'

(A letter about a champion)

Dear Tommy, Brie, Kathleen and Kim,

Here it is, September 1st again. This is the day Aunt Eileen and I got the call from Phelps Hospital that your Grandfather was gone. He was only 47. It was 50 years ago today.

I'll call Eileen later on today and we'll talk for awhile and then we'll go on about our daily business. Fifty years is a long time. Tommy, you missed him by only 19 months.

Usually on this day, I would come up with a story or two about him. I'm sure you've heard just about all of them. I have one which I never told any of you. I might have told you, Tommy, but I can't remember. I was thinking about putting this story in 'Is The Beer Cold Yet?' but I changed my mind. I didn't especially care for the language and I didn't want it in the book, but it epitomized your Grandfather. Whenever I think about how men should act and react about things, I always come back to the event I'm about to tell you. It's been 50 years. Maybe it's about time.

'Thomas Anthony Mc Guire, 47, of 400 Simpson Place, Peekskill, New York, passed away today after a long illness.' That was part of his obituary in the Evening Star, September 1st, 1961.

Those days were a blur. I was 22 and almost out of the Navy. His wake was up in Dempsey's Funeral Home. Nanny and Aunt Eileen held up pretty well. Uncle Ollie stayed by me the whole time. He and I were supposed to be heading to Spain in a few months. We didn't know it then, but we would never get there.

The usual crowd was at Dempsey's; Leo Palmero, Nookie Mc Caffery, and all the rest of your Grandpa's friends. The families were there, but the majority of the people were the Irish, obviously, and the Slovaks from Bleloch Park. There were some neighbors and some of his friends from work, and one black man.

He was standing over by your Grandfather's casket, talking to Tommy Burkiser. I noticed, that one by one, all of your Grandfather's pals would go over and talk to him. Joe Ravase gave him a hug. I saw Charlie Martin motion toward me as he was talking to him. I'd never seen the man before, but I knew he was supposed to be there at Dempsey's, somehow. Finally, when he looked over at me again, I walked over.

'You must be Chuck,' he said, smiling.

'Yeah, that's me.' I said, shaking his hand. 'Were you friends with my Dad?'

'Yes, I was. I saw his name in the paper so I came up to pay my respects.', he said. 'Name's Nat Austell. I was your Father's corner-man back in the '30's.'

I looked over at the 'boys'. Leo, Nookie and the rest of them were watching us, apparently enjoying the moment.

'I always wondered who his second was. He never told me.' I said to him.

My Father fought his way through the Depression, using the ring name, 'Tommy Butler', so my Grandmother wouldn't find out he was boxing. In 1934, he was only 20. But, at 20, he had already won the Diamond Gloves Sub-Novice Middleweight title in the competitions in New York City. By the time he and my Mother were married in 1937, he had given it up. I know he had 104 wins, but I can't remember the losses. I think it was in the teens.

Nat Austell told me he had lost touch with my Father after he'd hung up his gloves. Nat had a dry cleaning business in town, next to the Police Station.

'I tried boxing too, in the Navy.', I told him.

'How'd you do?', he asked me. (I was a middleweight too, about 160 pounds. I fought in the Second Fleet and in DESLANT (Destroyer Atlantic), but I only managed an 11-17 record.)

'Well,' I said to Nat, 'I was no Tommy Butler!' We both laughed. 'He told me a thousand fight stories, even about the time he was disqualified in the County Center for clowning.', I said.

Nat looked at me. 'Did he ever tell you about the Tarrytown A.C.?'

'Oh, yeah,' I said. 'Ossining too. All those places.'

'The three guys at the Tarrytown A.C.?', he said again, this time without smiling. I shook my head.

'Whenever I think of this, I think of your Old Man.', he said, and began to tell me.

It was 1935. My Dad was on the card at the Tarrytown Athletic Club one Saturday night in the summer. He and Nat Austell drove down to Tarrytown in Nat's old La Salle. They parked the car, gathered their bags and headed for the wide stairs leading up to the veranda of the club.

As they climbed the long stairs, Nat said, he noticed three men at the top. One was in a rocking chair. The other two were leaning against the front doors. They reached the landing as the two standing men moved away from the doors. The one in the rocking chair stood.

'Where you boys goin'?', asked the one from the rocking chair.

'What's it to ya?', my Father said. The three men moved closer. Nat said, all three were bigger than they were.

'I'll ask again,' said the rocking chair fellow, the biggest one, 'where do you think you're goin'?'

'I'm on the card. I've got a fight tonight.', my Dad said.

The big man looked at him. He said: 'Okay. You can go in, but not the nigger.'

'What?', my Dad asked.

Rocking Chair said: 'You heard me!'

Nat said they stood there for a few seconds and then my Dad motioned to him, to go back down the stairs. Back down they went, taking their bags with them. When they reached the bottom, Nat said he headed toward the car. My Father wasn't with him. He looked around and saw my Father take his wallet out of his pocket and put it on his bag. He took his ring off and put it in his pocket.

'Where you goin', Tommy? Don't go up there!', Nat said. He said my Father looked at him, turned, and started back up the stairs. Nat figured, he'd be driving home that night with my Father beaten up in the back seat.

'Up and up he went, eyes on the stairs. The three guys watched him come up.', Nat said. He went on:

'Your Old Man just about got to the top when the three men moved. They were too late. Tommy hit the first guy with a right that bent his whole head back, then put the other guy down with a left. The second guy fell against him but he pushed him away just as the rocking chair fellow came at him. Tommy stepped to the side and hit him good in the bread basket, then he crossed with a right and I could see the big guy's nose split from where I was standing!'

By then, Nat was laughing. I noticed we had an audience behind me. One of them was Nanny, stony-faced. Nat went on:

'Three men. Four punches. It was so fast it's a wonder I can still remember. I don't even remember if he won the fight inside that night. All I remember was your Old Man going back up those stairs.'

Nat said they never talked about it again. When Nat finally got to the top of the stairs with their bags, the three men were unconscious. He never remembered my Father telling that story to anyone. He guessed, he said, it was just something that had to be done.

'I guess I'll be goin' now.', Nat finally said. I clapped him on the back and thanked him for coming and also for the great story.

'I think about those three men and that night in Tarrytown all the time. Tommy was my friend. He was my good friend.', Nat said. He walked out and as he passed my Dad's casket, he waved to him. Then he was gone.

I never spoke to Nat Austell again. I saw him once, sitting outside his shop, smoking a pipe. I blew the horn and he waved back. Years later, they tore down the whole street for urban renewal. Nat's shop was torn down. I don't know whatever happened to him. I guess I should, but I don't. I'm glad I heard that story even though it took 50 years to tell it. Your Grandfather was never a Civil Rights-sort of person, but he wasn't a racist either. He was far from it. But, he did go back up those stairs that night in Tarrytown, didn't he?

What I think is; someone called his friend a name for no reason. It had to be rectified. So, he rectified it. He told me once; 'A bully will always go down when you hit him.'

Your Grandfather was a smart man.

Dad
(jcm 9/1/11)

Stress

Trying to fall asleep,
unable to turn because of the arrow in my chest.
Trying to button my shirt
leaving room for the arrow's shaft.

A day without stress
would be too simple, too bland.
Stress is daily combat
that becomes routine, habit.
It means never stopping as I pass under
the signs which say: ARROW REMOVAL.

When Death comes, it will have to be for something else.
It will be for disease, old age or lack of something.
I'll say to him; 'Look! I was stronger than they were.
I was able to handle it, right?'

But what if he says: 'I didn't come for them.
I came for you'.

jcm
2/18/84

'Je Pense, Donc Je Suis . . .'

Back in 1978, I decided to give college my third try and as it turned out, my last try. I enrolled at Mercy College in Peekskill to try once again for an English or History degree. I had a matchbox full of credits but those, and a dollar would've gotten me on the subway.

I enrolled in a Comp IV class, run by an honest-to-God hippie, a fellow by the name of Ron Rebhuhn. He was a hard case as we would all find out, but he knew his stuff. The first day in class I noticed all the bright-eyed and bushy-tailed students and I figured once again, I'd be the oldest one at 39. I was wrong. In the next row sat someone who looked like the Dowager Empress, or someone who lived in the Forbidden City. Her name was Helen Young, I found out later. She had the whitest hair, every one in place. Leaning against her desk was a very ornate cane. It looked like a blackthorn topped with a giant knob of ivory. I couldn't take my eyes from her.

She had a fur wrap hanging from her chair and the dress she wore looked like it had belonged to Evelyn Nesbitt when she used to dance with Stanford White at the Palladium on Broadway, back in the 1880's. It was all maroon and lace with pearly things sewn on. All she needed was one of those big English wedding hats. I smiled; I thought that I would stand out as the 'old guy'! I found later also, she was 88.

Professor Rebhuhn spoke and broke up my time travel back to the 1880's, with a challenge: He sad that most of the people in this class were here, not because they wanted the class but because they were made to take it. What?

'There are 29 of you today. Tomorrow, most of you won't be here. I don't want anyone in this class who doesn't want to be here. Don't think you're going to get three credits because I'm a good guy! I'm not!' And with that, two people got up and left. What did I get into, I thought? He continued on:

'I only want people who are serious about Composition IV, not the credit-collectors. That's two gone. The ones who don't want to be here, you know who you are. I don't want to see you here tomorrow!'

And with that, he started the class. I looked at Helen. She sat there, unmoved. I wondered whether or not she would be back tomorrow morning. Rebhuhn told us the class would culminate with a paper of 6-7,000 words, dealing with a subject of our own choosing. He would be a hard marker and if we were successful in completing the class, he would take us all to dinner when it was over.

After the class, I walked out with Helen Young. She was a bit tottery with her cane and didn't walk fast, but it gave us a few more minutes to talk. She took my arm with her cane-less hand and we walked up and out of the building. She was wondering whether or not he (Rebhuhn) would accept something in long hand because she couldn't type. I told her I would type her lessons for her. That made her happy. She asked me if she could drop me anywhere as we approached her car. If I remember correctly, it was a big, black Buick, driven by an unsmiling, black-suited man. I told her 'no' and helped her into the car. I could see Rebhuhn devouring her over the coming weeks.

The following morning, fourteen people showed up for class. That was a loss of fifteen. Rebhuhn, rubbing his hands over the destruction of fifteen people, was pleased.

'Now we can get down to work!', he announced. Almost from the first few minutes I could see what he had in store for Helen. He would call on her and when she didn't answer right away, he was on her, moving threateningly down the aisle, hands on hips, taking an offensive stance. She started off flustered but soon caught herself and gave it back to him in a small way. He kept telling her that she was 'slowing' him down. Helen had all the accoutrements for the class, her beautiful and intact, but old briefcase, her pads, pens and probably the first bottle of water I ever saw anyone carry. The more she came under attack from our vaunted 'Professor', the more I was drawn to her. I pictured myself as her Walter Raleigh, ready to smite the foe from the east . . . I knew we would both get through the course, . . . 'our minds being clean and our hearts being pure . . . 'There was the enemy, standing in front of his desk. Here we were, defending the castle walls! We would be fine.

After the second day, I hung back a little, while the other students filed out. Rebhuhn noticed me hemming and hawing around the door.

'Something on your mind?, he asked, coming toward me.

'Yes, there is something. I want you to get off Helen's back. She's doing the best she can and you're not making it any easier. There's no reason to pick on her.', I said.

Rebhuhn took his now familiar stance and pointed his finger at me.

'How I run my class is no concern of yours. You'd be smart to mind your own business!'

I looked at his pointing finger. 'Do you like that finger?', I asked.

'What?', he answered, dropping his hand.

'If you point that finger at me again for emphasis, I'll remove it from your hand. Now leave the woman alone. Try being a man and just teach. That's all you have to do.', and with that, I walked out.

The next few months were, I'll have to say, very fulfilling. Rebhuhn calmed down a bit and I typed away on my IBM Selectric II at home, doing Helen's and my papers. She wanted to pay me for all the typing but I told her to just give me the Buick! She laughed. We went through Kenneth Roberts and Bruce Catton and some other writers in the class. He had us criticizing everything we read and then attacked our critical analyses. He was a hard man, but I got a lot out of him.

The time came for our last paper, the big one. He went around the class, asking all of us what our theme would be. Helen wanted to do hers on Descartes Maxims which raised his eyebrows. He didn't have any trouble until he came to me. I told him I wanted to do mine on the Civil War. He threw up his hands!

'There's always one!', he yelled. 'There's always the guy who wants to glorify war and everything about it. I hate war! Everyone should hate war! You can't do the whole war. Pick something else.', he said to me.

'How about one battle, the Battle of Gettysburg?', I asked.

'No! No! No! That's too big. Make it smaller.', he said. Then, I dropped my 'Chuckie-Bomb'.

'Okay. How about just one regiment in the battle?', I asked.

'How about what the regiment did during the whole war?', he countered. I nodded. I did my favorite regiment of all time, of all wars, the famous 20th Maine Volunteers of Little Round Top fame, the regiment which turned the tide at Gettysburg. The regiment that kept America, America.

Rebhuhn said to me: 'And it'd better be good, Mc Guire. I hate war with a passion. It'd better be good.'

Helen told me later, she thought Rebhuhn and I would come to blows. No, I told her, we were just posturing, as banty roosters do. I asked her about Rene Descartes. She said she's been trying to pattern her life so far, after his beliefs and his outlook on the universe, etc. I told her when she was done with the paper, I would type it for her and put it in a nice folder. She thought I was such a gentleman, and I did a quick turnaround, as if someone was standing behind me. I loved to hear her laugh. She invited me up to her condo in Stonehenge, up in the hills of Peekskill. She said that she and her friends met once a week to read poetry and things and would I like to come? I told her no, thank you, and today, 33 years later, I can't for the life of me remember why I didn't go. I had hundreds of poems the little old ladies would've loved. I could've really been Sir Walter Raleigh, but, I declined.

We handed in our papers. We all passed the course and I, of all people, received the only 'A' from Rebhuhn. How could the 20th Maine NOT get an 'A'? He took us to dinner at a health food restaurant. We didn't know he was a vegetarian. We ordered some bean sprouts and boiled rubbish pie or something like that. Rebhuhn thanked us all for completing the class and glared at me and the Dowager Empress. When I typed up Helen's paper on Descartes, I was intrigued with her opening page, the page which was so important in introducing her paper. I kept it for all these years, framed and hanging at home, next to one of my bookcases. I hope you'll see why I kept a copy:

Reflections

. . . As I sit here, finishing my little term paper on Descartes, I remember the little hotel in the Latin Quarter of Paris where Victor and I lived and studied for a year. The bright red wallpaper, the high feather bed we had to climb into with a ladder, the little piano with the brass candle sconces and the collector in his tall silk hat coming for the $1.50 piano rent every month. The long windows looking out on the Boulevard de Montparnasse where funeral corteges passed frequently.

Three hundred years ago, along this very route, they took Rene Descartes to the cemetery of St. Germain de Pre' nearby, and here I am today, writing about it. I feel as if I had known Rene Descartes for a long time and I believe his spirit surrounds me now. He surely has influenced my life.

Helen Young
1978

There was a time when Helen Young and the memory of her Maxims which were so dear to her had gone a-glimmering. I don't remember when that was, but I remember her vividly as if she were here today. If I think hard enough I can see Victor, seated at the little table, drinking his tea. Helen would be at the piano, a very young woman. She would be on the keyboard, sending those beautiful notes through the window, out into the Parisian day, fluttering down on the Boulevard de Montparnasse like some tiny cloud of white goose feathers . . .

'I think, therefore I am.'

jcm 6/13/11

Another World Of Thought

I tell you only surface things,
alone, they're quite bizarre.
But I don't tell you inner thoughts
for fear they'd leave a scar.

I know you love the way I think;
Correction: most of the time.
I'd rather keep it just like this,
creating words in rhyme.

Other words I have, I'm sure
would leave you unblinking and still.
I know I should . . . I would and I could . . .
. . . But I don't think I will.

jcm
2/19/84

Joey, We Hardly Knew Ye

On February 5, 1989, Joe Morrison, head football coach of the University of South Carolina and ex-New York Giant, died.

He was the best football player I ever saw.

On Sunday night, the 5th, I watched Bill Mazer Sports, but it was a little too early to have a piece on Morrison. Mazer did a 'by the way' on the death of Morrison. The next day, the papers had a small blurb on the sports pages indicating the passing of Morrison. Today, the 7th, not a word in the paper. I was actually looking for a column, a small story about the man. There were none. Morrison wasn't a dinosaur. He was only 51 years old, but it was not the relatively young age which, I think, warranted a story on him. It was the quality he brought to the game for 14 years as a New York Giant.

There were all sorts of statistics on him; he never missed a game for 14 years, 5,000 yards rushing, 2,500 yards receiving, playing tight end, wide receiver, running back and doing just about anything he was called upon to do. Early in his career, Giant fans knew that Joe Morrison would never make the Football Hall of Fame because of his great diversity on the field. He wasn't a standout in just one position, rather, he was great at a number of them. During those days of the no-championship Giants, there were the Tittles, the Giffords and the Websters. But the heart and soul of the team was Joe Morrison.

They had blackouts then, meaning within a 50-mile radius the game could not be seen. My friends and I used to travel a few miles up the Taconic to a place called the Interlake, just outside the 50-mile ban and watch the games. Shoulder to shoulder, we urged the Giants on, yelling and screaming over our pitchers of beer. At or about halftime, Tucker Fredrickson, the Giant running back, became 'Freddie Tuckerson' to my inebriated friend, Carl. Larry, Gil, Ollie, Richie and all the boys screamed in vain for all those years, for the Giants never won a championship. There weren't many bright spots then, but drove we did, up the Taconic faithfully every Sunday, to the Interlake where we would watch our beloved Giants battle it out once again. Most of the time it was Joe Morrison we talked about on the way home. Today, I couldn't draw one play on paper or re-live one of Joe's runs or catches, but I wasn't alone in my reverie for him. In 1972, Joe Morrison's last season with the Giants, they retired his number '40'.

In all the years past 1972, I remained a Giant fan. I watched Dallas take them apart every year, and I watched them sign the only football player from Bermuda, Rocky Thompson. I watched Thompson fold up like wet laundry. Year after year I rooted for them, hoping against all hope that they would someday make it to the Super Bowl.

In 1987 they made it. I watched as they lambasted the Denver Broncos and sent them packing back to Colorado. My friends, before the game, started showing up with Giant T-shirts, sweaters and other paraphernalia. But my favorite thing to wear on that day was one of my own white T-shirts with a homemade '40' inked on it. Later that week, I read in the papers that Joe Morrison had remarked: 'It was a great game.'

It *was* a great game, Joe. It was always a great game and will continue to be. As long as people like you aren't forgotten.

Thanks for all those Sundays up at the Interlake, Joe. Thanks for giving all of us Giants fans something to remember as we head down that long corridor of time.

jcm
2/7/89

A German Car, A Swiss Watch, Scottish Horns And Thou

In tan contoured seats, a Ricaro design,
I cruise down the highway, hungry and lean.
A 944 at one-thirty plus,
my plum-colored, German racing machine.

Turning my Rolex so it catches the light,
stainless steel elegance that sings,
wristwatch no, chronometer yes,
a special timepiece made for kings.

A shrilly skirl from goat horn pipes,
a Scottish King, eyes downward cast.
Mist Covered Mountain, a lament I play
to hear that sound of centuries past . . .

Someday I'll have them, my favorite things.
Material fantasies may come true
but I won't mind if they never appear,
for the only real thing I want, is you.

jcm
2/20/84

Jacques Prevert, 'Barbara', and Friends

Anna—

Here 'tis. [translation by Sedulia Scott] It gives you the sense of what Prevert is saying, but I'm afraid it's much better in French—and I'm not just bragging. This is one I learned by heart just because I loved it so much.

Prevert—'Remember Barbara'

Remember Barbara
It was raining nonstop in Brest that day
and you walked smiling,
artless, delighted dripping wet
in the rain.
Remember Barbara
it was raining nonstop in Brest
and I saw you on the Rue de Siam.
You were smiling
and I smiled too.
Remember Barbara
you, whom I did not know.
You, who did not know me.
Remember,
remember that day all the same.
Don't forget.
A man was sheltering under a porch
and he called your name,
Barbara . . .
and you ran toward him in the rain,

dripping water, delighted, artless
and you threw yourself in his arms.
Remember that, Barbara
and don't be angry if I talk to you.
I talk to all those I love
even if I've seen them only once.
I talk to all those who love
even if I don't know them.
Remember Barbara,
don't forget
that wise, happy rain
on your happy face
in that happy town.
That rain on the sea,
on the arsenal,
on the boat from Ouessant.
Oh Barbara,
what an idiot war.
What has happened to you now
in this rain of iron,
of fire, of steel, of blood
and the one who held you tight in his arms
lovingly.
Is he dead, vanished or maybe still alive?
Oh Barbara,
it is raining nonstop in Brest
as it rained before.
But it's not the same and everything is ruined.
It's a rain of mourning, terrible and desolate.
It's not even a storm anymore
of iron, of steel, of blood.
Just simply clouds
that die like dogs.
Dogs that disappear
along the water in Brest
and are going to rot far away,
far, far away from Brest
where there is nothing left.

Minor American Poet—

I like the French translation. I go back and forth. 'Rappelle' is remember? What is 'toi'?

Anna—

'Rappelle' is really recall. 'Toi' is the 2nd person singular pronoun when it is stressed. It's use will become clear to you in the expressions that use it.

If I had been translating that poem, I think I would have started with: 'Do you remember, Barbara?' It's not literal, and 'rappelle-toi, Barbara' is a command rather than a question. I'm sorry I can't write more about this now.

Minor American Poet—

You can't write now? I'll just wander through the back alleys of these restaurants, looking for a morsel of 'word food' to sustain me.

Anna—

You could have quite a feast if your choice delicacies are the extra lines I write!

Minor American Poet—

I just received your message as I was consuming some old sentences behind the New York City Library. Apparently, some readers didn't need all their words and threw some surplus lines out. I managed to salvage some prepositions and a huge oxymoron to make a delicious salad and I dribbled a ripped up 'Happy Birthday' card on it.

Seriously, in 'Barbara', where do you put Prevert? Observer or player?

Anna—

Good question. I have no idea. He could fit in either position. What do you think?

Minor American Poet—

Prevert (I think,) put himself in the secondary position, the position of a man, meeting eye-to-eye with Barbara and in all the fear and crashing around them, he saw an absolute beauty. I would say this; not everyone would look at her as a 'beauty', but he did. Instantaneously. He made a move to cross the street when her 'friend' called to her. She ran over and embraced the second man. Prevert's attempt at a chance meeting went for naught and he became an observer, the secondary position.

The writing came afterward with Prevert wondering where the players were and how they were faring. Now that he would never meet or see her again, he was in love and would stay in love forever, chalking the whole thing up to 'chance', and 'chance' having a fickle nature, turned away from him. The thought would follow him for the remainder of his life.

The 'dogs' seem to me to have been the Germans, the 'Dogs of War'. ' . . . they rot now, far away from Brest . . .', meaning the Germans had moved on, further inland toward their homeland. The rain set the mood and also the nonchalance a heavy rain would have given, over the burden of wartime.

If that had come from my pen, that would've been my explanation, had I been asked.

Anna—

I think you are really a Frenchman, and you were Prevert in another life. Difficult, I know. You would have had to be two people at the same time. But you have explained what lies behind that poem.

jcm
3/28/12

View From The Parapet

South of Leander Castle the Reading hills began their undulating gallop toward the sea. Through his father's favorite long glass, Brendan could see the Weymouth-Salisbury Road winding away, between the hills for three miles until it disappeared toward the west for good. It was this road the Baroness would be appearing on, probably today, he thought. He lowered the long glass, staring out at the panorama in front of him.

He, Brendan Barnstable, the only natural son of Sir Lord Henry Barnstable, 9th Earl of Reading and the King's Protector of the District of Surrey here at Leander Castle, couldn't wait to see her. She, being Baroness Katyana Rouselle-Helmuth of Saxe-Coburg, was coming for the Royal Installation Ball at Leander, to celebrate the 20th Anniversary of Brendan's father as King's Protector.

'Watching the road won't hurry the arrival!', said Robert Dureth from the steps behind him, breaking Brendan's reverie. Irritated, Brendan turned, to see his friend grinning. Robert and he had been friends since childhood. They had both grown up at Leander and each matching the other's steps, became mirror images of each other. When they became young men, Brendan, through his father's influence, joined the staff of Marlborough and eventually fought with the Duke at the Battle of Cressy. He managed to distinguish himself when the French broke through and threatened to overrun the Duke's inner camp. The young Barnstable led a group of the Duke's artillerists in a cutting and slashing wedge which drove the French from the camp, enabling other English units to re-group and save the day. Brendan's story preceded him back to Leander and the family's name was showered with honor. When Brendan finally returned, he was a different man . . .

'Is it that obvious, Robbie?', Brendan asked. Dureth smiled, walking up to stand beside his friend at the parapet.

'Do you think the Count will be in her entourage?', Dureth asked, not looking at his friend, as well he didn't because Brendan glared back at him.

'You must be the instigator, whenever you're able!', Brendan shot back. Both men laughed, remembering the incident with Count Kristoph Tangermunde.

Two years before, the two men, Brendan and Tangermunde were vying for the attention of the Baroness in London while they were all viewing the races on the Thames at Chatham Cross. No one remembers how it started, but it ended abruptly when Tangermunde, astride his mount, started to challenge Brendan after he, Brendan, made jest of the Count's non-command of the English language. Brendan slapped the shanks of Tangermunde's charger and the animal reared, throwing the Count heavily to the ground.

'He'd have had you, if his shoulder hadn't dislocated.', said Robert.

Brendan looked at his friend and smiled: 'We'll never know who the actual swordsman would've been.' Then, still reaching back in his memory, Brendan said; 'I remember that she laughed when Tangermunde landed on his backside.'

'What is the date today, my friend?', Robert suddenly asked.

'It's the 29th. Why do you ask?', answered Brendan.

Robert Dureth pointed toward the end of the winding road as it came out from the winding hills. 'She'll be arriving on the 29th, you impatient dog!'

Brendan raised the long glass, focused the instrument and saw the coaches. There were two guidons leading the column. They both had long lances with the blue and yellow flag of Saxe-Coburg flying from their points.

jcm
12/29/11

View From The Parapet

(a snippet)

By the time Baroness Rouselle-Helmuth saw Brendan Barnstable that afternoon, he was re-introduced to her by Robbie, as, the newly appointed Man-at-Arms, which was for Barnstable a giant step forward toward knighthood. Sadly, they didn't have any real time together. There was the customary 'rest' period after the trip, then, the next morning was the trip through two nearby villages and the usual visits to the nunnery and the orphanages by the Baroness . . . another afternoon rest which consisted of what we would call 'kicking back'; the women sitting around, talking, taking tea; the men down in a nearby field, dressed down, splitting wood and partaking in the new autumn ale. Brendan looked up toward the castle once and saw the Baroness (we'll call her Katyana from now on . . .) looking down at the field, her long hair being slowly combed by one of the ladies. Brendan knew she was looking at him.

That evening was the dinner and ball. Count Tangermunde didn't arrive with Katyana's entourage. Later on, Brendan found out that he was 'told' to stay at home in Wannsee. The evening had an anti-climactic feel to it, just a great deal of eye contact but no direct conversation between Brendan and Katyana. In the morning the Saxe-Coburg contingent left with

Brendan riding along for a few miles on Robbie's roan gelding. He managed a wave to Katyana as her coach creaked by, and she . . . she blew him a kiss! A smile traversed his face from ear to ear! She smiled back, and was gone . . .

- Right about now, you may be wondering how I know all this? As I've told you before, I've had many 'lives', in and out of history. I was, at that time, an employee of Leander Castle. My name doesn't matter. It never made it down through time anyway. I happened to be a member of the small string quartet which played at banquets and other events at the castle. I saw everything and now, I relate it to you. It wasn't actually a 'quartet', but six men. I was in my usual spot, third chair from the left, second fiddle.

Mortimer Snee

jcm
1/10/12

Good King Wenceslaus

Anna,

Kim Jong Il of North Korea died today. And . . . ? Who cares.

But Vaclav Havel died today also. One of my big heroes, the President of Czechoslovakia. He was also a playwright. Standing up to the Russian Bear in those days was a precarious position to be in.

Did you ever hear his 'Wenceslaus Square Speech'?

When it was the eve of their independence and it was just about assured, Havel appeared on a balcony overlooking Wenceslaus Square in Prague. They said there were over 200,000 Czechs in the square. He made a rousing speech which is what they came for, but at the end of the speech, he pointed to the bronze figure of King Wenceslaus astride his horse, towering over the crowd. He said:

'Once, when we needed King Wenceslaus, he appeared with his army and saved this land!. Well, there stands King Wenceslaus,', and he spread his arms toward the crowd, 'and there stands his army!'

Goodbye, Mr. Havel. Thanks for everything.

jcm
12/19/11

Checking Out And Leaving Town

Don't ask me about then.
Ask me about now
because now, is what I know.
I don't know about then,
but it was fun, I suppose.
Good times came together
but not in series, just bunches.
There were big gaps which I can't recall.

I only know about now.
It comes to me in waves,
like Dreamtime.
The day you came to me
is when Now started.
Dreamtime began then, and only then.

I hope I've earned everything you've given me.
Sometimes I think not.
I don't know when it will be
when one of us Leaves Town,
but selfishly, I'd like to be first.

I'd like your face to be the last thing
in my eyes
when Dreamtime ends.

jcm
2/21/84

The Heroes of '75

Viet Nam was winding down,
tiring for the last time
our already tired bodies.
Those young faces on the seven o'clock news
are all older now.

Nine long years ago . . .
Twelve year-old Tom and I invaded Lexington;
The British are coming!

(Twas the 19th of April in '75,
hardly a man is now alive . . .)

". . . To April's breeze our flag unfurled!"
That was my personal plum day,
the best of all days,
a milestone in my current life.
I saw your face for the first time
in Nineteen Hundred and Seventy-Five.
Nine long years ago.

You gave me feelings of heroics, instant stardom
topped only by mingling with heroes.
But don't pin me down for my best of days
for I'd have to say—
I'm still riding that Lexington high.

jcm
2/22/84

'The Whites Of Their Eyes'

Dear Professor Lockhart,

I'm not quite finished with your book, 'The Whites Of Their Eyes', but I felt compelled to get a note to you now.

I just now finished the actual battle. Dr. Warren is lying face down in the dirt atop Breed's Hill. Putnam is a whirling dervish atop Bunker Hill and Mc Clary doesn't have long to live. I don't have much to read before I'm done, but I know I will have that same feeling I always have when finishing a book I wish had never ended.

I have, making a guess, 10 to 12 books on the Battle of Bunker Hill. I might as well stockpile them away in the face of your masterpiece.

I thought awhile before using the word 'masterpiece', but I think it's appropriate. Your research has left no stone unturned. You didn't miss a beat nor did you paint a scene that couldn't be mentally viewed. I am definitely in awe.

Of all my bookcases at home, I have one that's reserved for books such as this one. Needless to say, I'll find room for it there. I could say more, but I don't have to. You must've known what you had when you put your quill pen back in the inkwell when you were done.

Thank you for an enjoyable and educational read.

Yours,

James C. McGuire
Brewster, N.Y.

Mr. McGuire,

Not sure what to say but thanks! I'm fairly certain that that's the kindest e-mail I've ever received about any of my books. And it means a lot; I was genuinely touched. As you can probably tell, writing 'Whites of Their Eyes' was a great deal of fun for me. It's doubly satisfying to know that somewhere out there are a few readers to whom the book meant something.

Thanks again—sincerely—for your kind words.

Paul Douglas Lockhart
Ph.D
Professor of History
Wright State University
Dayton, Ohio

Professor Lockhart,

. . . And thank you for your kind words, though my own words pale in the face of; 'None of these men would be elevated into the pantheon of Revolutionary heroes; . . . They, along with the army they created and led, had served their purpose, and once that purpose had been fulfilled they passed into history.'

Artemus Ward, Prescott, John Thomas and the rest did what they had to do and 'faded into the mist' of time. In your own way, the way I looked at it, you called after them and when they turned, you thanked them. I took that idea from the book. I hope you don't mind.

In 1975, I took my son, Tom, up to Lexington to see the 200th Anniversary of Lexington and Concord. There were 130,000 souls in a town of 16,000 inhabitants. President Ford was there and so was Major Pitcairn and his Grenadiers. They arrived at 0415, the same as they did 200 years before. Captain Parker and his men came out of Buckman's Tavern and the war started. My son is 48 now. He's a teacher down in Arlington, Virginia. He tells his class about it every April.

I somewhat pompously tell people I'm an 'amateur historian' until I come across someone like you and your book. Then, I'm afraid, I'm not Twain's 'Great Indiaman, banked with sails and fragrant with spices from the Orient', but his 'tiny coastal schooner, *Maryann*, with pots and pans and nothing to speak of.'

I'll be looking for your next book, and once more, thanks for putting us all behind the earthworks on Breed's Hill, dry-mouthed, gripping our muskets and shaking in our boots.

James C. McGuire
Brewster, N.Y.

jcm 12/15/11

FDR And The HOUSTON

The USS *Houston* (CA-30) was FDR's favorite ship. He loved the Navy to begin with and everywhere the President had to go, he would go aboard the *Houston* and the ship would take him. He got to know the crew very well and made three trips on her. He had a picture of the *Houston* hanging in the oval office.

When the war started, the old *Houston* wasn't called back to the States because we needed all the ships we could get. The cruiser didn't have one anti-aircraft gun. Having been built in 1930, air power was still in it's infancy so they didn't put any guns on board to fight aircraft.

It was the end of February, 1942 and in the White House, in a conference room, FDR and his staff, along with about twenty other people, were having a meeting. One of his aides came in and whispered to Harry Hopkins, FDR's chief advisor. Hopkins slipped a note to FDR. The President read it and slumped back in his chair.

'We'll resume this, gentlemen, after a short break.', Roosevelt said. The room cleared, all except for Harry Hopkins. FDR looked at Hopkins and said:

'Harry, the *Houston* was lost this morning. She was sunk.' Hopkins went to sit down on one of the chairs and FDR said:

'Give me a minute, Harry. Would you?' Hopkins got up and left, closing the door. He said later, as he closed the door, FDR had his head down and his hands folded in front of him.

Hopkins wrote a short piece a few years later for Look Magazine. In it, he mentioned the story. He said they were all out in the hall for about 20 minutes before they went back in. The following day, Hopkins said, he went down to the Oval Office and the first thing he noticed was the picture of the USS *Houston* wasn't on the wall in its special place anymore.

It was perched on the President's desk.

Gore Vidal said once: 'There was a man who couldn't walk. He had trouble standing. Yet, he carried a nation on his back for 13 years.'

jcm
12/11/12

Just Visiting

Don't stay inside me too long
for fear of skin damage
as hot beach sand burns the feet.

I have labyrinths of endless corridors
populated by ghosts
who talk to me each day.

The times you reached down deep inside of me,
you laughed at what you found—
you confused drama with fact.
It was a little of both
but still,
it wasn't a laughing matter.

jcm
2/22/84

'Attention! Wake Island Marine On Deck!'

Everyone remembers Pearl Harbor, December 7th, but on the next day, December 8th, the next item on the Imperial Japanese government's list was Wake Island, a small dot in the western central Pacific.

The Japanese attacked the tiny island with a task force of 4,000 Japanese Marines and a Naval brigade. They also had two dozen warships complete with an aerial assault.

Defending the tiny islands, were the 449-man strong 1st Marine Defense Battalion, 68 sailors and 1,221 civilian construction workers. Their 'heavy' guns were six obsolete 5" guns which had been stripped from an old battleship, twelve 3" guns in various stages of repair, eighteen .50 calibre and thirty .30 calibre machine guns. Not much.

This tiny force held out for 15 days of continuous fighting. In the end, of course, the Japanese overwhelmed them, but not before losing two destroyers, one submarine and 24 aircraft. The USMC and Navy lost 78 men. All the civilian workers who had taken up arms against the Japanese were executed. The Japanese had just over 1,000 men killed. America didn't know what had happened there until after the war. The last radio message received from Wake Island before it fell silent came from Lt. Col. James Devereux and Lt. Winfield Cunningham. They sent:

'Send us more Japs.'

Wake Island ranks today among the greatest battles ever. In the book, 'Pacific Alamo' by John Wukovits, the opening paragraph, I think, should be repeated here:

'The aged man appeared to be in his eighties, but 'graying' and 'frail' were not the first words one would use to describe him. The bounce in his step was still there and energy shone in his eyes, carrying more than a hint of what a force he once was. He stood amidst the large gathering of Naval and Marine Corps officers, relaxing after a long day's schedule of reunion meetings. They sipped coffee and told tales of their service histories.

Suddenly, one of the officers recognized him, and a deep voice barked out above the din:

'Attention! Wake Island Marine on deck!'

"Everyone stopped talking.", said a Naval officer who witnessed the incident. "We stood at attention, faced the Marine and saluted. Those guys are legendary in the Navy and Marines for what they did. Whenever one is around, you pay him the highest respect."

Wake Island was 70 years ago, today. But to me, and others like me, it seems like yesterday. Like the Alamo. Like Guadalcanal. Like Omaha Beach. Like a lot of places and a lot of times. Those people will not come our way again. Let's hope we learned from them. Let's hope we can turn adversity into honor followed closely by triumph when the time comes.

Like they did.

jcm
12/8/11

Thanksgiving Message From A Voluntary Expatriate

More than any other, this is the time of year when I most miss living in America. No other land has a holiday quite like Thanksgiving. It has no religious connection, no ethnic connection, no underlying motive—just the idea that we all have a lot to be thankful for and that this is a time to remember that.

I always imagined I would live somewhere behind that white picket fence with lots of family and friends nearby who could gather for Thanksgiving. Instead, I live half a world away where no one has a white picket fence, far away from any family and with friends who would be likely to find Thanksgiving 'quaint'. How very odd!

This is not some plaintive cry for sympathy. It is really a wish for you to have a very happy day in the spirit that was intended for Thanksgiving. If I may never achieve that dream of yesteryear for Thanksgiving, I have achieved many others that would perhaps have been mutually exclusive with the white picket fence.

Have a good time tomorrow—and have a bite of pumpkin pie for me! This was always my favorite holiday too.

Thankful,
Anna

jcm
11/24/11

8 Kenosia Trail

. . . White hangers neatly stacked,
Hong Kong suitcase still unpacked.
. . . Unmatched coffee mugs in a row,
kerosene heater turned down low.
. . . Tons of peanut butter, skinny bread,
the broiler element burning red.
. . . Merwan's feathers filtering down,
the spare room closet's folded clown.
. . . 'Run the vacuum to and fro!
And scrub the bathroom as you go!'
. . . Apple magnets and boiling rice,
scents of bottled Joy and Old Spice.
. . . Instant coffee, 'The Breakfast Flakes',
apple crisp, chocolate syrup and carrot cakes.
. . . Now, two dirty plates instead of one
and we'll find a place for the Civil War gun.
Everyday habits, cemented with time,
routine things that we leave behind.
Our patchwork coat to keep out the cold—
we'll wear it together as we grow old.

jcm
3/4/84

There Will Always Be An Ark Royal

It was September of 1960 and my ship, the *Yellowstone* was visiting Plymouth, England. We had just come down from Greenock, Scotland.

Plymouth was a blue collar town if I'd ever seen one. The American carrier, *Independence* was miked out, beyond the harbor, so we knew there would be about 4,000 American sailors in Plymouth. Not good. The first night we were in Plymouth, we didn't get any further than one of the shipyard taverns. The place was bustling and I noticed the *Ark Royal* was in the yards, a group of cranes already assembled on her flight deck and arc welders could be seen working somewhere above on the superstructure. At the time, the *Ark Royal* was England's only carrier.

A few of us walked into the establishment, straight into a heated discussion between the two contingents of carrier sailors. There had to be about twenty of them, men from the *Ark Royal* and *Independence*, arguing until they were blue in the face, about the good and the bad of each ship. The *Independence* was at the time, was the state of the art in aircraft carriers. The *Ark Royal* had been laid down in 1943 right after the loss of the old *Ark Royal* in 1942. She joined the fleet in 1953 after work on her had stopped due to the ending of the war. After some austerity budgets, they started work on her again. Now, she was in the yards, an old but honorable ship with an honorable name.

My friends and I didn't get into the argument, not being carrier people, and one by one, the antagonists and protagonists started leaving, their diatribes having run out of fuel. I noticed there were four, maybe five British sailors still at the bar, so I went over. I made sure I told them I was off a destroyer tender which had just come into port and not somebody from the *Independence*. I bought a round for all of them and we proceeded to talk about their ship for the next hour or more. American sailors wore their ship tab on the upper right side of their arm and the British sailors wore theirs on their hat band. I asked them for one of their hats and they said 'no'.

Anyway, we talked and talked with the pints coming in full and going back empty. I told them of the *Ark Royal's* before and about their namesake sunk by the Germans. I gave them all the WWII stuff I could muster up and by the end of the night, we had gone through the HMS *Hood*, *Glowworm*, *Cossack* and *Hermes*. The *Hermes* was sunk off Trimcomalee, Ceylon. We all agreed that it was a pretty name! Then, of course, we had to toast all the men aboard the HMS *Prince of Wales* and *Repulse*. They wanted to know how come I knew so much about the Royal Navy and I told them that all great navies worked their way to the front of all conversations. More toasts! We toasted all the drowned sailors at Pearl, Captain Vian of the *Cossack*, and the *Exeter*, *Ajax* and *Achilles*, conquerors of the SKS *Graf Spee* in the River Plate. We managed to free ourselves from the tavern but instead of my heading across the yard to my ship, they took me aboard the *Ark Royal*. It was unforgettable. All four or five were talking at once and I got the Cook's Tour of the gallant carrier. I can remember the welder's smoke, the puzzled looks on some of their shipmates and the scornful glances from some of the officers. We were all talking at the same time.

There were no planes on the flight deck or the hangar deck because she was in the yards. The bridge was barricaded off so they couldn't show it to me. I knew all their names at one point and some of their addresses, but they've long disappeared from my memory. Before I left the *Ark Royal*, one of them pushed a flat hat in my hand. The band read '*Ark Royal*'. I was honored. So honored, that I wore it onto the *Yellowstone* when I returned. I saluted the flag then saluted the officer of the deck. He had his back turned toward me so he wouldn't have to say anything about my newly-acquired Royal Navy hat. I don't remember hitting the rack and falling asleep.

We were in Plymouth for two more weeks, but I never saw my new friends again. When the *Yellowstone* finally left, we were backing down with two tugs, turning to leave port. As we passed the *Ark Royal* (RO-9), our Captain had the whistle blow two short and one long. On the stern of the *Ark Royal*, I could see a few sailors. They were waving. We waved back. I always wondered if they were my pals. I guess I'll always love the Royal Navy.

jcm
2/28/12

The Play: Wolverine Scamper Left

'The outlook wasn't brilliant for the [Ole Miss boy] that day,
the score stood [17-15],
with only [minutes] left to play.'

'Fifty-Two! Fifty-Two! Hut . . . Hut!' and the ball slapped into The Kid's hands and he rolled back a few steps, looking, looking . . .

My beloved Giants were two points down to the Beantown Boys . . . not much time left.

But out to the left, streaking down the sideline from his own 6-yard line, Mario Manningham, the Wolverine from Michigan ran, just feet from the white resin. Sterling Moore and Pat Chung, the Patriot defenders were staying with him, step for step.

Mario Manningham, a standout at Michigan, was termed a bad apple. Not a good pick in the draft. Not a 'team' guy. He had a drug and alcohol problem. In and out of rehab twice. A bad risk so they said, but the New York Football Giants picked him in the third round.

'We'll straighten him out.', said Ernie Rondell. (Was Rondell at home, watching? Was he slowly getting off the couch and moving toward the screen?)

And Mario Manningham ran. And he ran.

Eli looked right, then the middle . . . nothing. Then he saw '82' in between two Patriots way over on the left. The clock was ticking. Eli Manning drew back his arm, knowing that it would be more than a 100-foot pass. He had to get it right! He had to thread the needle!

The ball left his hand and took off. Manningham saw it, arching, arching! Sterling Moore saw it. Patrick Chung saw it. One hundred and twenty million other people saw it. The clock ticked away.

Visions of Charlie Connerly and Emlen Tunnell and Andy Robustelli and all the rest came into view. And my all-time favorite, #40, Joe Morrison. They were all there, watching. They were watching.

The ball sailed neatly between Moore and Chung, nestling into Manningham's outstretched hands! He scraped both feet on the grass in front of the resin, just the edges. But the edges were enough. All three men crashed out of bounds and the Giants were halfway home. The football field was cut in half. They had a chance now. Sorry Mr. Kraft. Sorry Tom Brady. Sorry Gisele Bundechen, for these are the Giants, the New York Football Giants. They were playing football when the letters A, F and L were just that; letters. These were the people who signed Mark Bavaro from Notre Dame and Phil Mc Conkey from Navy. These were the caretakers of the Sport of Roughhouse. Sorry, Boston. Sorry, Mr. Revere. Sorry Old North Church.

Final Score: New York Giants—21, New England Patriots—17.

And, if I can steal a few lines from the famous Grantland Rice and grab some Super Bowl literary license:

'Outlined against the gray [February] sky, the Four Horsemen rode again. In legendary lore their names were Death, Pestilence, Disease and Famine. But in real life they're names were [Manning, Bradshaw, Tuck and Umenyora]. Once again they swept a brave [Patriot] team over the precipice.'

To reiterate for most of us, the famous words of Justin Ferate; 'I'm an American by chance, but I'm a New Yorker by choice.'

jcm
Peekskill (New York) High School Varsity Football
#19
2/6/12

The Last Few Leaves of Autumn

I've reached the end of this Sunday afternoon,
no more plums of thought
or structured lines,
only bits and pieces, a homeless group.
    I wish Harry Chapin was still alive
    and Stanley Baker and Hopalong Cassidy.
    No one remembers Dakota Staton.
Two hawks are circling outside.
I wonder if they're eyeing Dominic?
    Tonight I'll wash the car,
    have a drink with Kenny
    and rub my Lady's back.

Goodbye, Sunday.
Sometime tonight, sitting in this chair,
someone will turn the calendar page
and you'll be gone,
swept away as one sweeps snow
from a sidewalk.
Too bad.

jcm
3/4/84

Clarinet Glissando in B Minor

A few weeks ago, my wife and I were walking down W. 42nd Street, across from Bryant Park. Whenever I'm in that area, whether just walking around or sitting in the Bryant Park Grill with the greatest man-made Bloody Mary in front of me, I always look, for one nondescript building. That day, we stood in front of it; 29-33 W. 42nd St., just a few feet from 5th Avenue. Today it's the SUNY School of Opthalmology, but back in 1924 it was called Aeolian Hall. On the third floor was an auditorium of sorts where concerts and plays took place. On a winter night in 1924, an event took place which put a fingerprint, a birthmark on the City of Man. It was a night on which a man named George Gershwin and New York City became synonymous . . .

There were 850 seats in Aeolian Hall and every one was filled. Paul Whiteman's orchestra was on stage as the slender George Gershwin came out and sat down at his Baldwin piano. Whiteman's best clarinetist, a man whose name escapes me, launched into a glissando trill which riveted the audience to their seats, then Gershwin played. And he played. On the program, it said: 'Rhapsody in Blue', but in the layered air of the hall it was Manhattan the people heard. It was the Brooklyn Bridge they saw. It was the wheezing buses they smelled. It was a heart-stopping 16 minutes long and those gathered there hung on every note. It was supposed to be a piano concerto but the fertile mind of George Gershwin extended it and curved it into probably the greatest rhapsody ever written. At the end, the assembled music-lovers applauded and kept applauding. They had listened to themselves in the notes. It was a personal thing they heard. The rhapsody was them. Later on, when they stood outside on the sidewalk in the cold February air, they gathered in groups just to talk about what they had heard. The giant saloon Packards and Duesenbergs cut through the slush on the streets and those citizens who were not lucky enough to have heard Gershwin, rushed by, holding their coats tight against the cold. It was a memorable night, a night in which thousands of people would swear they were there, but of course they weren't. There were just 850 souls in Aeolian Hall that night. It was February 12, 1924. Eighty-six years ago today.

Twenty-five years later, E.B. White, in his great essay, 'Here Is New York', wrote his own description of the City of Man. He must've been listening to a recording of 'Rhapsody In Blue' when he finished the essay with:

". . . A block or two west of the new City of Man in Turtle Bay there is an old willow tree that presides over an interior garden. It is a battered tree, long suffering and much climbed, held together by strands of wire but beloved by those who know it. In a way it symbolizes the city: life under difficulties, growth against odds, sap-rise in the midst of concrete and the steady reaching for the sun. Whenever I look at it nowadays, and feel the cold shadow of the planes, I think: This must be saved, this particular thing, this very tree. If it were to go—this city, this mischievous and marvelous monument which not to look upon would be like death."

jcm
2/12/10

Bull's Bridge and Beyond

We do things on impulse and happenstance
but never too much on planning.
We went back to the weathered wood
on Bull's Bridge just once.
Did we find our initials?
The ones I cut with a key
for want of a knife?
If we decide to take a beach walk
at twi-light
and look for a galleon's gold,
we're bound to find it.
That's the way we are—
we stumble onto happiness
the way others stumble onto treasure.
You make me adventurous—
you make me want to carry
a penknife to carve our initials
in every tree, post and wooden bridge
we pass.
We must go back to Bull's Bridge one day
and find our letters in the wood.
Perhaps I'll draw a line in the dirt
and we can start again from there.

jcm
3/17/84

E.B. White's Tree

Dear Lo-lo,

Remember the story of the willow tree in Turtle Bay, in E.B. White's essay, 'Here Is New York'? Maybe you don't. I read a strange story about it in the Sunday Times.

It seems back in 2005, some NYC Landmark people started looking for the tree. E.B. White saw it in a private garden from his apartment window on E. 48th Street, in the Turtle Bay section of Manhattan. That was the willow tree in his essay. The Landmark people actually found it, but it was in sad shape. It was full of rot and some of the branches were split. They tried to save it by cabling and chemicals but to no avail. They had to take it down, so in 2009, an arborist from Brooklyn came over and took the tree down. The whole neighborhood was there along with members of the city council. E.B. White's tree was no more.

It so happened that the arborist brought some shoots home with him and planted them in his back yard in a corner of his garden in Red Hook and promptly forgot about them. Just this year, someone who happened to be in the Turtle Bay garden the day the tree came down, remembered the arborist taking the shoots and called him. He (the arborist) was speaking on his cell phone and walking down to his garden at the same time, the caller said. He had to wend his way through vines and such to reach the spot where he planted the shoots. The caller said the arborist yelled out loud when he saw the shoots. They were about eight feet tall, two of them! White's willow tree was alive. Now, they're thinking about transplanting them back in their original Turtle Bay garden.

Turtle Bay is about two blocks from both the East River and the front of the U.N. Building. It used to be an actual bay during the

Revolution, before New York started filling in the shoreline to make the island bigger. More land, more buildings.

The little tree is still alive, the same as the City of Man, the place the tree epitomized, to E.B. White. Personally, I'm thrilled. I hope to see the transplanted tree when and if they bring it over.

jcm
6/13/12

Over My Shoulder

Roads we drive down, rooms we pass through
no matter where they are,
places we've been to before, remind me.
        Some bars have changed their names,
        restaurants are no longer there,
        houses you lived in once
        have been repainted.
        Street corners too, where new people gather.
I look for that familiar couple,
the man, thinning on top, hunched over.
The girl, blonde hair flying, smiling.
        We were always smiling.
        Places we walked once, wooded paths,
        concrete sidewalks, asphalt lots,
        country roads.
I try to catch a glimpse of those two
but they're not in sight yet.
We need them now, to remind us of the way
it used to be.
They knew how to do it.
I miss them.
I miss you.
I miss me . . .

jcm
3/19/84

Aux Barricades!

Today, July 14th, is the birthday of our oldest ally. No, it's not England. It's France. Back when our tiny army were all in rags and we couldn't afford the proverbial pot, France was there. They were there at French Hill in Yorktown, N.Y. and they were there at Redoubt #1 in Yorktown, Virginia. They were with Washington's army as they marched down King's Ferry Road to cross the Hudson and they were with the Americans all the way down, on foot, to Virginia. When Lord Cornwallis looked out his window from the confines of Yorktown, he saw the white fleur-di-lis flag of France advancing on his soldiers along with the American flag. The French fleet under Comte De Grasse, outfought the British fleet just off the Virginia coast and the long revolution was over.

Americans always seem to turn up their noses at the French. We don't like their socialist form of government they seem to revert back to every few years. We seem to look down on them when it comes to combat. Even the British remind the rest of the world, in a subtle way of course, that the French use less hand soap per capita than the rest of the European countries. In America, I've found, most of the people who dislike the French, haven't even been there! There are voids in their minds sadly, where knowledge should dwell.

Here are some little known incidents concerning our first ally:

Spring, 1940. German panzer divisions were pushing the B.E.F. and the French 1st Army west, toward a little seacoast town named Dunkirk. The Allies would eventually be pressed in against the Channel and a herculean effort by the Royal Navy and civilian small boats would save 338,000 troops. Just outside of Dunkirk, on a ridge in a town named Roubaix, British tanks were beginning to leave the line, to head toward Dunkirk. There were three French tanks, Char B-1's, on the ridge. They weren't moving. To the east, German tanks could be seen, streaming over the hill toward Roubaix. Every time a

French Char scored a hit on a panzer, the two Char crews who didn't score a hit, would leave their tanks, and rush over to the third tank to congratulate their crew! The British tank crews yelled to them to pack up and get out, but the French stayed, scoring hit after hit on the German armour. 'They must be crazy!', the British said, as they roared off the ridge. Before the British left, they saw more than a dozen German tanks burning on the other hill.

On the last day of the Dunkirk evacuation, there had to be a rear guard, units that had to stay to fight or be captured, allowing the main body to escape back to England in the ships. General Molinie of the French 1st Army was about to board the last small boat to leave Dunkirk. He addressed the assembled troops, part of the 40,000 French soldiers who were ordered to stay.

'My brave boys,' he began, 'you have fought well. Now you are asked to fight more. I know you will do honor to France! We will meet again.' It was night and the fires from Dunkirk played on the shiny black helmets of the French poilus as they stood at attention on the last remaining quay. Other armies at other times would run, scatter to the wind, trying to avoid capture or death. But not the French that night. They stood at attention, unmoving except for the reflection of the fires of Dunkirk dancing on their helmets.

Molinie and his staff went down to the cutter to be taken out to one of the few remaining ships. One of the General's aides had forgotten something on top of the quay and climbed the stairs once more. He saw the long lines of French soldiers, still standing at attention in the dark. They hadn't moved, nor would they move until the last of the Allies had cleared the harbor. Until his dying day, the French staff officer said, he 'would remember the only things moving were the reflection of the fires on their helmets,'

Four years later, early on D-Day morning, American paratroopers came tumbling out of the sky, onto the sleepy French peninsula village of Ste-Mer-Iglise. Private John Steele of the 82nd Airborne came down onto the roof of the town church, the Church of St. Mary. His chute caught on one of the steeples and he hung there during the wee hours of morning. He watched most of his cohorts being shot while still in their harnesses as they came down out of the dark sky. Eventually, Steele worked his way into the tower, leaving his chute. All through the war, as the battles passed by Ste-Mer-Iglise and even France, the parachute hung on that steeple. Untouched. After the war, in 1946, on the anniversary of D-Day, an American officer came down to the French town from his base in Germany with a new parachute to replace the tattered one still hanging from the church steeple. Since then, on the anniversary of D-Day, a new parachute is delivered to the Mayor of Ste-Mer-Iglise. There's a parade in honor of the 82nd Airborne Division, a town fair and thousands of visitors. The old parachute is taken down and the new one is hung on the steeple. To this day, the citizens of the little town make sure the parachute stays there all year, through rainstorms and windstorms. It's always visible, day in and day out, reminding everyone of the morning 'those devils in baggy pants' came hurtling out of the dark sky to bring freedom to France.

Many stories can be found, up and down the countryside of France. One story, however, is never shown or told on American television and it happens every year. Every July 4th. It happened this year also, but we here in the States didn't get to see it.

On their own, each year, the citizens of the small Channel towns of Normandy, march. They shut the highway down and march, each citizen holding a small American flag. People from Arromanches, Ouistreham, Colleville-Sur-Mer, Vierville, La Cambe, Cabourg, St. Laurent Sur-Mer and many more, march down the highway with their flags. No bands. No government dignitaries. No newspeople of any kind, just long lines of French citizens remembering the birthday of one of the countries who came over and helped them. As 'Black Jack' Pershing said once at the Place de Concorde in Paris, after leading the first American contingent into the city during World War 1; 'We came over to help you, because a long time ago, you came over and helped us.' His actual words were: *'Lafayette, nous somme ici*! '(Lafayette, we are here!).

So here's to you, Pierre . . . Happy Birthday from the people over here. It would be nice if we all remembered because we won't know where we are going if we don't know where we have been.

jcm
7/14/12

The Traveler

Love brushes past me, unhurried
as groups of travelers
bound for other places.

Time is slow motion movement,
bent on going nowhere.

I'm afraid of the travelers,
they leave behind them spurts and squirts
of love, half teaspoonfuls of light.
If I take the time to know them,
they're gone by the time I get back.

All except for one traveler.
She came to me nine years ago . . .
and stayed.

jcm
3/22/84

The Sleep of the Innocent

I look down at your face on the pillow,
your eyelids flickering the dialogue
of the dream you are in.
What has changed?

I see the small army of Joy perfume on the dresser,
the flung nylon crumples
and the skirt neatly laid out on the trunk.
It's all the same, but it isn't.
Leroy lies dormant in his closet bed,
your electricity has turned into a brown glow,
blinking on and off.

Was it my crudeness?
Did I crowd your space, or,
not give you breathing time?
Will you be the same again? Someday?

Uncertainty stalks you like a mountain lion
and I can feel the fear in your voice.
The room is the same when colors abounded
but something has changed.

Come back to me when you're ready.
Not before because it won't count.
I'll know.
Standing here, I also know that I miss you
and need you.
    I've never loved you more than I do now.

jcm
3/22/84

Colonel Rol and Me

Anna,

Whenever I think of sharing wine or even hear the word 'sharing', my mind always goes back to one thing and one thing only.

The end of October, 1943. Paris. (where else?) I was in the F.F.I. at the time, the only remaining volunteer of my village, Grandcamp-Maisy in Normandy. Colonel Rol, yes, the Colonel Rol, and I were in a parked car on the Marche Neuf across from the Police Prefecture just east of the edifice of Notre Dame. Right across from us, the end sally port door had swung open. We knew that two cars, packed with Schlossberg's men would be coming out of that sally port fast, on their way to a pre-arranged attack on the Rue Saint Honore where we had a small cache of newly acquired Sten guns. Colonel Rol and I had been friends since April of the same year when I saved his life in front of the Basilique Ste Clotilde, but, that's another story . . .

'We don't have long to wait, mon ami.', said Rol. I nodded. 'While we wait . . . ', and his voice trailed off as he reached into his left boot and extracted one of those thin Montressor Estat bottles of Cabernet Blanc.

'Oho!', I exclaimed. A smile crossed his handsome countenance at my outburst and he pulled the cork with his teeth.

'No glasses.', he laughed and took a long pull on the bottle before passing it to me. There was only one place to get Cabernet Blanc in the thin bottles in all of Paris, and that was a tiny shop in the Vavin section on the Rue Delambre. I knew the place. The Cabernet was warm from Rol's leg but I drank regardless. I felt the warmth all the way to my toes. Then, following my appreciative sigh, I corked the bottle and just then . . .

'They come! They come!', Rol blurted out! I saw the two low-slung Martines flying toward the open sally port from inside the Prefecture! I jumped out of the right side of the car, cocking my Chauchat. Rol was already out of his side, in a wide stance, leveling his Sten gun. I ran to the front of the car but Rol didn't fire! What was wrong? The cars were on the street already!

I saw Rol's machine gun jam just as I instinctively raised the heavy Chauchat. It was a heavy machine gun from the Great War and had a bad reputation, but I treated it well. It had never let me down and it didn't this time.

I felt the rapid chug-chug of the 7.65's against my side and watched as the bullets tore into the two saloons. I saw a hat fall out of the rear window of the first car. The second car careened to the right and hit a light pole, its horn blaring like a klaxon! I emptied the entire drum magazine into the two cars with the first car catching fire.

'Let's go!', yelled Rol, and the two of us jumped into the small Puegot and sped away in seconds. Once across the Petit Pont, Rol slowed the car down. He clapped me on the shoulder and laughed. 'Wine!', he yelled and I handed him the bottle of Cabernet. He took a long pull and handed it back to me. I didn't drink. My mind was racing.

Many a night now, in the twi-light of my years, in the gray days of autumn, I can still recall Rol's face and his wide grin. I can still feel the thin bottle against my leg and the very hot barrel of the Chauchat on my other leg as the little car sped through the Latin Quarter.

I still remember him saying: 'The three of us did well, today, yes?' I must've looked at him questioningly, so he responded:

'You, me and the Cabernet Blanc!', and he laughed, that booming, all-teeth laugh.

You may tout the fame of Cabernet Sauvignon and laugh when I think of camaraderie, freedom and retribution for the good, but I think of that little bottle of sauvignon blanc and riding with Colonel Rol through the Paris night in that little Puegot, and every time, I think;

Liberte! Egalite! Fraternite!

jcm
3/3/12

Opening Up

Sometimes we have to open up our hearts
and let some of the hurt flow in,
mix in, swirl about
if only to keep ourselves honest.
 Old loves are a good shot of 'instant hurt'.
 All of us have to know
 if we still feel.
We can't shake the memories of old loves
because we don't want to.
 We manufacture times and places
 to build up the things that weren't there.
Some say it makes us appreciate things more.
I don't know.
Memories of old loves should be taken
out, shaken out and fed once again.
Good, bad or indifferent, they all
must have a place,
a spot for remembering.

First loves are easy, the middle ones come hard.
But when it comes to my last old love,
I always think of you.

jcm
3/22/84

Walking With A Friend . . .

I watched 'Midnight in Paris' again last night. I can't describe how much I miss that town. I can't stop picturing myself by the metro in Montmartre, looking at the dome of the Sacre Couer through the trees. Even if I had to partake in red wine the whole time, I have to get my tired, old body back there.

I would trade everything I've ever seen and almost everything I've ever done to spend just one summer in Paris with McKuen, a younger McKuen, and similarly, a younger me. He and I could start in Maxim's as the sun started its downward plunge and we could map out the evening, searching for . . . her. The 'face, form and footfall' girl, he left behind, or, who left him behind. I would walk the darkened side streets until dawn, looking at every shuttered window, every darkened doorway and every minor garden. He and I would wonder which window was hers.

It would be a needful thing, an important thing. I would give up an entire summer to walk with him. We wouldn't find her of course, but we would feel her, smell her, hear her. She would be all around and eventually, he would tell me about her. I would be jealous. Not of her, but the way he would and did write about her. All of us who love life and have loved life, have found that person. When and how and for how long doesn't matter. The fact is, we did.

And we would talk. And talk. I would listen, mostly. I would listen and try to remember that summer for the rest of my life.

And, as the broom clears the doorstep in the morning, you can sweep this away. It was just a thought that I wanted to share, but a very big thought, whittled down to a minute or two of side street ramblings.

jcm
7/6/12

From May to May

All things considered
this has been the roughest of years.
It gets harder to bounce back
from direct hits.
Good things abound too,
but they don't want to listen.
They only want to know about the bad things—
they remind me every chance they get.
    But I'm bringing this ship in
    to the safe harbor it deserves.
    Everyone on the bridge is dead;
    I'm down to half power
    and I'm taking water.
My wounds will heal, they're not fatal.
I wonder if the other's wounds are?
    Am I worthy, God?
    If there's a penance,
    lay it on me—

    Say ten Our Fathers and a million Hail Marys.

jcm
3/22/84

3 A.M.

I rise up on my elbows
like a great sea monster
shedding water from my sloping back.

The streetlight shimmers from the heat
my mind sends out—
a dream so real, far from where we live.

You come to me in sections;
a 'V' of a leg, then an arm
carelessly thrown.
You murmur as your eyes open to me
and your fingers curl.

You taste of cinnamon sticks in hot rum
complete with Cuban sun
and delicate palms, salty to the touch.

I follow myself to your heart
and see my reflection on your face.
. . . You say my name.

jcm
3/22/84

The Story Of The R.F. CAPRICE or 'How Come We're Sinking?'

In the mid-60's, a bunch of us tried to resurrect an old river ferry. She was 36' long and had a narrow beam. She had a 150-hp diesel, a head and seats for 36 people. Her name was *Caprice.*

There was a bar we used to frequent down near Verplanck's Point, on King's Ferry Road, named 'Bap' Mitchell's. Mitchell, the fellow who owned it, had an old river ferry he wanted to sell, down at the marina. It seems the old ferry was sort of a legend and a landmark in the area. It had been taking people back and forth across the Hudson since 1900. When the Bear Mountain Bridge was built in the '30's, the old boat was hauled up on land and there it sat. Mitchell sold it to the guys for $900 and told us he would sell it if we kept the same name for her. It was bad luck anyway to rename a boat, so the name stayed. We had all been in the Navy, except for Ollie Thompson. But, having been in the Navy didn't mean we could manage to maintain and run a wooden boat. There's an old saying that goes; 'There were three things that didn't belong on a yacht; a cow, a lawnmower and a Naval officer.', or something like that.

The skipper would be a fellow named Richie Manderville. 'Skipper' meaning we picked him to go down to Manhattan to get his Master's License. Someone had to because the boat was registered commercially and it was over 35' long.

The other fellows were Gil Fredrickson, Navy. Larry Lent, Navy. Andy Zsiday and Ollie Thompson, construction carpenter. Manderville, of course, had been in the Navy. And then there was me; professional Naval helmsman and adult beverage procurer. How could we possibly miss?

While Richie was getting his certification, the rest of us started getting the old girl back in shape. The *Caprice*'s hull was sound. It was oak, and 'clanged' when we hit it. It was clinker-built and had the sweetest prow you ever saw. The cutwater was just that; a very thin 'knife' that hardly moved the water when it slid through. The cut of the bow was the best feature of an otherwise functional ferry. She was low-slung, with a very low cabin which used up 28' of the boat's 36'. The cabin itself had seats arrayed along each side which we outfitted with cushions.

(I'm getting ahead of myself.) The entire boat, inside and out, had to be scraped down, sanded smooth, re-painted, re-varnished and literally brought back to life. Every weekend we were down at the Montrose Marina. We had a crowd every weekend. It seems the *Caprice* was a 'town character', sort of like the drunk who hung around outside of church on Sunday. All the other boat people had suggestions for us and of course, beer. Beer was our fuel. It kept us going, rain or shine.

There were mice in the engine compartment, bats in the cabin and all sorts of living things, things that had a carapace, in every corner. We had to re-caulk the entire hull. Thankfully, after all that time, we didn't have to replace any below-surface wood. The cabin consisted of windows, windows and more windows. Two or three had to be replaced but the rest were fine and went up and down smoothly. We re-covered the roof and then covered that with deck tread. We spent a lot of time on the roof, during break-time of course.

On the weekends, the women of the *Caprice*'s crew came down. All except my Janie. She didn't want to have anything to do with it. Andy's girlfriend(s) was (were) there. Gil's wife, Eileen, Ollie's girlfriend, Mary Lou, Larry Lent's girlfriend and Manderville's wife, Doris. It seemed as if a crowd was present all the time. As time went on, we started to make the newspaper. Stories started to appear about the little ferry. There was one story in the paper about a lady who rode it every day, during the period around the 1st World War. Another fellow rode it to visit his girlfriend in Stony Point. More and more people started showing up, some to just give us a hand.

A marine mechanic had to come down from Poughkeepsie to try and get our recalcitrant engine to turn over. That was expensive. Getting the head in working order was expensive also. We managed to find an old gas marine stove for our galley and got it working with bottled gas. Needless to say, I didn't go near that! Once we got the cushions in, some of us would sleep on the boat when the weekends came. I think Janie came down once, pooh-poohed the project and left.

The day finally came when we put her in the water! They announced it in the paper and there had to be a couple of hundred there. They had photographers there too. It seems that, back in 1783, Washington and Rochambeau, with their American and French troops, came down the King's Ferry Road and used ferries to cross the river to Stony Point, on their way to Yorktown and the meeting with Cornwallis which ended the Revolutionary War. They played the crossing in with the launching of the *Caprice* in the newspapers.

. . . So, here comes the big yellow crane with her slings. Our ungainly 'lady' gets lifted free from her earthly shackles and heads toward her element, about 60 yards away. The crane lines herself up on the rails over the water and the *Caprice* just hangs there, unmoving. Richie Manderville steps forward with a bottle of champagne, says a few words which I can't remember and cracks the bottle on the bow. we all rushed up

and poured beer on her prow as she was being lowered into the Hudson. What a moment! Everyone was clapping; boats were stopped outside the marina, cars were stopped on the causeway . . . It was great!

As soon as the slings went slack, we piled on, and on, and on. There were people shoulder to shoulder on the poor old *Caprice* when Gil Fredrickson yelled out:

'We're sinking!'

Then, just as fast, people were scurrying off, girls were falling down on the pier, everyone was shouting, what a mess. The pumps, naturally, decided not to work and it was a harrowing few minutes before the crane retrieved her out of the water. She was down by the stern when she started to come up. Water poured from her for a long time. It was our 'Steel Navy Inferior Caulking Job' which was the culprit.

She hung there in her harness, water seeping out of a dozen seams. The people started to drift away. The boats left and after about an hour, it was just the six of us. And the crane operator.

'I told you so!', said Janie. And her Mother. And her Sister. I think it was two days later, or three days, we started again at the marina. We managed to find some old river salts to show us how to do a better job with the caulking. We managed to get the pumps running perfectly and in a matter of weeks . . .

Here comes the crane! Back in the water but this time, no crowds. No newspapers and no bad luck. Well, almost . . . She still leaked, but the pumps worked, and the engine sprang to life in a cloud of white smoke! Leaking, sputtering and with a lot of beer on board, the *Caprice* tore away from the pier at about 1 knot . . . We cruised around the marina only, then came back to where the crane plucked her out again. More work.

The rest of that summer and the next, the *Caprice* was the belle of the ball. I think her top speed was 6 knots and that's just a guess. We'd be going up the river and a sleek cabin cruiser would pass us, complete with the pair of bikinis on the forecastle. The boat would turn around and come back up abeam to us. They would just stare and then the questions:

'What is that?'

'What's her name?'

'Where did you get that thing?'

'Need any help?'

Every marina we pulled in to, the people would come around. She was a throwback to another age and the modern-day stink-potters wanted to know all about her. They had their pictures taken with her. They posed at the wheel. With their kids. With their martini glasses. The Coast Guard would stop us and come aboard now and then, just to look at her. They were amazed.

It was a good party boat. We were sailors! Hadn't we survived the Italian attack on Pearl Harbor. Hadn't we beaten the Norwegians at Normandy? I remember Larry Lent telling Janie once, at the marina, that his first wife was named Jane. He said:

'I drowned her.' He didn't, but she was always afraid to come after that.

The old-timer served us well, but at the end, marina fees, the cost of upkeep and so on, forced the guys to sell her. Richie Manderville found an Honest-to-God Sunday school teacher in Haverstraw who wanted her. He sold the *Caprice* to him, but I don't remember for how much. The first summer the teacher had the boat, he was coming back into the Haverstraw Marina and hit an underwater spar. The *Caprice* went down in minutes. It didn't even get a mention in the paper. No one else was on the boat at the time and the teacher just swam away when it foundered.

Going back to the days of repair at the Montrose Marina, one of my jobs was the wheel. It was a beautiful wheel, inlaid with brass, six spokes. I shined it up to a sparkle and put a few coats of spar varnish on the wood. It was beautiful.

Richie Manderville borrowed some SCUBA gear and dove on the sunken *Caprice* the following summer. He managed to get just one thing off her. The wheel. He kept it in his house, on the wall, next to a picture of all the 'crew', standing on the roof of the *Caprice.* Richie Manderville died some years afterward. His wife, Doris, moved away, supposedly taking the wheel with her. Larry Lent died also. Liver problems. Ollie survived liver cancer and is doing fine now. Gil Fredrickson and Andy are gone also. They moved away.

So that leaves me. Down in my workshop at home, there's a ship's wheel hanging on the wall. It's the wheel from Barbara's Dad's boat they used to keep on the Connecticut River. All that's left is the wheel. It has burnished brass fittings and six spokes, fanning out to every point on the compass. Every now and then I look at that little wheel and think of the *Caprice.* I think of her churning upriver, her thin wake trailing astern. There's Gil, asleep in the giant cabin. Richie is at the wheel, a grin from ear to ear.

'Is that you behind those Foster Grant's, Richie?', I'd say. And the little ferry, her engine thrumming, would continue up the river, in the shadow of Dunderberg and we would be sailors once again.

jcm
7/5/12

My Own Line

I wish I'd written; 'This is the winter of our discontent',
or Kilmer's 'Trees'
or Catton's '. . . The Iron Brigade came swinging
up the hill into their last, great battle . . .'
        But I didn't.
        I never came close
        though I keep trying.
Their audience is vast
where mine is minimal.
        I write for a select few
        as most minor writers do . . .

I'm thinking, 'Love is here'
on this chilly Spring day
as sure as the amber stare of a squirrel
outside my window—
as sure as today's gray pulpy clouds
will give way to swirls of white—
as sure as I know there's a faraway beach,
waiting, waiting.

        'Love is here'.
        I can't write more importantly than that.
        I don't think I have to.

jcm
3/23/84

'USS FITCH . . . On Station!

I received a catalog in the mail the other day called 'Military Issue', all models, paintings, books, etc. On the cover for this month is a painting of a destroyer firing its 5-inch guns toward a beach. Normandy Beach. It's the USS *Fitch* (DD-462). It was one of five destroyers that cruised up and down Utah and Omaha Beach, peppering the German positions during the invasion.

The 4th (Ivy) Division landed on Utah on 6 June 1944, with the 8th Regiment of the 4th to the left. It was a bad position because of a perfectly situated German pillbox on a small hill which commanded the beach. Units of the 8th Regiment couldn't move and they were taking casualties. They noticed a *Gleaves*-class destroyer patrolling off the beach, about 2,000 yards out. The ship was contacted and it turned toward the beach, inching in until it slowly grounded, bow-first, about 400 yards out. Right away, the Germans started shooting at and hitting the destroyer's bow with their PAC-40 and MG-42's. The ship was the 1,600-ton USS *Fitch* (DD-462).

Right here is where the stories of the *Fitch* and the 4th Division combine for all time.

The *Fitch* couldn't use her 5-inch guns for fear of hitting some American infantrymen, so, as the soldiers watched, a lone Gunner's Mate, apparently, came walking up the port side of the ship. As the years went on, a coffee mug was added. Then, it was said that the sailor had his hands in the pockets of his foul weather jacket. All agreed afterward, that he nonchalantly climbed the ladder to the port side of the bridge where a 20 mm gun was mounted. They said he lifted a 60-round drum of ammunition, spun it into the receiver, unlocked the carriage pivot and started blasting away at the pillbox. The soldiers said the sailor walked the 20 mm cannon fire up the beach and right into the firing slits of the pillbox. In seconds, smoke and fire came out of the embrasure of the pillbox and it was silenced.

As the men of the 8th Regiment watched, the sailor locked the gun in position again, turned and went back down the ladder, disappearing through a hatch. The destroyer backed down and freed itself from the Normandy mud. The *Fitch* episode was mentioned in all the reports and in the personal report of the only General officer on the scene, Major General Theodore Roosevelt, Jr., son of President Theodore Roosevelt.

After the war, unit reunions were held every year by American Veterans, the same as they're held today. Whenever the 4th Infantry Division held its reunions, crew members of the USS *Fitch* were always invited. They would call the roll and the USS *Fitch* was called last. A crew member would always pipe up 'Present!', or, 'Here!'. As the years went on, the numbers of the veterans dwindled, as they do from every war. By 2004, all the original crew members of the USS *Fitch* were gone. They had made their final roll call. The *Fitch* itself was gone too. The Navy had sunk it intact in the Bahamas to be used as a makeshift sanctuary for fish. For the past six years, USS *Fitch*'s family members of the old crew have been invited to the 4th Division's reunions. When the roll is called, the USS *Fitch* is still called last. At that point, one of the family members stands and announces:

'USS *Fitch* (DD-462)! On station!'

Duty, Honor, Country
J.C. McGuire
Gunner's Mate Third Class
USN

7/2/12

The Fleet-Footed Toes of Time

Time doesn't move faster,
it's our legs that slow down.
        Your back spasms linger,
        you worry about smile lines
        and root canal
        and muscle tone . . .

I shudder at the sound
of a new bone creak,
heat loss from my dome
in Winter
and settling for a single
when I hit a double . . .

Time can be scary, a foreboding thing
to ruin a life or two.
        But what is time anyway?
        It's the period we spend together;
You can tell me of my bones creaking
and I can run my finger along
your new smile line.
At least we can do that together;
        for the rest of our time.

jcm
3/23/84

No Photographs, Please!

Most of my friends have put me down
as the Big Disappearing Act.
I've lost complete circles
and parts of others
but picked up new ones.

The new circles are smaller,
fewer,
but more meaningful.
I'm working harder to be more
meaningful to them
though I had a late start.
I hope I can create
my own importance
instead of points.
I hope someday I can go back
with an imaginary rake and scrape
the old circles for a few more.
I'll need all I can get when it's time
to fight off the oncoming end.

jcm
3/23/84

Anchors Aweigh, And Away, And Away . . .

Yesterday, Saturday, December 1st, 2012, the USS *Enterprise* (CVN-65) had reached the end of her journey. She was taken off the Active Vessels List by the Navy. Her tenure had ended after fifty-one years. The only ship that has been in commission longer than the *Enterprise* is the USS *Constitution* in Boston Harbor. This, unfortunately, is the way of all ships. They're taken off the high seas, then later on, sold to a scrapper for a fraction of what they cost. A few old sailors show up as the ship is being towed away, to solemnly wave their blue embroidered hats to their home for so many years. Maybe there'll be a reporter there. Maybe not. Some stories are swapped about the ship, then one by one, the few members of the crew file off to the parking lots. Another brick in the defensive wall of the United States is gone.

The U.S. Navy is 'down' to ten carriers now. New ones are being built. They will be the new *Gerald R. Ford* Class. CVN-80, when it's built, will be named the USS *Enterprise.* That news was announced by the Secretary of the Navy to a waiting crowd of carrier sailors and their families. That was only a tiny consolation to the behemoth carrier directly behind the SECNAV. There she was, all 90,000 tons of her, longer than three football fields and capable of carrying and launching 90 aircraft. There were only a few of her 4,400 crew still aboard as the painful and long shutdown began.

In 1959, my ship was in Norfolk, Virginia. Across the bay, that summer, they were going to have the keel-laying ceremony for the new nuclear-powered carrier, *Enterprise.* I took a ride over to the shipyard in Newport News to see it. I'd never seen a keel-laying ceremony before. The place was crawling with Navy brass with politicians and dignitaries every few feet. Down below, on the floor of the shipyard, where the carrier was to be built, I could see the keel, the spine of the new ship-to-be. I remember not believing something could be that big and still float.

CVN-65 was the eighth ship in the Navy to be named *Enterprise*. The first *Enterprise* was an armed sloop on Lake Champlain in 1775. It was part of a little fleet of ships, commanded by General Benedict Arnold, which fought the U.S. Navy's first battle, the Battle of Valcour Island. Every war the United States has been in after that, there has been a ship named *Enterprise*. In the early part of World War II, the USS *Enterprise* (CV-6) was in the Battle of Coral Sea. In that battle, the Navy lost a carrier, USS *Lexington*. With the loss of *Yorktown* at Midway and the *Hornet* at Santa Cruz in the Autumn of 1942, the *Enterprise* became the only operational U.S. carrier in the Pacific until the arrival of the new *Essex* (CV-9). The Imperial Japanese Navy at the time, had 28 aircraft carriers. The *Enterprise* went into battle after battle after that, sometime with yard workers aboard, still repairing the ship from the previous fight. In the Pacific war, the USS *Enterprise* held the line until *Essex*, leading 35 other new carriers came to bend back the Japanese until they broke.

CVN-65's first conflict was the Cuban Missile Crisis. She went out after the Russian missile-laden freighters as they tried to get to Cuba. I was out of the Navy then, but cheered the big carrier on when I listened to the news, much like cheering for Notre Dame going after Alabama in the Sugar Bowl. I always imagined the Russian sailors, looking up one day and seeing the big *Enterprise*, coming over the horizon, her two-stories high bow waves hunching up, and her planes, like angry bees, coming off her flight deck! No wonder the Russians turned and fled home.

Wherever she was asked to go, she went. Whatever the Navy asked her to do, she did. There must be thousands and thousands of sailors who served aboard her during the last 51 years, sad about hearing of her last trip home.

There was a Navy band in Norfolk the other day as the *Enterprise* tied up for the last time as an active ship. 'Anchors Aweigh' was probably played a dozen times for the assembled people, those stirring lyrics and tune that will never leave my head:

> 'Anchors aweigh, my boys, anchors aweigh.
> Farewell to college joys
> we sail at break of day-ay-ay-ay.
> Through our last night ashore,
> drink to the foam,
> until we meet again, here's
> wishing you a happy voyage home.'

When the ship, later on in 2013, is towed to Philadelphia where the breakers await, maybe there'll be a cabin cruiser or two following it. There'll probably be some old crew members aboard those boats, looking up at her slowly moving stern where those black letters, '*Enterprise*' will look back. Old stories will rattle back and forth among the old crew members and maybe, as the ship, pulled and pushed by her tugs finally slides ignominiously into her last berth in Philadelphia, the old sailors will retire to a nearby tavern for some adult beverages. The sun will probably be down by then, leaving the Delaware River just a gray ribbon in the dusk. The sailors, one by one will leave, each one waving toward their 'old friend'. Then, the light will rush away toward the west, leaving the giant ship alone, unlit, gray blending into the gray. And hopefully somewhere, somewhere along the East Coast, in some tiny gin mill with a sailor or two leaning on the end of the bar, someone recites the lines of John Masefield's 'Sea Fever'. I'd like to think that will happen. I'd like to think the amateur orator's diction will give Masefield's last stanza justice with:

> '. . . and all I ask is a merry yarn
> from a laughing fellow rover,
> and quiet sleep and a sweet dream
> when the long trick's over . . .'

jcm
12/2/12

The Speed of Sound

Sometimes I think
if I ran fast enough
and far enough
I'd lift from the ground
in a low level flight.
No grace or speed involved,
but more like a gooney bird
lifting awkwardly from a Pacific atoll . . .
All of us have wounds,
from good things turned bad
or bad things that turned worse.
We try to block them out,
keep them behind us,
flying ahead of the hunter's gun.
I'd like to make some of those short flights,
to fly ahead of some of the things
I never talk about.
Some of the wounds I have from words,
no one will ever hear about.
They have set me apart and alone
from everybody else.

jcm
3/28/84

Line After Line

From the very beginning,
from that very first key tap,
my last and final poem was near.
Each one was a step toward you
but only a step.

Trying to make you understand me
was always unfair.
You understood to a point—
Everything after that became lost.

I don't strive for that anymore.
I take things in stride.
Nothing bothers me.

I even lie to myself . . .
Maybe loving you would have been easier
if I loved myself a little more.

jcm
4/3/84

‘. . . And My Boat Is So Small’

It started somewhere south of Spanish Sahara, toward the east, toward the shimmering vastness of the Sahara Desert. It probably began as a dust devil, swirling for an instant, throwing sand out from its center. Hot air from the desert floor drove it westward as it rose and fell, resembling a small dust storm at times. It became an unstable depression, winding it's way into Mauritania and the Adrar Mountains. Following the sinking dry air on the western side of the mountains, it mixed with the deep humidity near the Mauritanian coast, riding the Saharan Air Layer out over the water until it found a cooler area of low pressure. Northeasterly winds started the heat layers turning in a clockwise motion as it made its way west. Right here, meteorologists would say later, it became a Tropical Wave.

Praia International Airport in the Cape Verde Islands was busy on that September day. Baggage handlers were winding their way through parked aircraft, driving their luggage cargoes toward the terminals. The equatorial sun was blazing overhead as it usually did on the tarmac, boiling the top of Poriforo's bald head. He was used to the heat, having been a handler at the airport for the past six years. It was a wide open area with not too many places for shade. As he drove his electric cart toward the gray doors of the Brasilia Air terminal, a blast of hotter than usual air engulfed him. He stopped the cart.

Other handlers looked toward the sky. They had felt it too. What was it? The air seemed to suck the oxygen from around them. Then, as soon as it came, it was gone. The men continued on with their work and quickly forgot about that odd hot air blast . . .

Once free of the islands, the tropical wave, pushed along by the prevailing winds continued it's clockwise motion, gathering strength from the relatively flat ocean surface and the heat. The following day, September 17, 1958, weather stations in the northern hemisphere would announce a new 'tropical depression', the eighth one of the season. The tiny Saharan dust devil had now grown to a 45 miles per hour swirl, one hundred and fifty miles across, checkered with thunder and lightning and growing whitecaps. It was too far away to worry about, the meteorologists said, but they gave it a name anyway.

Helene . . .

Norfolk Naval Base was the biggest naval base on the east coast of the United States. In 1958 the Chesapeake Bay Bridge-Tunnel hadn't been built yet. To get from Princess Anne County to Norfolk, one had to take the Kiptopeke Ferry. It was a well-protected anchorage and port but when hurricane season arrived every year, the smaller ships would clear out and run for cover to some other port, out of the hurricane's path.

As a ship would come into port, they would pass the carrier piers. At times, there would be three, maybe four aircraft carriers in port at one time. That was the 'brown shoe' Navy, floating cities, bunk lights, air conditioning and escalators. Then came the cruiser piers. The cruisers were the 'Limo Navy'. We would watch them painting the sides of their ships in whites! 'steamer' whites but white uniform nonetheless. Admirals loved to have cruisers as their flagships. They were the spit-and-polish Navy, the carriers and cruisers. They didn't bother with us.

'Us', I liked to think, was the rest of the Navy, the subs, fleet tugs, oilers and logistic ships. Most of all, at least to me, the majority of the 'us' were the destroyers. The Tin-Can Navy. The destroyer was a ship in the true sense. There were few amenities if any. There seemed to be a magazine full of explosives wherever you looked and your bunk seemed to be situated right above it. The magazines were a must because of the abundance of guns. There were all sorts of weapons and weapon-systems on board. The destroyer was a fighter. I looked on the tin can as an armed yacht with a college education. The crews of the destroyers loved their ships and the ships, oddly enough, loved them back. If you took care of your ship, she would take care of you.

A good mile or so from the shiny cruisers, the destroyers were berthed. On any given day in Norfolk, the destroyers numbered twenty, twenty-five or more.

The *Fletcher* Class destroyers were the true greyhounds, the sea wolves. They were WWII craft and would soon be phased out and decommissioned, but right then, in 1958, they were the lightweight champions of the fleet. *Fletcher*'s like the USS *Beale, Bearrs* and *Bache* were the sleekest ships I've ever seen. The USS *The Sullivans* (DD-537) was also a member of the *Fletcher* Class. She was named after the five brothers who went down with the light cruiser, *Juneau* at Guadalcanal in 1942.

There were other destroyers at Norfolk; *Gearing* Class and two new *Forrest Sherman*'s. We called those the '900' Class.

Then, way near the end of the piers, tucked in behind the big tenders, were the 'small boys', the poor man's destroyers. The Destroyer Escorts. When they were developed in the beginning of WWII, the need for the small ship was paramount. The Europe-bound convoys were being decimated by the German submarine wolf packs and protection for the cargo ships was needed. Enter the Destroyer Escort.

The DE was a smaller version of a destroyer. It was 40' shorter and 1500 tons, 750 tons lighter than a DD, destroyer. The diesel and slower version DE was recruited for convoy protection, while the oil-fired geared turbine DE was faster and supplemented the bigger destroyers of the fleet.

On that September day back in 1958, moored behind the destroyer tender *Sierra*, were four such geared turbine *John C. Butler* Class destroyer escorts. They were side-by-side, all wearing the crest of Destroyer Division 21, DESDIV21, on their single stack. The furthest outboard ship was USS *Tabberer* (DE-418), alongside the USS *Blackwood* (DE-219). Second from the pier was USS *Tweedy* (DE-352). Moored next to the pier with all the lifelines of steam, electric power and water for herself and the other three ships was the USS *Robert F. Keller* (DE-419). My ship.

The *Keller* was a good sailer and a decorated veteran of WWII. She had been through the bad storm near the end of the Pacific War, the storm they called 'Halsey's Typhoon', the same storm in which the U.S. Navy lost four destroyers and their crews. Very few survivors were picked up, the *Keller* herself, rescuing only one man. The destroyer escort's role back in 1958 consisted of picket duty up and down the East Coast, keeping an eye out for Russian submarines on patrol. When not on picket duty, the ships would ferry Naval Reservists on two-week cruises down to the Caribbean.

Every summer, during hurricane season, at Navy bases up and down the East Coast, the bigger ships battened down the hatches, so to speak, while the smaller ships made a beeline for the open sea. The thinking was, bigger ships could ride out a storm in port but the smaller ships would just get knocked around, beaten senseless against the pier. The bigger ships had protection from just their weight and the insertion of 'camels', sort of long, double-thick telephone pole-shaped 'shock absorbers' between their hulls and the piers. Destroyers, not having an ounce of armour and thin-sided, were subject to their side plates changing shape from a pier or pilings pressing in or the crushing weight of a rogue wave. The resulting rib exposure gave the 'greyhounds' a hungry-dog look.

All four DE's of DESDIV21, that September, were getting ready for a cruise to Bermuda. The talk then, was, would we start our cruise early because of the tropical storm down south or not? We'd seen it before because the storm brewing east of the Leewards was the eighth one that summer. We had plenty of time because the storm, named Helene, was up to 50 miles per hour and just northwest of Dominica and the British Virgin Islands. Chances were, it would hit the east coast of Florida as a huge rainstorm with a little wind. It had happened before during the summer. No one was worried. It was our first miscalculation.

By September 24th, the usual traffic around the destroyer piers had doubled, then tripled. Our division was leaving soon. The hurricane, which is what it was now, had reached 76 miles per hour in wind power and had moved up the coast without coming ashore. It was 80 miles off the coast of South Carolina and heading toward landfall in North Carolina. It was too close for comfort, so the Navy was sending us to Bermuda early. Supply trucks were lining up on the pier and the feeder lines were being disconnected one by one. The dozen telephone booths on the pier were filled with men calling home. All non-essential gear on all the ships was being piled up on the pier; boxes and crates of things, even a canoe. I can remember a German Shepherd tied to a cleat, barking non-stop. Signal flags on the USS *Sierra*, a destroyer tender forward of us, the flagship of SOPA (Senior Officer Present Afloat) were being hoisted and dropped continuously but I don't think anyone paid attention. The *Sierra*, all 19,000 tons of her, was staying put in Norfolk, but she was sending her 'children' out into the maelstrom. Clumps of sailors lined the *Sierra*'s rail, watching the proceedings down below, probably glad they weren't going with us.

That evening, I was on the bridge lashing equipment down and securing lock bars on the chart drawers of the Navigator's table, when the door of the Captain's sea cabin across the passageway opened. There he was . . .

Edward J. Steffen, Lieutenant Commander, USN. Skipper of the *R.F. Keller*. Unsmiling, stern-faced, square-jawed, unblinking ice-blue eyes, poker-faced and looking straight at me.

'Hello, Captain.', I said. No answer. He just stared. I could say that he was 'all business' except for the fact he was wearing khaki shorts, shower clogs and a white T-shirt which read 'OHIO U.' But his LCDR hat, perched on his head, was squared away and straight as an arrow. From the neck up he reminded me of Steve Mc Queen. During WWII, he was in the Pacific, in the U.D.T., Underwater Demolition Teams, the forerunner of today's Navy SEALs. The gold braid on his officer's hat had taken on a green patina and he had most likely earned it.

I should interject here; there were three men aboard the *Keller* who, without any malice aforethought, seemed to give Captain Steffen a rough time. I never knew how old the Skipper was, but I'm sure some of his white hair came from us. There was Ron Bramblett, a Sonarman from Hannibal, Missouri. The second man was Doug Drabin, the honest-to-God best Helmsman in the Navy. The third man was a Quartermaster-soon-to-be-Gunner's Mate. That would be me. The three of us weren't bad people by any stretch of the imagination, but we liked to have fun, ashore and on board. It was peacetime and our only 'enemy' (they told us) was the Russian Bear. It seemed every time we turned around, the three of us, singly or together, would be up in front of him for Captain's Mast. 'Mast' was sort of a shipboard court where punishment for infractions was dealt out. Between the three of us, Bramblett was the least offensive to Captain Steffen. Ron turned out to be our 'ringleader'.

Ron Bramblett and Me 1958

Doug Drabin and Me 1958

Once, my friend, Ollie Thompson, sent me a pair of his sister's panties. The *Keller* was in Washington, D.C. and we were leaving for Cuba the following morning. That night, I climbed to the top of the mainmast and hung the panties on the top of the surface search radar net. They weren't detected by any of the officers until we were somewhere off the coast of Georgia. When the Captain went out on the wing of the bridge and looked up, the rest of us were down on the fantail, watching. He stared at the fluttering panties for what seemed like a long time. Then, he did a slow turn and looked straight at me! He knew I had hung them. I don't know how, but he knew. Nothing ever happened to me but they were taken down immediately. I never saw the man smile. His face could've been on Mount Rushmore. Years later, however, I knew I had loved the man. He was a good skipper.

We worked through most of the night with our Executive Officer, Lieutenant Bartlett, riding herd on us. In the morning it was hot, very hot. It was a super-humid day that only seemed to crop up around the Tidewater area now and then in the summer. Captain Steffen had the word passed over the 1MC that the uniform for leaving port would be dungarees and T-shirts! We cheered. We didn't have air-conditioning like the carriers and cruisers so this was an early Christmas present.

Just before 0800, the destroyers started backing down from their piers. One by one, with whistles blowing, yard workers on the pier waving and the rails on the bigger ships manned with spectators, the spectacle ran it's course. Out into the channel they streamed, gray-brown water billowing up at their sterns as the twin screws stopped, then churned forward, sending the tin cans lurching ahead to the open sea and their various destinations.

Low on the totem pole, finally it was DESDIV21's turn. I was at my usual post, the quartermaster's desk with the daily log. Doug Drabin, our helmsman extraordinaire, was the Sea Detail Helmsman and Ron Bramblett was in the sonar shack at the rear of the bridge. We watched as the *Tabberer* backed down. We would be the last to leave. Just then, a signalman came onto the bridge.

'Captain! Signal from *Sierra*!' Captain Steffen ignored him. The signalman held out the paper but Steffen wouldn't look at him. The Skipper knew what it was. We all found out later on, it was a message from SOPA, wanting to know the reason for *Keller* not adhering to the Uniform Of The Day. The Skipper chose to ignore it. All the other destroyer crews wore their whites leaving port. We had our T-shirts. Good for you, Skip!

'Single up all lines!', Bartlett bawled from the bridge wing. 'Starboard back one/third', and the annunciator man yanked the brass handles back. 'Let go all lines!', and the line handlers on the pier dropped the mooring lines from the bollards and they were hauled aboard. We swung out into the channel, the very last ship to leave Norfolk.

'All ahead two/thirds! Come right to 010!', said Mr. Bartlett. We felt the screws stop in reverse, hesitate, then rumble forward, pushed by the 12,000 horsepower of the geared turbines. We were on our way, hopefully leaving voracious Helene behind, in her vain search for *Sierra*'s children.

The long easy swells started just off Little Creek, as we passed a fleet tug to port. Our signalman was finishing up 'talking' with the tug's signalman by morse light when I came walking up.

'C U', the signalman flashed. The tug answered: 'C U 2'.

'I give up, Tom.', I said. The signalman, Tommy Tetreault, told me he sent 'see you' and his buddy on the tug sent 'see you too'. The fleet tug was already peeling away to the north, on it's way to New York, trying to put as much distance between herself and the hurricane. The rest of DESDIV21 were off toward the east with the *Keller* catching up. There was a chill in the air and the sky to the south was a flat gray. The last we'd heard, Helene was barreling toward the North Carolina coast with the Outer Banks in it's sights.

Soon, we were just out of sight of land when the worst news of all was transmitted to the ship, and our tiny radio shack all of a sudden, became the center of attention.

> ". . . A destroyer is a lovely ship, probably the nicest fighting ship of all. Battleships are a little like steel cities or great factories of destruction. Aircraft carriers are floating flying fields. Even cruisers are big pieces of machinery, but a destroyer is all boat. In the beautiful clean lines of her, in her speed and roughness, in her curious gallantry, she is completely a ship in the old sense."
>
> John Steinbeck

By the time I got my hands on the message it was dog-eared to death. Radioman Bill Bedell was at the console in the radio shack and the message was alongside him. I picked it up. From what I can remember, it read:

> 'From: DESLANT NORFOLK
> To: DESDIV21—NWMU, (DE call letters) NTIO, NTZB, NKLR-(us) trop storm 80 kts—hdg chg 010 ENE. speed 25 kts"

There was more, but that was all I needed to read. 'Has the bridge seen this?', I asked Bedell. He nodded. Helene, fickle Helene had changed course almost opposite to what she had been heading. The storm had been 60 miles off the North Carolina coast and heading almost due west, when the speed picked up to Category One and it changed course to almost due east. Helene was heading for us. Bedell and I looked at each other.

'A little wind, Bill?', I said to him. He turned back to his console.

I walked out onto the bridge. John Brockman was at the wheel. The Captain and Mr. Bartlett were in conference out on the port wing. Charlie Rex was at the Quartermaster's desk.

'We're in for it, Mack.', Rex said to me. I nodded. There was no way we could outrun it. This was to be my first hurricane at sea. Before I left the Navy in 1961, I would be in two hurricanes. Looking back, it was two too many. I went out on the starboard wing. No wind which meant we were steaming with whatever wind there was, probably 15 knots. The sun had disappeared, leaving different shades of gray; water, sky, clouds and us. Off to starboard, about a mile, another DE was positioned, her staccato morse light blinking. The four DE's of DESDIV21 were steaming abreast, a mile or more apart. We were 600 miles from the U.S. Navy seaplane base in Bermuda and Helene was coming.

The *Keller* was a frenzy of activity. Down in the forward and after magazines, 5" projectiles and powder cans were being strapped to their bulkheads and cradles. The 40mm magazines, hedgehog projectiles and depth charges were being tightened down also. All normally opened lockers were being locked up. The mess decks were securing tables and benches and preparing sandwiches and pots of slumgullion for later. Slumgullion was a stew-soup made from every conceivable edible the cooks could find. It was always tasty, yet none of us ever knew what was in it. I'd been in storms before and if I found one thing true, no matter how much things were secured, the cacophony of everything breaking and tearing loose was just a matter of time. I had never, however, been in a hurricane at sea. We all had an education coming, and it was coming up from the southwest, faster than we could steam and packing winds so far, of 100 mph. Helene was searching for *Sierra*'s children.

A little while later I happened to be on the mess decks when the *Keller* rose in the air suddenly, hung there for an instant then dropped down with a crash which buckled the knees of everyone around me. It was the first of many swells that would torment us from then on. We all looked at one another. Just then water came cascading down the mess deck ladders and flooded the deck. A wave had apparently come through the midship hatches topside . . . . And so it began.

I went topside to witness the dramatic sea change. Helene was reaching out for us. The wind had picked up considerably and significant waves were coming in from every direction. We didn't know how big the hurricane was, where the fringes of it reached to, but we were being hit with 80 mile per hour winds. Down below in the sleeping compartments, things were starting to come apart. Already, the bunks were being filled by their inhabitants, piles of life jackets littered the deck and most conversations had ended. My compartment was under the fantail and directly under the after 5" gun. The rising and dropping of the ship was more pronounced here, at least 150 feet from the fulcrum of amidships. All non-essential crew had already hit their bunks, some of them chaining themselves in. Some already had life jackets on. I didn't want to stay in our sleeping compartment I wanted to get to the bridge but my turn at the wheel wasn't until the late afternoon. Doug's bunk was empty. He could be at the wheel but I didn't know. I made my way forward, toward the center of the ship where the pitching and yawing was lessened, listening to the crashing of equipment throughout the *Keller*.

Word was passed over the 1MC to stand clear of the weather decks. If we went topside, out on deck, we ran the chance of being swept away like chin whiskers in front of a razor. Noises began which I'd never heard before. The sound of the side plates changing shape as waves slammed into them was a rending sort of screech. The yelling of crewmen as something nearby fell over. But the sound that will stay with me for the rest of my days was the sound of the twin screws coming out of the water. It sounded as if the stern was about to shake itself free from the rest of the ship. It was a metallic groaning, the screws uncomfortable without the pressure of water, shaking the entire skin of the ship, then stopping as the stern dropped down again. In little more than an hour, the sea had turned into a hunting thing, seemingly reaching out for us. 'We were as long as a football field', I would tell people. All of a sudden, the 300 feet of the ship didn't seem so big after all. We were being tossed about like a rag doll. I had to get to the bridge. I had to know what was going on.

Climbing the interior ladder was an experience. Not knowing when the ship would lurch required both hands and both feet. Usually we went up and down the ladders like monkeys but it was different now.

The bridge was a mess. Brockman was at the wheel, but he was sick. He was just hanging on. Captain Steffen was entwined in the flying bridge ladder, locked in place. Charlie Rex, the quartermaster was gone, his desk empty. The lookouts had been called in and sent below. Through the string of portholes in front of the wheel, it was a scene of anger.

The only color was a dark, dark gray. There was a sun somewhere but not here. Instead, the sky seemed backlit and showed as yellowish-gray, outlining heavy swells coming in from the port quarter forming mountains of water. The wind had many notes in its chorus, deep and sorrowful as if the whole world was in pain. There was hardly any surface at all, just clouds of spray, spume and rain whipping across everything, obliterating any chance of a line between the sky and the sea. If Hell had an ocean, I thought, this was it.

I glanced at the annunciator. We were making turns for 10 knots. Steffen was keeping her bow into the parade of swells. Every time the bow went up, it kept going up then hung for a moment before falling at a dizzying speed downward. As the ship hung, I could see hands reaching out for something to hold on to, to keep from pitching forward as she dropped. Every time the ship nosed down, I noticed, Brockman leaned against the wheel, and stayed leaning as the ship rose again.

John was slate-gray and not long for the upright world. I was standing inside the chartroom hatch, not really on duty yet, watching. Mr. Bartlett went over to the wheel and said to Brockman:

'Steady on 350, not 340! Come right to 350, Damn it!' But Brockman had reached the end. He was finished. I was due on the bridge to steer in about two hours, but I stepped over the combing onto the wet bridge deck. Steffen looked at me, expressionless.

'Mc Guire!', Mr. Bartlett bellowed. 'Take the wheel. Brockman, get outta here!' John, more or less fell away from the wooden grating and staggered through the hatch leading down past the radar room. The next time I would see John Brockman would be three days from then.

The wheel was wet as I gripped it. I hoped it was sea water and not Brockman's lunch. I yelled over my shoulder toward the Captain:

'I've got the wheel! Bearing three-five-zero!' To my left, Bartlett said:

'That's a late news bulletin.' No one liked Bartlett.

It didn't take much for the day to disappear, light-wise. The sun could never fight its way through the clouds and rain, so the daytime sort of drifted away. The last thing we saw was the foam being blown off the tops of the tall waves as if a giant were blowing the suds from his beer mug. Now we had to rely on radar to give us the height and direction of the incoming waves. In a hurricane, it's a clock-wise, swirling motion with the wave and wind direction changing constantly. The heavy seas would always come in from the north or northeast, sometimes east. The least of it would be from astern in our case now. It had just darkened up a bit when the *Blackwood* called over the GERTRUDE, the ship-to-ship communication net, used mainly for anti-submarine warfare.

Four men had been swept off the deck of that ship! They had gone out, against orders, to take pictures before the light went away. They were gone. No one could turn back and try to retrieve them. It would've been suicide. They could only survive for a few minutes in those seas.

'What the hell were they doing?' Bartlett yelled, 'What the hell . . . . ', and his voice trailed off. Captain Steffen got on the GERTRUDE and spoke with the Captain of the *Blackwood.* I couldn't hear what he said. No one spoke after that except for the low monotone of Steffen.

'Left a bit . . . Right, right . . . steady on 355.'

'Aye, Sir!' I must've spouted 200 'Aye, Sir's!' that night.

(My Father, back in Peekskill the following day, saw in the New York Daily News that four men were lost from a destroyer escort on their way through hurricane Helene. He buried the paper in the kitchen garbage so my Mother wouldn't see it.)

The night wore on, the seas and the wind intensifying if that was possible. The radarman (I forget his name) would stick his head out of the hatch and yell toward Steffen:

'45-footer, bearing 345 degrees, one mile!' Instantly, Steffen would say to me:

'Come left, 345.'

'345, aye!', and I would spin the big wooden and brass wheel left. A minute later;

'Steady on 345, Sir!'

It went on like that, over and over again, for hours. We would wait and brace for the wave. Sometimes it would hit and other times it would roll by but we could almost 'feel' it, out there somewhere.

The biggest wave I ever saw was a 78-footer, years later, but my ship then, weighed 16,000 tons, not 1,500. It didn't matter how big the ship happened to be. Those waves looked like the end of the world coming straight at us.

There was no let-up, no respite in the storm. Our anemometer, the wind gauge read 100 miles per hour not too long after sunset. During the night, it reached 135 but we were too busy to notice. Things started to disappear also. The tampion, the plug for the 5" gun on the forecastle was forced out and water was cascading down the barrel, through the breech and onto the deck of the mount. It would find its way to the brass exit scuppers and spew out onto the deck. Lots of work for the gunners would follow. Our air search radar above us on the mainmast was torn loose and lost over the side. So was our searchlight on the stack. Stanchions were ripped off like matchsticks and the whaleboat was starting to take a strain on the steel cable securing it to the davits, by filling up with water every time we heeled over to port.

If we went over too far, water would enter the smokestack and work it's way down to the boilers, extinguishing the fires. We would slide into a trough and we would be goners, so we couldn't let that happen. All eyes had been on the list gauge on the after bulkhead. We watched it swing back and forth and finally we stopped looking at it. I noticed Bartlett was in the corner, sitting on a pile of life jackets, sick. It wasn't too long before he left the bridge, mumbling something to the Captain. It was just Ed Steffen and Florence and Tommy's boy. Without saying anything, the Captain assumed control of the annunciator, if a change of speed was needed.

It wasn't long after Bartlett had gone below, that Captain Steffen came over and hung a life jacket on one of the annunciator arms next to me! Uh-oh! I turned to watch him walk away back to his ladder perch. He had put on one of the orange life jackets.

In a short while, radar called out, for what seemed like the 100th time:

'Captain! . . . 60 feet! Bearing 010! Two miles!'

They that go down to the sea in ships, that do business in great waters;
These see the works of the Lord, and his wonders in the deep.
For he commandeth, and raiseth the stormy
wind which lifted up the waves thereof,
they mount up to the heaven,
they go down again to
the depths . . .

-Psalm 107:23-26—

'Fine. Fine.', Steffen said and came up alongside me at the annunciator. 'Brace for this one.', he said.

'Yes, Sir.', was all I could get out. Forward of us was just blackness and the wailing wind. Somewhere on the bridge, the Captain had picked up a pair of sound-powered phones. He called the engine room for the Chief Engineer to warn him of the wave. This was the biggest one so far.

He let the phones dangle and grabbed for the brass arms of the annunciator. The compass hung on 010. We were ready. I hoped so because just then the bow started to rise. It rose and hung, as if on the edge of a shelf . . . then dropped. Before we could try and cushion the crash with our feet, the big wave struck. All the air was sucked out of the bridge and we instinctively ducked. The portholes squirted water for an instant as the green water enveloped everything forward of us and the bridge too. Then, as if someone had placed a hand grenade outside the porthole in front of us, the brass ring and glass blew inward, a thick jet of salt water hitting the two of us square!

It was like being punched in the face with a fire hose. My left eyelid had curled under and now was scraping my cornea. I ended up on the deck behind me, on my back. Steffen had been knocked down too and he was starting to sit upright. The red glow of the night lights showed each of us that the other had a bloody nose. Water was everywhere, sloshing over our legs and sending the wooden grate I had been standing on, to the starboard side of the bridge. I scrambled to my feet and grabbed the wheel. We were turning to starboard slowly, starting to fall away into a trough. We couldn't do that. Already the deck had canted to the right as the *Keller* yawed. I spun the wheel to port just as Steffen called:

'Hard a-port! Hard a-port!' We stayed where we were, steering control almost gone. The bow rose again, then settled. We were nudging past 030 and I started to wonder if we were ever going to come left again. Steffen was yelling into the voice trumpet to the engine room. His sound-powered phone was gone.

I had the wheel all the way over to left rudder, right to the stops. Was this it, I thought? Is this all we were going to have in this life, stuck in a trough, waiting for the end? I thought of the Brown Shipyards in Houston, the people who built the *Keller*. I wondered if they foresaw any of this? I was stretched to the right side, my legs lying along the deck, when Steffen reached the annunciator. He rang for All Back Full on the port screw and All Ahead Full on the starboard, yelling into the voice trumpet at the same time. We slowed for too long, it seemed, water pouring in through the starboard wing hatch as the ship staggered. If I let go of the wheel I would slide down the deck, so I hung on for dear life.

The ship vibrated, gained a few degrees to upright, then slid down again. Another wave came up and over the port wing and into the bridge space. This, I thought, will not sit well with my family. I couldn't stand. I had no strength in my legs.

'She's coming up!', Steffen yelled. I could feel the deck vibrate like a jackhammer as the port screw started backing in reverse. The starboard screw, at All Ahead Full, bit into the trough and the *Keller* righted a few more degrees. Steffen was holding onto the annunciator.

'Come on! Come on, good girl!', he called out.

We were still listing at 15 degrees when the Captain said: 'Amidships!' I complied, bringing the wheel around to zero.

'Amidships, Aye!', I called out, as the *Keller* returned almost to centerline, at the same time rising up on another swell. Steffen waited until the last minute then rang for All Ahead Two/Thirds on both screws. We hesitated, waiting for the surge. When it came, the Captain said:

'Come to 010, Mack.'

Mack? Did Steffen call me 'Mack'?

'010, Aye!' and I brought the wheel right, to the proper course. The ship, during all it's contortions, had sounded like a moving van on a bumpy road. Noises I never heard before were filling the air between the sound of the wind. Lieutenant Hogan, the Gunnery

Officer, appeared in the hatchway. He looked sick too. He was panting heavily when the Captain looked up.

'We've lost the whaleboat, Sir.'

'Damn!', exclaimed Steffen.

Hogan continued: 'The port stern rack is gone, with all the depth charges. There's some damage to the K-guns but I can't get to them, Sir.'

'Thank you, Mr. Hogan.', Steffen said. He was slumped against his raised chair over on the starboard side of the bridge. He was sick. It seemed the whole ship was sick but me. I was never seasick, ever. Not even close. The ocean would drop the ship on me before I ever became seasick. I made a rough guess when we finally reached Bermuda, only four out of one hundred and twelve men did not get seasick. I was one of them. The Captain, however, had just about had it. It didn't stop him at all. He stayed on the bridge all night. Just he and I. Occasionally another officer would come up. He and the Captain would talk, then the other officer would leave, on some sort of errand. I found out later, Steffen had sent Mr. Miller to get another helmsman to relieve me but there were none to be had. They were all sick.

The *Keller* was being hammered unmercifully by King Neptune, but he never forced us into another trough, thanks to the Captain. It became a routine; first, up one side of a swell, tipping then sliding down the other side, hoping a wave's punch wasn't in between. I was soaked. One of my shoes was gone and my waterproof Zodiac watch my Father had bought me the day before I went into the Navy, was still working. My miraculous medal, miraculously, was still around my neck. We had emergency lighting from battle lanterns on the bridge and I could see the life jackets sliding aimlessly around.

'Captain?', I heard, and turned. It was Alapinario Kelly, the Filipino mess steward who handled the officers wardroom. He looked like a drowned rat and very nervous.

'Captain?', he said again. Steffen, half in his chair, half out, looked up. 'Can I get you anything?', Kelly asked again.

Right here I should explain why I can remember the name of the Filipino mess steward, especially one who only dealt with the Officer's Wardroom. Alapinario Kelly was unique on the *Keller*. Alapinario Kelly had a tail.

Right at the base of his coccyx bone, Kelly had a four-inch appendage. A tail. Every new member of the crew was marched up to Officer's Country where Kelly would drop his pants to show the 'newbie' his tail. No one knew why he had one, but there it was, in living color . . .

'Get this man whatever he wants!', rasped Steffen and Kelly looked at me. He had a terrified look on his face, hoping I wouldn't ask for too much because there was really nothing to be had. The wind almost took Kelly down the ladder again and he hung on with both hands, all the time looking at me.

'Got any coffee, Kelly?', I asked. He nodded and disappeared down the ladder again.

Radar was still singing out the directions of incoming waves and we kept making slight course changes, all the time the ship's hull ringing with the tossing about of broken equipment. Ensign Roberson arrived on the bridge reporting all magazines secure and no loose ordnance. Five-inch rounds weighed 55 pounds each and their cartridge shells, loaded with powder, weighed 27 pounds. The depth charges we lost weighed 350 pounds each and we didn't know what the 27-foot whaleboat weighed when it finally broke loose because it was full of water and sea water weighed one ton per cubic yard. I figured, one of those monstrous waves must've weighed about as much as Philadelphia. There was a lot of weight being pushed and battered around. I was wondering again about the Brown Shipyard in Houston and how well the welders laid the seams of my ship in. All this twisting and turning must've taken a toll on the 14 year-old hull. The *Keller* had already been in a typhoon in 1944 where four destroyers were lost. There were only about 70 survivors out of 1300 men. The other three ships in our formation, or what was left of it, were heard on the GERTRUDE, their crackling voices coming out of the speakers.

Kelly arrived back with a mug of semi-warm coffee. He had his thumb in the mug as he handed it to me. He handed Captain Steffen as silver thermos bottle, presumably with coffee inside. Kelly scurried down the ladder before anyone asked him for something else.

For the rest of the night the only sound out of the Captain was for a course change. That, and the occasional visit to the starboard wing to vomit. It was becoming harder and harder to concentrate on the compass. With the swinging of the binnacle, the sloshing of the water back and forth and the jarring of the hull, it almost lulled me to sleep, and still the night wore on.

Somewhere toward morning, I can't remember the time, we saw a light gray line to the east. It was the next day arriving. We were on course 015 and 020, back and forth. The false horizon was lumpy and bumpy but it was a horizon nonetheless. The waves were still house-high but they were fewer and far between. Helene had none too quietly, slid off to the northeast. We would make it to Bermuda. The other three ships were still chirping but a pall had closed over the day with the loss of the four men on the *Blackwood*. Steffen called for 12 knots. Mr. Miller, looking fine, had the annunciator. He had crisp khakis on and I wondered where he managed to get them. Mr. Miller, as I recall, had also refused to look at Alapinario's tail when he first came aboard.

There was a commotion behind me and the happy face of of T. Douglas Drabin confronted me. He looked gray and drawn, but he was here.

'Drabin reporting for duty, Captain!', Doug said. As soon as he said it, without any hesitation, Steffen said:

'Mc Guire. Get below. You're off duty.'

Stepping away from the wheel, I said to Doug:

'Course 020.' Then, under my breath; 'I'm whipped.'

'I have the helm. Course 020, Sir!', said Drabin, and the watch had been relieved. I walked the few feet to the ladder leading to the 01 level and started down. Before I got down to the level of the bridge deck, I turned on the ladder. Captain Steffen was watching me. Our eyes met. I almost said, 'Good job, Skipper!', but I didn't. When he turned his eyes away, I continued down.

At that time, I weighed 160 pounds. I had a body ache that weighed 160 pounds exactly. I was trying to figure out what to do first, visit the head or crash. I made my way through the shambles, the mayhem that once was a sharp destroyer escort. It was a mess now. Everything from broken glass, clothes and the usual splashes of semi-digested food littered the passageways and bulkheads. It was like picking my way through a minefield. Everyone was in a daze. We were still on the carnival ride of the storm but much less so. I made my way into my sleeping compartment under the fantail. It was a junkyard. I couldn't see the deck for the clothes and broken lockers.

Everything was soaked. My rack was missing the mattress so I found a pile of life jackets and pea coats in the corner. I flopped down on that. I had no thoughts in my head, and having none of those impediments to sleep, that's what I did.

"... 'Shipmate' is an honorable word that is earned, not given. Being called a shipmate is the highest compliment one can earn in this life. Shipmate is a word equal to none in the English language. It is filled with courage, love, hate, duty, honor and country. It is a bond forged in storms, battles, adversity and victory, and is equalled only by a man's love for his wife and family. It is formed at sea in a ship with a captain of character who causes a 'can-do' spirit to pass down the line: captain to executive officer to junior officers, chiefs, petty officers and crew. Weak links are cut loose and replaced quickly and cleanly without fanfare by a wise captain. We were lucky. Everything happened like a well-written script, that is, the good ship, the good crew, and a bonding forged so strong it can be broken only by the death of the last shipmate. This bond, this ship and our great good luck are the reasons we survived and won."

E.J. Jernigan

A search was taken up for the four missing crew members of the *Blackwood.* PBY's and PBM's from Bermuda and Norfolk did pattern searches to no avail. They were never found. When Helene subsided, the *Blackwood* requested time to go back and look for her missing men but they were told to proceed to Bermuda. All four destroyer escorts arrived at the U.S. seaplane base on the west side of Bermuda at the same time. All of *Sierra*'s children had made the crossing. The other three ships looked beaten down also. The *Tabberer* had lost her air search radar net too. The *Tweedy*'s stack was canted. We were missing half our topside gear. Our Hedgehog anti-sub weapon on the forecastle was smashed. The cover was gone and the launchers were askew. We had two out of eight K-guns, depth charge-firing weapons, missing their cradles. Our lifelines and stanchions were a mass of spaghetti. We'd lost two Kirby rafts plus our whaleboat. The one-inch steel cable hung limply from the davits, frayed like thread. Big patches of paint were gone on various points on the hull and superstructure. Rust had already started to form. All canvas covers were missing and two out of four antennae were gone.

The mess decks were operational again and we ate like a band of carnivores. There were just sandwiches and the dependable slumgullion stew-soup, but we didn't care. There were a few of us, the usual bunch, who searched for some loose 'Torpecker' but we couldn't find any. I don't think there was a ship in the Navy that didn't have a few mason jars of Torpecker.

Ah, Torpecker . . . This was a concoction developed long before any of us joined the Navy. No one knew where it had come from. Some say it went all the way back to the 1890's, but I tend to think Torpecker came about out of necessity, when it was found that torpedoes ran on fuel. Denatured-alcohol fuel.

Nowadays, torpedoes run electrically. They're homing devices now, shorter and deadlier. For almost a century, the 18 and 24-inch torpedoes ran on fuel to reach their target. The fuel was loaded with additives and impurities and it fell to the sailors of the time, to turn the needed fuel into the famous 'Torpecker'. Our torpedoes and two torpedo launchers amidships had been taken off years ago but for some reason, we still had an abundance of torpedo fuel.

A new batch of Torpecker would materialize when a quart or more of fuel was drained from the stainless steel tanks on the main deck amidships. We would get one of those long, wax paper-encased pullman loaves of white bread (it had to be white bread) and cut the ends off, the paper and the two heels. Through the top of the loaf, we would pour the reddish fuel, the white bread slices acting as a filter. In a few minutes, clear alcohol would come dripping out of the bottom into whatever container we had, most of the time, a canteen. We were convinced all the impurities were out of the fuel. It was a clear solution coming out of the bottom of the loaf, the red color gone. Sailors, long gone, had come up with this idea. Who were we to argue? To complete the famous Torpecker, one more ingredient was needed. Purple Death. On the mess decks of almost every ship in the Navy was the big urn of a purple Kool Aid-like drink. Very sweet. Very awful. But when mixed with the filtered fuel, the seaborne adult beverage, Torpecker, was born. It was fit for kings and explorers. Ulysses and the crew of the ARGO would've loved it. It was also in the realm of public knowledge because every time a new batch would appear, so would Ensign Schmidt and Chief Corpsman Tomilla, with their clunky white mugs. The first and only important thing was to get rid of the heavy, red-tinted loaf of bread. It was quickly jettisoned over the side and would sink like a rock. Before we left Bermuda, two batches of Torpecker would be made.

At the seaplane base, we cleaned up the ships as best we could. Later on we would procure another whaleboat but as of now, the davits hung empty. The missing stern rack gave us the look of someone with a 'missing tooth'. The 1,400 pounds of explosive amatol in the depth charges was now lying off the Atlantic Shelf, 7,000 feet down. Some injured men were taken off the *Tabberer* on stretchers. They wouldn't be making the trip back. Later on we found out that hurricane Helene had gone from a 135 mph terror to an autumn breeze somewhere south of Nova Scotia. She had done her damage. The *Keller* and Ed Steffen had held her at bay, however, using our 12,000 horsepower Westinghouse turbines and good seamanship. On October 1st, we weighed anchor and headed west, toward the United States again.

For all intents and purposes, this was the end of Helene versus DESDIV21. There were some other incidents indirectly related to our experience at sea which should and can be told here.

They began two weeks later, in Washington, D.C. One afternoon, my division officer told me the Captain wanted to see me on the bridge. What did I do now? Mr. Miller, my division officer, came with me which in itself was a little strange. Captain Steffen was standing at the chart table with one of the yeomen when we arrived. The Captain was dressed in his full uniform and right away I thought I was going to have another Captain's Mast, sort of a 'court' for infractions and things. In the Marines they call it Office Hours.

'Stand at attention.', said Mr. Miller. I did, and with that, Steffen started reading from what looked like a parchment of sort, he was holding in his hands. It was a Letter of Commendation. For me! He droned on about my control of the helm for 17 hours straight, during the hurricane. The Chief Engineer had received one too. This was immense. The Captain and I had always been at odds. My shenanigans aboard ship hadn't solidified our friendship in any way, but apparently during the mayhem Helene put us through, we had become shipmates. He finished reading and reached his right hand out. I shook it, then saluted. He saluted back. I took the letter down to the Ship's Office where there was a copier. The original had to go to St. Louis where the Archives for the Armed Forces was. The Archives . . . Imagine! The Letter had pressed seals and a big U.S. Navy Department Seal on the bottom. My name was in bigger type than the rest of it and on the top and bottom of the paper, images of porpoise and sea gulls and ships abounded. It was the prettiest thing I'd ever seen. Well, almost.

I sent the copy to my Mother. I thought it was time she heard something good the Navy had to say about me. It was a good thing I did. The Letter of Commendation was only the beginning of a strange turn of events, events that alter and illuminate our lives, where in the end, whether good or bad, seem to make our lives worth living.

Aftermath

Autumn, 1958-Summer, 2012

One month after the Letter of Commendation ceremony on the bridge of the *Keller*, almost a month to the day, I found myself in a jail cell in a police station in Southeast Washington, D.C. I had spent the night as a guest of the Washington, D.C. Metropolitan Police. It seems the night before, outside an establishment named Johnny's Rebel Room, on the corner of 8th and E Streets, I was involved in an altercation which warranted my overnight incarceration. I didn't think it was necessary but the local law enforcement apparently did. I expected an officer from the *Keller* to arrive sometime that morning to take me back to the ship where Captain Steffen was most probably waiting.

Just before noon, Lieutenant Hogan showed up. He had a dour look on his face as we walked out of the station house. As we climbed into the jeep, he said:

'The Captain is waiting for you on the bridge. It'll probably be a Mast.'

We drove the short distance to the Naval Gun Factory on the Anacostia River, through the main gate and down to where our ship was tied up. Next to the *Keller* was Eisenhower's yacht and next to the yacht was the small turn-of-the-century steamer, *Sequoia*, the Secretary of the Navy's ship. I had swum across the Anacostia River that summer and the driver of the jeep, Mr. Hogan, had caught me. I received one week's restriction for that. I couldn't leave the ship for one week. There wouldn't have been any punishment had I not been on duty.

As I climbed the ladder to the bridge, I noticed my dress blues needed a pressing. Too late. Steffen was looking out of a porthole, smoking, when I entered the bridge. His yeoman was motioning me to stand over by the wheel. There was a podium set up near the Exec's chair and Steffen moved over to it.

'Ten-hut!, yelled Mr. Hogan. The yeoman and I came to attention.

Captain Steffen spoke: 'I have your service record here. It's not what it should be.' He thumbed through the pages. 'Where were your two buddies last night?', he asked, meaniing Drabin and Bramblett.

'They had the duty, Sir.', I answered.

'You should've stayed aboard with them.', he said, still studying the folder in front of him.

'Yes, Sir.', I said.

'Your vocation seems to be the embarrassment of the Navy uniform, Mc Guire.', Steffen said, but I didn't say anything. I just stood there, at attention.

'What do you suppose I should do with you?', he asked, not looking for an answer. What could he do to me that he hasn't already done, I thought? Restriction? He couldn't bust me, I was just a Seaman. Anything less means I couldn't be on the ship. They usually didn't do that. Only petty officers were busted down as I was to find out years later. My 'inside' face started to develop a measured smugness.

'What's this?', Steffen said loudly. He was holding up a copy of my Letter of Commendation! My blood froze. It was a big piece of paper, not the usual 8x11 sheet. The original was safe in St. Louis, in the archives, or so I thought. The ship's office told me later that day, the Navy makes provisions for everything. It boils down to this: The individual or outfit who awarded you the Letter, can take it back, or rescind it if the need arises, and can only be done by the one who awarded it. It's also taken from the Archives in St. Louis and destroyed.

. . . Captain Steffen ripped up the Letter. He didn't just rip it up, he ripped long pieces off, starting at the top and ripping all the way to the bottom until my Letter was a mass of paper strips lying on my service record. It was impossible to mask the horror on my face. It was definitely the worst thing that could've happened to me. The yeoman, his name escapes me now, had a smirk on his face. I remember him lying in the passageway the day after the storm when I was relieved on the bridge. He was so sick he was unconscious, lying there in his own regurgitated mess. I suppose he got the last laugh.

'These proceedings are at an end. Dismissed.', the Captain said and with that, he stalked off the bridge. Mr. Hogan left and so did the yeoman, carrying my service record and the wooden podium. I was left on the bridge, by myself. I went to the wheel and stood with my hands on the teak rims. The surface of the Anacostia seemed so far below. The bridge seemed so high. It was all quiet now, here on the bridge of my ship.

'If you could talk!', I said to the wheel. I should've been angrier than I was, but I wasn't. Captain Steffen, I knew even then, had done the right thing. It broke my heart, but he'd done the right thing. There was a man who was in the Underwater Demolition Teams in

WWII. He swam up onto the beaches of Peleliu, Tarawa and Rabaul at night, mapping the terrain for the upcoming invasions. He had a chest full of medals, along with probably saving countless lives in the invasions. He was a better man than I. I was so glad my Mother had a copy of the Letter. I never told her it was bogus and she showed everybody.

Up on the starboard side of the bow, I could see through the ports, two stanchions hadn't been replaced yet from the storm. The North Atlantic almost won that day or two, but it didn't. The North Atlantic is the toughest body of water in the world. But we were tougher. I gripped the finger curves of the teak and brass wheel.

'We were tougher!', I said aloud, then turned and left the bridge.

The following September of 1959, the USS *Robert F. Keller* (DE-419) had come to the end of the channel. She was to be de-commissioned. The Navy was cleaning house again and they were crossing out certain ships from the Naval Register. They did this every now and then. It was a necessary evil and was usually the older ships that went first. It was a sad thing to us because the little destroyer escort had been our home for two years. It had taken us out and brought us back, in one piece. She had done everything we asked of her and all she asked for in return was, a fresh coat of paint and a long drink of fuel oil now and then. All the ships of DESDIV21 were scheduled to go also. We had a framed picture on the quarterdeck of *Keller*'s namesake, Ensign Robert F. Keller, USN. His thin, unsmiling face looked down on us whenever we went through the midships passageway. Destroyers are usually named after Navy or Marine Corps heroes and the *Keller* was no exception.

Ensign Keller had been a PBY patrol plane pilot in World War II. When the Japanese invaded Kiska and Attu in the Aleutian Islands, we didn't have many forces up there. Ships had to be rushed north to meet the invasion. Ensign Keller was based on Attu with his PBY squadron. The Consolidated PBY was a slow, unarmed, two-engined float plane. it could stay aloft almost all day. It's top speed was something like 140 mph. It was by far, not a warplane. The Navy had to use anything that was available, so they rigged two torpedoes under the wings of Keller's PBY, with release lanyards which came through the side windows and were controlled by the co-pilot. The idea was, to get close enough to the Japanese landing ships, pull the lanyards and release the torpedoes. It had never been done before and the base commander asked for volunteers. All the PBY pilots stepped forward, including young Bob Keller. He was last seen skimming across the water in his lumbering amphibian, bringing the war to the Japanese. He posthumously received the Air Medal. In 1944, his mother cracked a bottle of champagne on the cutwater of DE hull #419 at the Brown Shipyards in the Houston Ship Channel and the USS *Robert F. Keller* went to war.

By August of 1959, Doug Drabin had already left the Navy. Ron Bramblett was going to his next ship, the destroyer USS *Laffey*, as a Sonarman. I was headed to newport, Rhode Island to be a Gunner's Mate on board the destroyer tender USS *Yellowstone* (AD-27). De-commissioning bells were breaking up that old gang of mine.

Much to our delight, however, the *Keller* was to be saved from the breakers. The Navy decided to give the entire ship over to the Naval Reserve of the Washington, D.C. area. Reserve units would handle the ship and take it themselves on two-week cruises, for training exercises. It would still be out of commission, but it would be afloat and not turned into packs of razor blades.

There was to be a ceremony on board, officially handing the ship over to the Reserves. None other than the Chief of Naval Operations, Admiral Arleigh (31-knot) Burke was to be in attendance, along with numerous politicians and Naval personnel from the district. It was to be a big deal. They even planned to have a band on the pier. There was to be an official change of command, that is, the handing over of the ship by Captain Steffen to his counterpart in the Reserve unit. They were going to present the original commissioning pennant to Lieutenant Commander Steffen, the last Captain of the ship.

The commissioning pennant. This was a two-inch wide, yard-long strip of cloth, a pennant. It was made up of two red-and-white stripes with a blue field at the hoist. Seven white stars graced the blue field. There was also a grommet at the hoist. This little pennant flew at the very top of the mainmast for as long as the ship was in commission. If it was shot away or damaged in war, so be it. Whatever was left, even if it was the brass grommet, was always presented to the last Captain the ship had. It was like preserving the 'soul' of the ship and taking it with us, or in this case, Captain Steffen taking it.

I was given the job of climbing the mainmast and retrieving the pennant, bringing it down and holding it until the ceremony.

So now, the former Letter of Commendation recipient pondered; What goes around, will certainly and enthusiastically come around again.

The night before the ceremony, I climbed the mainmast and plucked the pennant from the topmost part of the mast, 84 feet above the water. The pennant was dirt-streaked and had numerous holes throughout its length. It had been flying from the tops for the last 15 years and looked it. I brought it down and showed my division officer, Mr. Miller. I told him I would stow it in the flag locker until the ceremony the next day. That night, I got a new commissioning pennant from the flag locker and spent a few hours making it look like the original. I dirtied it up, soaked it, dirtied it up again, made holes in it then frayed the the hole edges. I ran it through the dryer down in the laundry a few times, soaking it each time. After awhile, I had a reasonable facsimile of the original pennant. It looked the worse for wear and would even fool Mr. Miller, the only other person who had seen it.

The next morning, the honor guard, about 15 of the crew, including me, donned our best dress blues, complete with white leggings, white gloves, white web belt and a Garand M-1 rifle each and went up to the quarterdeck. We lined up on the port side where the Admiral could inspect us as he headed toward the ceremony on the fantail. Mr. Miller came up and took the doctored 'pennant' from me. I had it rolled up and held together with a rubber band.

We hadn't waited too long when a black limo arrived on the pier and '31-knot' Burke stepped out. There he was, the Babe Ruth of the Navy! I'd never seen so much gold. He and his entourage came up the brow and strode past us, nodding. He was taller than I was.

Halfway through the ceremony, the honor guard wandered down to where they could see the proceedings. Burke made a speech and some Maryland politician made a speech. The Undersecretary of the Navy was also there but he didn't speak. Captain Steffen looked like he wanted to be somewhere else. The band played, the speakers droned on and on and I watched Mr. Miller put his hand in his pocket a dozen times to make sure the pennant was there.

Finally, the time came for Steffen to get the pennant. Mr. Miller handed the rolled up red and blue ball to one of the Admiral's people who gave it to Burke. The Admiral went before the microphone again and recounted the *Keller*'s wartime patrols, her four rows of battle ribbons and her exemplary record. He said it was a sound ship. He was right. It was because of Mr. Brown and his welders down in Texas. He walked over to our Captain and handed him the rolled up pennant. Steffen looked at it, then put it in his pocket. He looked resplendent in his uniform and had just about as many medals as the Admiral.

Afterward, after everyone had gone, I saw him standing on the 01 level, smoking. He saw me and I yelled up to him:

'Congratulations, Captain!' (I wanted to call him 'Skipper', but I didn't.) He gave me an imperceptible nod and then walked away. That was the last time I saw him. He was gone the next morning, on to his next duty assignment.

I always wondered what he did with the pennant Admiral Burke handed to him. It's probably in a drawer, or hanging on a wall somewhere. He probably showed it to a lot of people.

The *Keller* sank one Japanese submarine in WWII. She rescued scores of downed pilots and saved just one man from Halsey's Typhoon of 1945. She operated on the east coast from Maine to Florida, on picket duty, watching and listening for submarines from the Russian Bear. She was the last American warship to visit Havana, Cuba and she was a witness to the very first Polaris missile launch. She was in a number of hurricanes and always brought her crew back, including the one I was in. She was my ship too. The *Keller* was my ship and I loved every bolt and fleck of rust on her.

The USS *Keller* (DE-419) went to the breakers in Philadelphia in 1971. There was no fanfare, no bands playing and no crowds. She was just a little destroyer escort who, at the end, must've been very tired. She served her country well and stood up to every evil thing that came her way. She was a good ship and now she doesn't exist, except in the hearts and minds of those who sailed her. And of course, in the bottom left hand drawer of a mahogany desk in my dining room at home. There, her real commissioning pennant resides.

The *Keller* was a little too big to be my Shipmate, but nevertheless, that's what she was.

I'm not a big computer person. Whenever I see the word 'download', I have this vivid picture of a dump truck at a landfill. I'm still in the 'look it up in the encyclopedia!' age group. Not really, but I struggle through the electronics when I have to.

It was Autumn again, only this time it was 1988. I was on the computer and came across a list of ship reunions on some nondescript website. I also found some old ship rosters. Just for the fun of it, I typed in my old ship, the *Keller*. Up popped some names, and there he was! Edward J. Steffen. His address at the time was 422 E. Ravine Ave., Lake Bluff, Illinois. No e-mail address came along with it. That night I sat down and typed a letter out to him. I had no idea if he remembered Ron, Doug or me. I told him a little about myself and of the other two, as much as I knew about them. I mailed off the letter the next morning. I figured this was a good time to call him 'Skipper', but instead, I had written 'Dear Captain Steffen'.

Almost a month went by before I received a letter back from him. It was postmarked October 20, 1988. He told me he retired from the Navy in 1964 and started teaching at a junior high school. I had asked him if he remembered the three of us, and he wrote back:

'Yes! I remember you and Bramblett and Drabin. You guys made the *Keller* a great ship to serve on and command. We had our good and bad times, but we can always look back and say we gave it our best shot, and the target had to take a fall.'

It turns out that Steffen's son was a Naval aviator and his daughter was in the Navy too. I never heard from the Captain again. I thought about sending him the real commissioning pennant but I quickly changed my mind. Working on the premise, 'It was my ship too.', is the reason it's still in the desk. I'd like to think, if I was supposed to have the pennant and the Captain held it, he would send it to me. Then again, I suppose that's why Ed Steffen was Captain of the *Keller* and not me.

In September of 1995, I drove down to Vicksburg, Mississippi to see the only Civil War ironclad ship, the USS *Cairo*. On the way down, I made a left turn at St. Louis and drove 40 miles to Mexico, Missouri. Ron Bramblett lived in that town.

It was great to see him again, to say the least. He looked the same, just a little older. We both wondered where Doug was. I told him I'd been trying to find Doug for years. Ron was a personnel manager at a brick refractory plant in Mexico. He told me that all the people in his office were talking about 'Mr. Bramblett's New York friend' who was coming to see him. We met at his office and before we went downtown to have coffee, he told me he had to go to the head. He went in the men's room and I was behind him. When I had my hand on the door handle, I noticed all the secretaries were staring. It was central Missouri. I had to do it. I stopped and said to all the upturned faces:

'Mr. Bramblett and I always used to go to the men's room together.' I smiled. Ron's wife, Sandy, was back in Hannibal, taking care of one of the mothers who happened to be sick, so I never got to meet her, but I did get to meet his beautiful daughter, Rhonda Lee. Ron and I had a good afternoon but I couldn't remember a word of our conversation. All I know is we laughed a great deal.

Ronald Lee Bramblett, Sonarman Second Class, USN, died in May of 1999. We'll meet again someday. Somewhere up ahead.

That left the elusive Theodore Douglas Drabin. My wife, Barbara, told me to get on Facebook. It was the end of the summer, 2012. Reluctantly, I joined Facebook. In a matter of days, there he was! He was dressed in a tux, with his little head popping out of the top of his shirt! To shorten this already-too-long story, I contacted him, got on a plane and flew down to Florida. I landed in West Palm Beach, saw my daughter, Bridget, and drove across the state to North Venice.

I got out of the car. He was standing on the sidewalk. He turned and yelled back into the house:

'Honey! There's an old sailor in the driveway! Hide anything of value!'

I hadn't seen him in 53 years. No description could follow that initial meeting. No narrative. it would need the likes of Stephen Ambrose or Mark Twain. His wife, Candy, was a perfect human being. I think that's a good description. Seeing him, felt like the tying up of two loose ends, two 'Irish pennants' if you will.

That evening we drove down to Sarasota Beach. As we walked along on the white sand, when one of us took a breath, the other one would chime in with another question or story. If he said: 'Chuck, I'm glad you came down.', once, he said it ten times.

We met three girls from Austria, who were enjoying the sunset. We had them take our picture.

'Chuck, take that shot of the sun!', he said. The sun was a pot of gold, just sitting on the clear horizon of the Gulf. I took a great shot and we just watched, as it sunk slowly out of sight. Doug turned and smiled.

'I wish Ron was here.', he said. I nodded and for some reason, I heard once again, the crushing, all-enveloping sound of a wave, coming out of the darkness and slamming into the side of our ship. We had spoken about the hurricane before and it was probably about to come up again, I thought. But, that wasn't the case. The World's Greatest Helmsman turned to me again smiling, and said:

'Ya know,' he nodded toward the Austrian girls on the blanket. 'There was a time when we wouldn't be standing here, watching the sunset. We would be over there, on that blanket.'

(Doug Drabin and Me 2012

END

jcm
7/8/12

Self-Appraisal

Knowing everything there is to know
has its high points.
Being smug and cynical
toward other opinions is acceptable
only in the short run.
The low point in knowing everything is,
There comes a day
Every now and then,
When knowing everything means
You don't know anything at all.

jcm
4/3/84

Playing For Keeps

Who goes home alone anymore?
We go out as one
and come back as two,
pumping out make-believe life blood
to keep the night going
until we crash,
only to wake in the harsh light,
smiling benignly at each other
and groping for sober conversation.

Some of us cry out for human contact
while others keep it a game still,
having had more practice
in the art of catching others' eyes,
promising Nirvana and sweaty sheets.
(Just cruising, sailor?)
They can automatically relax their standards
or put them out of sight entirely.
I've never admired those who play
the game of love,
only those who love.

Waking up alongside an actress
makes you the actor
and the smell of popcorn
stays on your hands all day.

No matter how much we take
we always give back something.

'I'll put the coffee on.'.
(Anything to get out of that room!)
Trying to check my watch
without her seeing me.
Sunlight has a way
of making vibrant nudity
an object of naked embarrassment.

Whatever we take,
we have to give something back,
or worse yet, something is taken from us.
No one goes home alone anymore.
No need to,
unless,
we demand self-quality.

Is there time for that?
There used to be.
I have no time for playing,
no time for eye contact—
the contact I seek is much deeper than that.

I'm readying myself for a journey.
It may end tomorrow morning
and it may not.
If you want to come along, you can.

jcm
4/4/84

Plot A, Row 40, Grave 13

The road from Nancy to Epinal was straight as an arrow. It was nice to be on an 'N' road, what we would call a super-highway at home, but here in France, most of the roads wound through the countryside, especially the ones we had been taking. N57 was easy to reach, on the Nancy city map but we became lost anyway. It took an extra hour to find our way through the herds of milk cows and tiny villages. Our route was supposed to have taken us from Nancy, up through the Foret de Paroy and on into Strasbourg. We were following Barbara's Dad's route in WWII and this was our 5th day of the trip. This 40-mile side trip to Epinal had been planned from the very beginning. The entire plan was to have followed her Dad's division, the 44th, all the way to the end of the war, in Austria, but this was the 5th day. On the 5th day, I had a mission to perform. In Epiinal. That's where we were going.

There were two exits for Epinal and we took the second one. We had our eyes peeled for a certain sign, but we didn't see it. The land had become hilly for we were deep in the Vosges Mountains. All we knew about Epinal was the Moselle River flowed through it. Down into the town we drove until we saw two ladies walking along with groceries. Barbara got out of the car and tried her French out. She told the ladies what we were looking for and they pointed south, across the Moselle. We drove toward the river and over a short bridge. Down below, the Moselle glistened. It was late in the day and a chill had come into the air. We drove across the bridge and immediately saw two signs. One sign read 'Dinoze', the little hamlet across from Epinal. It was the second sign we both stared at. Barbara said; 'There it is.'

The sign was green with white letters, with a white arrow. 'Militaire Cemeterie Americain'.

In January of 1945, the U.S. 397th Regiment of the 100th Division was on a low ridge just east of Epinal. The Germans were less than half a mile away. E (Easy) Company consisted that day, of 82 men. Two of them were friends, buddies if you will. They were Robert D. Burlison of Lockport, New York and Phil Ellsworth of Ohio. Both were PFC's and both were 20 years old. They had been in the front line for 31 days. Ellsworth later on recounted that he had never been so cold. The two young men talked about home, their families and what they would do after the war, the same as all soldiers in all wars do.

On the 23rd of January, German armour surprised Easy Company and the rest of the 397th. It was a mismatch; infantry against tanks, and the regiment started pulling back, off the ridge. Easy Company had failed by a few minutes to get the word about pulling back. They were about to be surrounded and started running for it, over an open field. Phil Ellsworth said he turned to see where his friend, Burlison was. He saw him, standing up in his foxhole, firing a Browning Automatic Rifle at a German tank and the German foot soldiers behind it. The tank had stopped and was starting to train its guns on the single soldier. Easy Company made it to the safety of the woods behind them. It was the last time Burlison was seen alive.

Phil Ellsworth fought through the rest of the war and made it home. He always thought, he said, he would make it back to the cemetery at Epinal to see his friend, Robert Burlison. But it was not to be. Ellsworth wrote a poem for his friend in 2005, when he was 80. It was entitled 'Epinal'. He told his son that he would travel to Epinal soon, and read the poem over his buddy's grave. But, as I said, it was not to be. Phil Ellsworth passed away in Ohio in 2007. I read the whole story on some webpage on the internet. I was looking up information on the cemetery of Courville-Sur-Mer at Normandy and came across the one at Epinal. There was the story about Phil Ellsworth and Burlison. I never forgot it.

We followed the small road lined with brick walls and drove up the hill. On a bluff overlooking the Moselle, we found the cemetery, the Marble Gardens of Epinal. As far as one could see, it seemed, the crosses and the Stars of David stretched away, in perfect symmetrical lines. The sun had slunk down over one of the mountains to the west and if a needle fell on the grass, we could've heard it. There was no one around. No caretakers and no visitors except for us. There were, of course, the 5,524 American soldiers and the one soldier I was looking for.

Barbara walked toward the well-groomed walkways while I went into the Visitor's Center. No one was there. I knocked on the office door but there was no answer. They must've gone home for the day. There were easy chairs and a couch with a table in front of it. On the table was a big ledger. I knew what it was. I looked through it until I reached the B's and there he was; 'Burlison, R.D.—Plot A, Row 40, Grave 13.' I walked out and found Barbara. We walked over to the first few acres of crosses, Plot A. We waked down the rows until we reached the stone marker that read '40'. I walked down the line, not really counting, just looking for his name.

Robert D. Burlison
397th I.R. 100th Div.
New York
Jan. 23, 1945
PFC U.S. Army

Barbara walked up and we both stood there for what seemed like a long moment. 'All these men.', she said, then said it again. 'Oh, all these men . . .'

I wasn't quite ready to do what I had come to do. It was one thing thinking about it but quite another to actually do it. Finally, I took

Wendel's '44' hat off, dropped it on the grass and reached into my back pocket. Words were very hard to come by but I managed to get them out.

'Hello, Robert.', I said, opening the folded paper. 'Our names don't matter, but we took it upon ourselves to come here today to read you something your buddy, Phil Ellsworth wrote for you. It's a poem. He wanted to come back himself and read it to you, but he couldn't quite make it, so we've come in his place. (as I type this now, I still don't know how I managed to get those words out on that quiet afternoon at Epinal.) So, Robert, here it is. It's entitled 'Epinal', and I started to read:

'EPINAL

It seems unfair,
considering all,
that I am here in this place now
with eighty summers on my brow
and you are there in Epinal.
Among our comrades sleeping there,
that I can hear the robins sing
and see the almond tree in Spring
and you are there. It isn't fair.
Flowers, if you grow in Epinal,
grow near where Robert lies,
I will dream that he has eyes
and sees some fairness after all.'

I folded the paper again and knelt by Robert's cross. Between the marble column and the earth, I slid the paper down next to the stone, out of sight. I put the '44' hat back on, walked to the front of his grave and came to attention, the way I remembered from way back when. I hope I gave him my best salute. I wanted it to be my best one.

As Barbara and I walked back down the line of trees, the sound of 'Taps' came from the loudspeakers on the Visitor's Center. I looked at my watch. Seventeen hundred. Closing time. Over the trees, about eighty feet in the air, our flag flew. No, it wasn't the Land of the

Free and Home of the Brave, but it was the closest one could get to America over here in Europe. The last notes of 'Taps' sounded . . . Go to sleep soldier-boy, God is nigh . . .

Hitler told his soldiers before Normandy, the American soldier was coming and not to be afraid of him. He said that Robert Burlison and his friends were ill-fed, scrawny, uneducated and worn down physically and mentally from the Great Depression. He told them the American soldier would be no match for them. Stephen Ambrose wrote that in his book, 'Band of Brothers'. Ambrose also reminded the reader, and in an ironic way, Hitler, that the American soldiers were survivors of the Depression, and they turned out to be the toughest soldiers on the face of the globe, the kind of soldier who would stand up in a foxhole and empty his weapon at an enemy tank to save his buddies.

We got in the car, not needing to say a word. The sun had completely disappeared as we started down the hill, leaving the mission behind us and the dream ahead of us. I thought of Ernie Pyle's words as he visited the Allied Cemetery in Oran before going on to Sicily:

'There is nothing we can do for those who lie beneath the wooden crosses, except to pause and murmur . . . 'Thanks, Pal."

jcm
10/7/12

Spin Cycle

The white, pulpy mass that was in my pocket
could've been a note,
a saying,
profound words of love,
or hate.
What was it?
It didn't survive the wash
but it was important enough
to have lived in my pocket for a week.
A phone number?
A message from someone?
An invitation from Ed Koch?
What!
The wet, white goo
was already in its first stages
of decomposition,
at the starting gate,
already heading for the plastic kitchen garbage bag
to disappear in a land refill;
and I would never know.

jcm
4/4/84

Time In Cubic Feet

I have truckloads of time,
all the time I need now.
We can wing it—
never checking the clock or calendar,
never worrying about lies.
    We have time to watch sand castles
    crumple in the tide.
    I want to tackle you in the snow
    and bury you in crispy leaves.
Whatever kept me from you before
is gone.
I want to watch the beans
force their way to the surface,
watch the green tomatoes redden
and the lawn come to life again.
    I want to sleep, waken.
    sleep and wake up again
    without ever knowing what month it is.
I want to do all things with you.
But now that I have
all this time,
I can't find you.

jcm
4/5/84

'44th! Give 'em Hell!'

The winding road from Embermenil down through the hills to the main highway was bordered by farmland and probably the richest earth I'd ever seen. We were on the edge of the Foret de Paroy, the wooded area Barbara's Dad and his Division had camped back in 1944. We were almost half-done with our trip, the one we'll always call, The Long March.

Her Dad, S/SGT Wendel Kokll, had been a medic with the 44th Division in World War II. He and his buddies fought from the middle of the Alsace in France, all the way into Germany and finally into Austria where the war, for them, ended. We decided in 2011, the year before, to follow his steps, or the steps of his regiment, the 71st, and eventually his battalion to the very end. There was a mountain in the Austrian Alps called Mt. Wanneck. He was on that mountain when word came that the Germans had quit. That was our quest; to find that mountain. We had a few scotch miniatures and his hat with the Backward Fours on the front. We had plans to find that mountain and leave the hat and the scotch bottles there. I had done the background history of the Division and Barbara had done all the harrowing logistics. We'd started in Portsmouth, England, riding a jet ferry across the Channel to Cherbourg where the 44th Division had debarked. From there, they wound their way through France to the edges of the little town of Embermenil in the Alsace, between Nancy and Strasbourg. There they stayed for five weeks until they were ready to move the few miles to where the war was raging. We followed the same path they did, through Fougeres, the Falaise Pocket, into the outskirts of Paris, Bar-le-Duc, Nancy and finally Embermenil. Embermenil had been the only little town he'd mentioned, down through the years. I remember him calling it 'Ember-mill'. It was a tiny town with pristine little streets and an equally pristine little church. It was a Sunday, so no one was out and about as Barbara and

I walked around. She was saying things like; 'I can see him in this town. He would've loved it.'

When it was time to go, we said 'goodbye' to the small village and started down toward the highway to Strasbourg.

I like to think of myself as a 'history buff', or an amateur historian. History and I had always seemed to go hand-in-hand. What was tedious about history to other people, came easy for me and enjoyable at the same time. I hoped a little of it might rub off on Barbara, as we followed that unmarked path across France. I remember telling her as we left Embermenil, this was where the 'shooting war' for her Dad started. In 1944, this is where it became serious. So serious in fact, that her Dad was wounded not far from Embermenil. He had been attending to a wounded soldier when he was hit with shrapnel in let's say, the 'back of his upper thigh', a scar he was always ready to show people, much to my Mother-in-Law's chagrin.

I was trying to keep it interesting for Barbara, knowing full well it might just grow tedious for her, somewhere along the way. For me, this was where every detail in my maps became important; every stream, every hill. If I thought hard enough, I could almost hear the sounds of the war itself . . .

We had gone about twenty 'clicks' south of Embermenil, heading toward, if I remember correctly, N12, the highway to Strasbourg, a city about a mile or two from the German border. I was driving and I wanted the camera so I pulled off the macadam onto the shoulder, by a field of hay. I had just opened the back door of the car and had my hand on the camera strap, when I heard it.

It was the kind of sound you'd hear on a deathly quiet night, no breeze outside, no oil burner humming, no dog snoring. The kind of whispering rubbery noise a Selectric II typewriter used to make in the next office when the space bar was held down. I looked back up the road toward Embermenil, half expecting to see some rickety old French moving van, huffing and puffing down the hill. But no moving van came. Instead, through the morning mist on the other side of the hill, emerged a column of four olive-drab jeeps, packed with helmeted soldiers! Down the dirt road they came, followed by a two-ton weapons carrier. Behind the weapons carrier, rumbled a long Conga Line of 2 1/2-ton troop trucks, commonly called '6 x 6's', swaying and trying to keep up with the jeeps. More and more vehicles came up over the hill and started down toward us; two Sherman tanks, a huge tank retriever, an M-3, jeeps pulling bouncing 105's and an endless column of troop carriers. As the first jeeps approached, I looked back in the car. Barbara was reading the itinerary in the passenger seat. Why doesn't she turn to look?

The first jeep passed and I could see the gold circle on the door with the blue fours in the middle, one of them backward! One officer, on the passenger side was angrily waving me off the dirt road. The officer behind him had a cigar in his mouth. The trucks roared by, soldiers peering out at me from under the canvas tops. one kid smiled. One of his front teeth was missing. The two Shermans roared by, throwing up gritty dust. The second tank had 'BRONX BABY' painted on the side. The road was a storm of noise and just then, three one-ton ambulances came by, their white squares and red crosses sticking out in the dusty clouds. I searched the windows for a familiar face, but all the men looked alike. They all looked at me. Some smiled, some didn't. A French family had stopped their wagon in back of me and some of the soldiers were throwing candy bars to them. The family's teen-aged daughter, amid the whistles and catcalls, tried to pick up all the candy.

For 30 minutes the convoy passed by. The dust hung on my clothes but I couldn't stop watching as vehicle after vehicle roared by. It was the 44th, heading into their first great battle. Up ahead of them, lay the Simserhoff Fortress and Sarraguimes, both German strongholds. A 6 x 6 came by and the driver blew his horn while looking at me.

'44th! Give 'em Hell!', I yelled as loud as I could. He blew his horn again.

Soon, the end of the line appeared, in the form of a camouflaged, brown and green tanker truck. The tanker found its way to the turn up ahead and disappeared around the corner. All the sound melted away. I turned to see the French family but as I turned, I kind of knew they wouldn't be there. They weren't. As I walked back to the car on the macadam road, I noticed my shirt and shoes weren't dusty anymore. I leaned on the driver's door and looked in. Barbara was still poring over her itinerary. I started to tell her about the 'convoy' but decided against it. She probably wouldn't understand. I got in the car.

'Babe, if we stay on this road, we're bound to hit N12 sooner or later.', I said to her. Barbara looked at me and for an instant, just an instant, I saw her Father looking at me. She looked at the road up ahead, then without any hesitation, said:

'Jimmy, why don't we just follow those Army trucks?'

. . . Past her beautiful face, past the passenger-side window, down the hill and out in the hayfield, the stalks began to move as a breeze pushed them along.

jcm
10/7/12

Architecture in Sugar

I have all intentions of doing the day right
but my imagination takes over
and that stone pony
goes galloping through my head again.
        I'm frozen under the blanket,
        afraid to move
        as my mind colors
        and puts shape to the new scenario.
There you are again,
in my thought.

It's always the same
every morning,
every noon
and evening too . . .
I never get it out of my head.
It stays with me, looking me in the eye
and lying.
It never blinks, it just smirks.
        I have the foundation, the stone, the cement,
        but the rest is fragile sugar candy,
        beams and studs of milk chocolate
        and caramel for the roof.
I'll have to wait for the next rain
to wash it away again.

jcm
4/5/84

Middle Kingdom

That path,
        the one we're about to walk
        is treacherous;
        it winds and dips
it's way through the leafy corridors.
I'll have to rely on you
to find the way;
I'll be too busy showing you things
like ice crystals
glazing over the bark of trees
and fat, gray squirrels eyeing us.
I'll be telling you of woodpecker nests
and the double eyelids of frogs.
I'll be very busy
pointing, emphasizing and talking too much.
Too busy in fact, to keep on the path.
If I wander off,
a slight tug on my sleeve
will bring me back on.
I'll rely on you to do that.

jcm
4/5/84

I Got 'Em, Pa!'
or
It All Came Down To The Brachioradialis

My Grandfather, James J. Mc Guire, had been Fire Chief of Centennial Hose #2, in Peekskill, New York. That was many years ago, nearly one hundred. He kept his position as Chief of Centennial up until 1948 when the City of Peekskill made him 'Chief of Chiefs', the titular head of all six companies.

Centennial's little red firehouse used to be nestled under the Route 9 overpass until 2008. It had been abandoned years before in favor of a new firehouse up on Washington Street. A firehouse can't move with the population when a city shifts it's center, so they had to leave the old structure where it was. It stayed there until 2008 when the state decided to put in a new overpass bridge. The firehouse was doomed. The City of Peekskill, however, managed to hire a building mover. They intended to move the firehouse across Water Street to the area in front of the Lincoln Train Station. Abraham Lincoln made a speech there in 1861, on his way to Washington, D.C. for his inauguration, fifteen years before the little firehouse was built. It took months of preparation, leveling, digging, balancing and bracing, then finally, they were ready. The five hydraulic four-wheel lifters started working, but one of them failed. Before anyone could do anything, the old firehouse, circa 1876, collapsed in a cloud of smoke and noise!

I managed to get down to Peekskill a week later when the area was cordoned off and guarded. The city filed a lawsuit against the mover for negligence so the bricks and debris were off limits to any souvenir hunters. The men and women of Centennial were devastated and tried to get mementos but were thwarted by the pending lawsuit. My Sister, Eileen, asked me to get a brick for a keepsake but I couldn't get near the debris pile. In time, the pile was moved inside the Lincoln Station fence and that's where it lies to this day. Well, not exactly . . .

Centennial firefighters in front of the "ghost" of the fire house

The firehouse collapsed over a year ago, in the summer of 2008. Grass had grown up around the brick pile and a new Anchor fence had been built complete with U-shaped fence bolts to hold it down. I would go down to Peekskill every now and then and when I did, I would drive down to the old site to check on the bricks.

They tore down our old high school which had been built in 1931 and a few friends of mine who lived out of state, Mike and Lo-lo, asked me if I could get a few bricks as a remembrance. Mid-October of 2009, I drove down and got a few bricks from the high school which was in the process of being torn down. While I was there, I decided to go down to Water Street to see the new construction and to check on the Centennial bricks again.

The brick pile had been moved. It was closer to the inside of the fence.

My Sister's words rattled in my head . . . 'Chuck, can you get me a brick?' (I should interject here; my Grandfather and I shared the same first name, James and/or Jimmy. He had the seniority, so in the house where we both lived, I was called by my nickname, 'Chuck' and he went by 'Jim'. To make matters worse, he always called me 'Jimmy'.)

Back in 1939 they say, my baptismal party was held on the second floor of that little firehouse. Their engine answered many a call in the city, including the Standard Brands Granary fire, the Young Apartments fire and hundreds more. The annual Fireman's Parade back in the old days is and always will be, fresh on my mind. We would wait and wait for the boys of Centennial to come marching by with my Grandfather at the head and cheer our brains out. We would all yell to him: 'Hey Pa! We're over here, Pa!', but he would always keep his eyes straight ahead. He took the Fireman's Parade very seriously. Centennial Hose would always stop at the Enterprise Press and my six year-old sister, from her pre-arranged spot, would run out and hand our Grandfather a bouquet of flowers. He would put them in the horn of his hailing trumpet, pat her on the head with a white-gloved hand, or give her a peck on the cheek and the parade would continue on. I can still see George Strumke, Louis Cole and all the others, waving to the people, joking. But not my Grandfather. Not Jim Mc Guire, the Chief. They were OUR fire department. Whenever there was a fire, here would come that beautiful apparatus, bell ringing, siren sounding, men hanging on the back like bats on a ledge . . .

I had to get a brick.

There was a line of cars in front of the fence, enough room for me to slide in sideways. I could only use one arm. I'm left-handed (like the 'Chief') so I could only use my left arm. There were two surveyors watching me, but no one else. I walked back to my car and put my camera away. There were no work gloves in the car. Then, I walked back to the narrow space between the cars and the fence.

Leaning down, I grabbed the lowest part of the fence and pulled upward! Nothing. I called on my 70 year-old deltoids and left bicep. The fence didn't budge. The bricks were only a foot away. I remembered from high school baseball where I couldn't throw as far as the rest of the infielders. In the Navy, I had an 11-17 boxing record. So much for the left bicep! I went back to the car.

Standing by the car, I looked across Water Street. Scores of construction workers were hanging off the new bridge and dismantling the old one. Where the firehouse once stood, a new granite bridge support grew. I wondered how many of those people knew that a firehouse once proudly stood there? I went back to the fence.

I reached down again. I grabbed the fence and called upon my forearm flexor and even my elbow muscle, the brachialis. I pulled. I pulled again! Nothing. I stood. I looked at the bricks inside the fence. An honest-to-God snake crawled across them!

Snakes be damned! Underneath my unused chest muscles, the triceps, was a quadruple by-pass and seven (count 'em) stents. The triceps had to be employed. Death before dishonor, as I asked the USMC and the Navy for help. Triceps don't fail me now. I pulled. I pulled. The fence didn't move. The skin was coming off my second and third finger as I walked back to the car and got in. I felt a pinch in my back, where in 1990, I had a laminectomy. My neck was getting stiff also.

The surveyors had gone. No one had noticed me in my failed recovery of the bricks. I reached in my pocket for my car keys. It was time to go. There will be no joy in Mudville . . .

Then I thought of the Union Hotel only a block away, and my Father as a teen-ager, changing sheets and getting rid of the detritus in the guest rooms. I thought of Patsy Coffey, my Great Grandfather, wrestling a deer which had crashed through the front window of the hotel bar. I thought of the nuns at St. Joe's, coming up the hill to see my Grandmother who was bed-ridden near the end. I thought of 'Johnny McEldoo', the GPO, '. . . He rose on Sunday, we rise on Monday!' . . . I got out of the car, slammed the door and made my way to the fence.

There was just one muscle I hadn't called upon yet, the brachioradialis in my forearm. I employed it now as I reached down between the car and the fence and gripped the bottom of the wire. I put my right hand on the bumper of the parked car and with my left hand, pulled as hard as I could. I focused on the fence bottom in the grass and directed everything I had into the upward pull.

. . . My Grandfather, his marine collar crisp, white hat down over his eyes, hailing trumpet under his right arm, stood at rigid attention as the parade stopped, right in front of the Enterprise Press on Washington Street. My baby sister was running out with her bouquet. He slowly turned, and looking at me with those Irish-blue eyes said:

'For Christ' sake, Jimmy! Get that damned brick!'

.The curved anchor bolt moved. The fence began to lift. It started to come up . . . one inch, three inches!

'. . . If you love me in September as you do in May, if you love me in that good old Irish way . . .'

The fence anchor bolt popped out, along with another one. The fence came up another five inches!

'. . . On my knee, a pretty wench,
and on the table, a jug of punch.'

The edge of the fence rose, just enough. I reached in and slid two bricks out!! I turned and walked back to the car, the two bricks in my hands were as light as the down of a Lough Innis duck! I heard the roar of the Gaelic kings and the clash of the claymores and the joining of the shields against the hated Cromwell. I was euphoric. I was Admiral of the Ocean Sea. I was Padraic Pearce and Michael Collins all in one.

As I reached the car, I looked over my shoulder to where the old Centennial firehouse used to stand and said aloud:

'I got 'em, Pa!'

Author's Note: The reference to the anatomical make-up of mostly my left arm and the multiple sinew thereof, are of course, fictitious. Those muscles, that I know of, were probably of no consequence. But, the fence DID come up. I have to give all the credit, not to the muscle-absence of the author, but to the very distinct and my very true recollection of Eileen J. (Mc Guire) Dilley, running out to our

Grandfather, the Chief of Centennial Hose, with those bouquets of flowers, on those long-ago summer days when the firefighters marched.

She made the fence come up. My little Sister.

'So let the memory ring true,
down to that last bottle of beer,
to that last wave 'goodbye',
down that long and narrow corridor of time.'

jcm
10/22/09

My Sister's Brick

(In 1876)

Dear Queen Lo-lo,

That's all true, about Centennial, the baptism party, the fence, the law suit, etc. My sister's B-Day is November 27th and I'm going down to Jersey with her brick. My Wife's friend is coming in from Maine for Thanksgiving and the two of them are going down to see 'South Pacific' on that day, so I'm going to Jersey by myself. I glued the brick to a nice piece of wood, varnished the wood and had a brass plaque put on, explaining the brick. She should be surprised. She has an antique shop in Maplewood and has a ton of Hudson River Day Line paraphernalia on display. Her husband, John, is a retired Army Colonel and he helps her out in the shop. She knows everything about antiques.

Just before I closed the box with the Centennial brick for her, I noticed pieces of cement on the top of the brick. I pictured a bunch of brick workers in front of a half-finished firehouse down on Water Street. Water Street wasn't paved yet, back in 1876. All the cement was mixed by hand. The hod carriers probably stood around the giant mixing pan while the strongest worker of them all, the one who had to continuously mix the cement, went back and forth, turning and re-turning the gray mixture. Motorized cement mixers hadn't found their way into the work place yet, so this was the way the cement was mixed. His name could've been Tyrone McGahee. They probably called him 'Rory'.

They were horse-drawn steamers in those days, the fire engines of the past. They consisted of a great boiler, smoke billowing out of the top as the six horses swung the steamer around the corners of the town, on their way to the fire. Imagine . . . The bells clanging, the giant wheels grinding and crashing, the teamster driver swearing and screaming, the steam cascading from the boiler, dogs running, children waving, women screaming. The boiler would run a piston pump which in turn would bring water to the fire, once it got there.

But all those things were in the future, until the little fire house was built. The bright red steamer was on its way from Rochester. The horses were up on Nelson Avenue at the stable, and Rory kept on mixing. The hod carriers waited. The bricklayers on the scaffold waited. Time stood still on Water Street that hot afternoon. The mosquitos buzzed and the sound of the hoe scraping the bottom of Rory's pan carried across my workshop as I closed the lid on the box holding my Sister's brick.

That's a story for another day.

jcm
10/31/09

Sinister Assumption Stories

Dear Loretta,

One time, I was in the 1st Grade at the Assumption and two nuns, God bless them, put me in a metal garbage can on the 3rd floor. (There were no plastic garbage cans then.) They put the lid on and tied the lid down with a cord, running from the handle of the lid down to the handles. They turned the garbage can over on its side and rolled it down the stairs! I hit the wall at the landing and heard them coming down the stairs after me. I thought they were going to let me out (I was crying about then.) but they didn't. They rolled the garbage can across the landing to the next set of stairs and over I went again, down to the second floor! This time they let me out. I was skinned from my eyebrows to my knees. I remember, I had striped shorts on and a cream-colored shirt, both covered with blood spots. I walked home back then, no buses, and I remember my mother and my father were mortified. My father, who had been a prizefighter a decade before, didn't do anything. He had gone to the same school and figured I had done something horrendous. I don't even remember what I did. That sounds like a 'story', doesn't it? It happened. I swear on all four of my children. The Assumption School in Peekskill was about the worst place I've ever been in and I'm including a jail in Naples, Italy.

Another time, Lance Cables (do you remember him?) was sitting in front of me in class. We were in the 2nd Grade. Lance used to wear suspenders. I reached over to his back and snapped the suspenders. We were reading at the time and the nun (Sister Marie-something) told him to stop snapping his suspenders. The worst thing anyone could do in those days was to rat another person out, so he didn't say anything. I snapped them again. The nun looked at Lance and Lance started crying. That's when I should've stopped, but I snapped them again. The nun, as quick as a flash, threw her hardcover book at Lance's head. Lance was about eight feet from her desk. The book hit him full in the face and I remember his glasses breaking in half, each half flying off at 90 degree angles. Glasses weren't plastic then, they were actual glass. Then, the nun came over and smacked him! He cried the rest of the time in class. I think it was the day I knew I was going to Hell. Lance became a driver for Mr. Katz. Remember him? The blind fellow? Lance and I became good friends after that but I haven't seen him in decades.

Another time, I was chewing gum in class. Sister Virginia made me spit the gum out in her hand and she proceeded to knead it into my hair. She then took me to every class on the second floor, interrupted whatever class it was, bent my head down and said to the other kids:

'Children, this is what happens to you when you chew gum in class!' We went to every classroom. When I got home, my mother had to get the gum out of my hair with naptha. No wonder I'm bald.

There are other stories, like the time I brought a water pistol to school and they made me hold the pistol in two hands while they proceeded to beat my hands with their fists until the gun actually broke. The times Sister Columbo (Remember her? Mother Superior?) skinned our knuckles in her office with the 18-inch ruler with the metal edger until our hands bled. The time Danny Ryan punched a nun on the 3rd floor and a Brother came down the hallway out of nowhere and beat Danny, I mean, beat Danny! Danny had to go home after that beating, but before he did, he tried to get his chair up to the window to push it out. I helped him. It went out of the window and crashed in the parking lot. The Brother and the nun had gone out into the hall just before.

I don't know how any of us survived, but we did. I guess the only consolation for us is when those nuns died, they went straight to Hell. They didn't pass 'GO' and they didn't collect $200.

Anyway, how are things in Georgia?

jcm
9/29/09

Changing Horizons

Good or bad,
dull or rosy,
exciting or indifferent,
each day with you
is never the same
as the one before.

No matter what it brings,
things good, bad or indifferent,
I can't wait for tomorrow
to spread itself
across my face.

jcm
4/5/84

Rocky Mountain Billy Goat

Under the sign of Capricorn I am.
The goat.
    Plodding, methodical
    and deep in thought is the goat.
    But above all is his sure-footedness.
    He knows where each hoof goes.
    He never makes a mistake
    as he nimbly moves along in
    his precarious and lofty domain . . .
I would have preferred the sign of Yield;
to be humble,
not so sure,
willing to believe
that other opinions are just as good
or maybe, better than mine.

jcm
4/5/84

Ogden, Utah and No Further

The troop train ground to a halt just outside Ogden, Utah. The unit on the train, the 71st Infantry Regiment of the 44th Division, United States Army, was on it's way to San Francisco to embark for the Western Pacific where they were to become part of the invasion of the Japanese mainland. The date was August 15th, 1945.

Six days before, August 9th, a B-29 named 'Bock's Car' dropped a 21-kiloton atomic bomb on Nagasaki, Japan, hoping it would force the Japanese government to finally call a halt to World War II.

The soldiers of the 71st climbed down from the train and made their way down the embankment to the Red Cross doughnut and coffee trucks parked nearby. The 71st had landed in Cherbourg, France over a year before. They had fought their way into Germany, then down into Austria where the war ended for them. Or so they thought. They came home and left almost immediately for the west coast where they were to travel off to war again. One of the soldiers, a combat medic, S/SGT Wendel F. Kokll was in one of the lines to get a mug of coffee. He didn't know it then, but 40 years into the future, his unborn daughter-to-be would marry me, in Danbury, Connecticut. I'm sure he wasn't thinking of those things as he slowly moved forward in the line. The soldiers hardly noticed the commotion up on the tracks to the west.

A man was running down the tracks from Ogden, yelling at the top of his lungs. The soldiers turned, one by one, and strained to hear what he was yelling. Finally, he came within earshot of all of them:

'The Japanese have quit! The war's over! The war's over!' It was like an electric shock to the men by the trucks! They threw their equipment into the air, laughed, screamed, dropped to their knees and prayed and grabbed each other. I remember asking Wendel: 'What did you do?'

‘I didn’t do anything,’ I remember him saying. ‘I just stood there and stared at the wheels of the train. I knew they weren’t going any further.’ And they didn’t.

Years later, at the Thanksgiving table in his house, with the family all around, he and I were talking about Harry Truman. He loved Harry Truman.

‘He saved my life, you know.’, Wendel used to say. Not only his life but everyone at the table. If the 71st Infantry Regiment along with a million other men ever invaded Japan, he might never have come home. There wouldn’t have been a daughter, Wendy. There wouldn’t have been a daughter, Barbara. My wife. Subsequently, our daughter, Kimberly would never have been born. His son, Richard, also. No ski instructor. no lawyer. No Richard. There would’ve been no other grandchildren either; no Cathie, no Greg and no Devin. Emil Nigro, Wendy’s husband, might have become a doctor without her. Maybe not. Richard’s wife, Josephine, would be living in New Jersey somewhere. My Mother-in-Law, Josephine would probably have married a sailor. That leaves me, but without Barbara. I would have been dead 16 years ago.

So, because of Harry Truman and his bomb, that table was brimming with good people that November day. Wendel came home and we all lived happily ever after . . .

I loved Harry Truman.

jcm
8/9/09

Too Big For a Band-Aid

It would be hard to remember the faces
or write down all the names
of the people I've damaged
while clomping through life
with my big feet.

Some damage was intentional,
most were not,
but the lines remain—
creasing faces
with frowns of disbelief
and damp pillows like tombstones
on unmade beds.

Too late to change opinions
and too late for a new coat of paint.
Damage is damage—
scarring the brain beyond repair
no matter how hard I try to reconstruct.

Once I took the four-dollar raincoat
out of its neat little bag,
I couldn't get it back in.
Hours of folding and re-folding
could never get that exact
and compact shape again.

jcm
4/10/84

August 6, 1945

They're having another memorial service in Hiroshima today. They'll probably float lighted candles down the river past the rusted remains of the observatory again. They'll have big crowds there and I'm sure all the non-combatant crowd and anti-war people will have bad things to say about the United States. It will be the same as it is every year in Hiroshima. There wasn't too much left in Hiroshima after the Enola Gay dropped the first atomic bomb on the city that day. Seventy-eight thousand Japanese citizens, give or take a few, never made it home for dinner that evening. I'm sure there will be thousands of other people paying homage to those citizens and there will be a number of people watching the proceedings on the evening news tonight.

Commander Ernest Evans won't be watching. He's not here. He was killed aboard his destroyer, USS *Johnston* in Samar Strait while trying to protect his baby flattops in TF58 from the Japanese super battleship, IJN *Yamato*. Admiral Isaac Kidd won't be watching either. He's still aboard his flagship, USS *Arizona* at the bottom of Pearl Harbor along with 1,076 other crewmen. SN1 John James of Peekskill won't be watching his television. He's with Admiral Kidd, somewhere inside the *Arizona*. Sgt. Harold Schubert, U.S. Army, from Montrose, New York won't be watching either. He was my aunt's boyfriend. No one knows where he is. After his tank destroyer was hit in the Huertgen Forest in Germany, all they found was his raincoat. Four hundred and ten thousand other Americans never came back home either.

Today, when they show the lighted candles floating down the river in Hiroshima, I hope most people remember that it didn't have to be that way. Not very much thought is given to the future Nobel Prize winners who never made it back to Altoona, White Plains or Sacramento. Two future Presidents came home, but maybe there could've been three. Or maybe four. We'll never know.

On Hiroshima Day, I'd like to see four hundred and forty-thousand lighted candles floating down the Hudson River. One of them could be for Harold Shubert. Or one for John James. The scene on the Hudson wouldn't have to take up much time on the evening news, just a few seconds. Just enough time for Americans to remember how we managed to arrive here, today.

jcm
8/6/09

'Hold Until Relieved . . .'

Dave,

Sixty-five years ago today, as a matter of fact, now, B and D Companies of the Ox and Bucks dropped down out of the sky in their Horsa gliders and landed in the field next to Pegasus Bridge over the Orne.

It was D-Day plus one hour. Lt. Den Brotheridge of B Company led his men onto the bridge and flushed the Germans out. In minutes, the bridge was theirs. Lt. Brotheridge couldn't report to Major John Howard because he had been hit in the neck by a German machine gun. He lived for a few minutes then died. The Ox and Bucks, their formal name being the Oxfordshire and Buckinghamshire Regiment, had secured their objective and all they had to do was wait for Lord Lovat to come over the hill from Sword Beach to relieve them. Howard's orders were: 'Hold until relieved.'

Around 0300 two German Tigers came down the road but one was taken out with a Piat anti-tank weapon and the other turned and ran. Lord Lovat arrived a little later and the Ox and Bucks took a well-needed rest.

The action at Pegasus Bridge was small but important. It took place before the American Airborne dropped from the sky, before the Rangers clambered up Point du Hoc and before Omaha Beach saw any LCVP's or any members of the 29th Division. It was the very first action on D-Day. Lt. Den Brotheridge was the very first Allied soldier, in a long list of Allied soldiers to lose his life on that day.

Sixty-five years ago, right now.

jcm
6/5/2009
2001EST

The Curtain of Midnight

Over my left shoulder, midnight sits;
aquamarine bordered in black,
hanging between a smirk and a smile.
        Ahead lies dawn,
        somewhere over the hills
        in striped pajamas and morning-mouth.
The calendar tells me the new date
for my mind is still on yesterday,
but midnight closed the gate on me-
I'm cut off from the useful hours
I threw away.
        I'd trade tomorrow
                to get another hold on yesterday,
        but it's out of reach.
        I didn't have enough time
        and I can't even think about it
        because dawn is coming on with a rush.

jcm
4/10/84

Demons

I can move a mountain
if given enough time.
Or, drain the Adriatic
if I had a deeper valley.
    But I can't seem to corral
    those demons you threw down on me.

Maybe it's better
that you don't understand,
if you don't comprehend
my illogical logic.
That way I can blame you
to my heart's content
and let the demons eat me away.

  I can blame you daily
  and watch the wonderment
  blossom on your face again,
  because I could <u>never</u> blame myself.

jcm
4/10/84

In Flanders Field . . .

'In Flanders fields the poppies blow
between the crosses row on row . . .'

Another Memorial Day is gone. I watched the Yankee game yesterday afternoon with each team wearing red caps. The Mets had a flyover with Marine Ospreys and small town after small town had their mini-parades. It was Fleet Week in the city and all the sailors with their shapeless new white hats were all congregated in a freshly-scrubbed Times Square, snapping away with their phone-cameras. There were the usual clips on the news of the pretty girls with face-painted American flags on their cheeks, not really sure why the flags were painted on. There was the President laying wreaths at Arlington, at the Tomb of the Unknown Soldier. All the old scenes so familiar to me now.

I tried to remember when I was a youngster, growing up in Peekskill; watching the parade and the sight of a waving Jack Buhs, a paratrooper who was crippled on D-Day when he landed wrong in a field outside Ste. mer Eglise. Up at Depew Park Pond, the veterans always launched a metal boat filled with flowers. Each year the boat was pushed out onto the pond and promptly turned and stopped. I always thought that strange. The moment of silence. It was a somber day once, a day of actual national pride. I don't remember the military-hating Leftist people then. I don't think they were born.

The day wore on with the Yanks pulling away from the Texas Rangers, when Barbara walked in. She started to ramble on about her day then said to me:

'I stopped up to see my Dad today, to say 'thank you'.' Then, she started to tell me about a woman she met at the same cemetery who had lost her husband two months ago, another World War II vet, but I wasn't listening.

Barbara's Dad was a combat medic staff sergeant in the 44th Division,'The Backward Fours'. He landed at Cherbourg, France and walked all the way to Germany. I was thinking about the story he told me once when he cut an orange with a Ghurka soldier's knife. He got in trouble because he wasn't supposed to touch the Ghurka's knife. Wendel lies beneath the lilacs now, on a hill overlooking a beautiful creek which empties into Diverting Reservoir.

I thought of what the great English writer, Barrie Pitt said when he tried to explain the appearance of the 'men of action' in times of trouble.

'It is good for us, good for this nation of ours that in between wars when things grow quiet, this spirit does not die. It only sleeps.'

And so ended another Memorial Day. 'Thanks' from me too, Wendel.

> 'In Flanders fields the poppies blow
> between the crosses row by row,
> that mark our place and in the sky
> the larks, still bravely singing, fly . . .'

jcm
5/26/09

The Spider

There he was
clinging to the bathroom wall
like a black burr.
'Get him!', you said,
panic creeping into your voice.

We saw the robin last week
hopping on the driveway.
'Spring is finally here.', you said.
Once the wash went back on the line
our clothes smelled of pure oxygen
and sunlight.

Spring.
The crocuses are peeping out to see
and the buds are blossoming,
but it wasn't Spring to me
until today.
    The bugs are back,
    the spider proved it.
    I wrapped him in a toilet paper coffin,
    Galahad in denim I was.
        Spring is finally here—
        We've reached another plateau.

jcm
4/11/84

The Value Of Things

Whenever we see a setting sun
nestling down among the mountains
and pushing it's feet deep into the trees
to gather all the warmth
for the night ahead,
we say to ourselves;
  'Give us another day, like this one.'
Another day follows that,
then another,
and another.
  But what if that day was the last?
  We would have no more days,
  just an hour or a minute.
  What would we do?
If I knew, deep in my heart
that this day would be the last,
the setting sun was setting for good,
I'd try to write something
more profound than I'd ever done.
Or, I'd try to say something to you
that you've never heard before.
  I would have just one minute
  to think, to ponder, to get an idea.
And nothing would come.
It would all have been said, written and done.
  I would look at you and just smile.
  That's all. Just a smile,
and you would know.

jcm
7/5/84

Marching Through Old Southy

St. Patrick's Day, 1960, Boston.

They passed the word on my ship, the USS *Yellowstone* (AD-27) that all men of Irish extraction, on a voluntary basis, report to the quarterdeck if they wanted to march in the St. Patrick's Day parade in the city. Naturally, I went down to the quarterdeck in my dress blues where we were issued M-1's, white gloves, white leggings and white web belts. They bused us over to Boston proper and we lined up to march. There were soldiers and marines there also. The Navy, never known for their marching ability, were positioned last.

St. Patrick's Day, in Boston, is never called that. It's called Evacuation Day because that's when the British left Boston, in 1776. On March 17th. The bands came, the dignitaries came, the county associations came and the parade was off and marching. One of the first areas we marched through was South Boston, heavily Irish. The people were in front of their homes, waving the tri-color and yelling as we marched by. Finally, we stopped for a respite and when we did, women came running over to put green carnations in the muzzles of our rifles. And that's how we marched off a few minutes later, those green carnations swaying like a small green sea on the tips of our M-1's, up through Old Southy and beyond with the sons and daughters of Erin, cheering us on.

. . . Many a time, when the day turns bad or a calamity or two strikes, I reflect back to Evacuation Day, 1960. I thought of those carnations just before the coalition jumped off in Desert Storm. I thought about those carnations again when the terrorists hit the World Trade and again when we went into the Afghan maelstrom. Whenever things or events tend to get me down, I always think of those marching carnations and the men who were under them. Then, everything seems all right. It will be okay. All the smiling faces in Old Southy, clapping their hands red, the swaying green carnations, a free celebration in a free country. They were shipmates all.

jcm
3/17/09

The Witching Hour

Will our merry-go-round ride
ever come to a halt?
Will the referee
ever blow his whistle
ending the game?
Will there ever be an end to us,
a witching hour?
        Will we argue so badly one day
        that we crack like an egg?
        If that happens
        and we fight to see
        who leaves first,
        will one of us look back?
        Or both?

The first one to look back
will have had more feeling
                for the other.

jcm
7/1/84

Periods, Commas And Puns

Way back when,
back when the last dinosaur
had fallen into his tarry grave,
and back further
when Eve offered a Golden Delicious
to wimpy Adam.
(Didn't Eve say:
'You're always ribbing me!')
Back, centuries ago
when we worked in Valhalla,
I always thought
that just being loved
was not enough for you.

    To love or not to love,
    being in love, falling in love,
    loving me, loving you, I love,
    you love, we all love.
    There had to be more emphasis,
    at least, this time.
    This last of all times.

        Enter Conan the Typist!

What a job it was to scrape
that glaze from your eyes.
I thought that daily frown
on your face was polyurethaned on.

    The Most Beautiful Woman in Minsk,
    Alfred Lunt and Lynn Fontanne.

They were all there
at one time or another.

Remember the parade down Broadway
when you came to see me off?
Was I in the Seventh Regiment
and your father was a carriage maker?
The Baltimore bard
scribbling over a trying note
to the fancy dolly
who lived across town?
Those crazy characters
running back and forth across the paper.
The clown and the equestrian sweetheart
in the circus on that dewy morning.
'. . . but morning found the breeze
a hundred miles away.'
The couple dancing to no music
on the bandstand.
Was it in Cincinnati?
There were more,
they're all in the box on the shelf.
Were they worth it?
Was I right in saying,
just being in love
was not enough for you?

jcm
6/30/84

343 Honor Company

Dear Friends, Cohorts and Enemies,

I'm watching the St. Paddy's Day Parade from Manhattan today. I was waiting for one division to pass by, the 343 Honor Company. Three hundred and forty-three probies, each carrying an American flag, representing the 343 firefighters who lost their lives on September 11, 2001. It was a sea of flags, carried by brand new probies, just out of the academy.

There are other things I wait for in the parade, but this is the one I look forward to seeing each year as they pass by the cathedral and the Cardinal takes his hat off and holds it over his heart until the last flag passes by. The greatest fire department ever, in the greatest city ever, in the history of the world.

Now, I'll put on my old jeans, take my watch off and make sure my claddagh ring is turned around so I can see it, and if I run into one of the Islamic terrorists, he can see it too. Of course they're not around Brewster, but I look under every rock and in every garbage can where they usually hide. I wonder where they're cowering?

'. . . We came down the stairs that day,
through the smoke and fire.
We noticed as we were going down the stairs,
the fireman was climbing higher.'

Up County Clare!
Up the FDNY!
Death to Terrorists!

New York for Honest Abe and the Union!

Jcm
3/17/12

Conference at 3 A.M.

It will be one of those nights
at Milepost #19—
not too windy—
clear as a cat's eye—
air soft and warm—
surf whispering and rolling.
 I'll silently leave the bed
 careful not to wake you
 and tip-toe outside.
The sand will be cool,
the clouds surrounding the moon
will be waiting like
the College of Cardinals.
I'll walk a ways down the beach
until I find an open and smooth spot.
 I'll wait until it's just right,
 when I feel alone and shut out
 from everything and everyone around me.
 Then we'll talk. He and I.
I'll tell him of my plans,
maybe make a confession or two,
explain a few things that have been
confusing to most, and make some promises,
most of which I intend to keep.
 I know He'll listen.
 He always does.
 He knows it's the only time I talk to Him.

jcm
6/21/84

Message In a Bottle

If I came home one day
and found you gone,
I'd initiate my contingency plan.
You may have been kidnapped,
or snatched away,
or have wandered off.
It wouldn't matter.
You may have even left of your own accord.
If that was the case,
and you grew tired of new surroundings
or broke free of your captors,
just send me a message in a bottle.
Wherever you may be at the time,
you would have to be near water.
The Earth is covered mostly by water,
so,
send me a message in a bottle.
I promise to walk every shoreline
from Namibia to Patagonia
and from the Scilly Islands
to Zanzibar and back.
I'll walk every beach.
I'm not saying that I will find that bottle.
I'm saying that it will find me.

jcm
6/20/84

March 11th

To all my children,

Well, here we are again. March 11th. Now it's two years since Nanny left. The time starts to speed up after awhile but the memories remain. They'll always be here. I remember how distraught the boys were in church and how Kim was trying to herd them in; that awful snow storm and all of us pushing the hearse up the hill in the snow with Coby yelling: 'Aunt Florence! What are you doing to us?' Tom's show-stopping reading at the grave site, not from any bible but from his heart. The silver dollar story at the restaurant. All those things and more; poignant memories from a great life.

Update: The people renting Nanny's condo, Tom and Alicia Mann and their baby daughter, love the place. They might renew their lease in May. I don't know. They're nice people. Kathleen is coming down today and we're going to make chili. Kim is here too.

None of us are as religious as Nanny was. She told us all she was going to meet us 'up there' one day. Wouldn't it be funny, one day when our time was up and we boarded that big bus to take us out of here, if she was waiting at that bus stop? Wouldn't that be something? I can see her now, as we step off the bus, shaking her finger at us as if to say: 'See? I told you!' Who knows. I guess we're all going to find out one day.

But, it's today. March 11th. I look at the clock and it's 9:10. She was just getting ready for 10:15 mass, to go to St. Patrick's to do what else? To pray for all of us; to pray for her family.

I hope your day today is pleasant and not too rainy. I love you all.

Dad

jcm
3/11/09

The idol of the moslem world is dead

My Fellow Enablers of Freedom,

Abraham Lincoln used to call them 'Uncle Sam's Webbed Feet'. The British Admiralty back in 1812 told the Royal Navy: 'A fast frigate of the United States will now only be confronted by our ships in squadron force.' General Kuribayashi on Iwo Jima said: 'When the U.S. Marines get here, we will see that they all die!' Commander Ernest Evans called for All Ahead Flank, as he headed his destroyer toward the IJN *Yamato* with a .45 in his only good hand. Lewis B. 'Chesty' Puller, while pulling his Marines away from the Chosin Reservoir said: 'We're just attacking in a different direction!' For all of them; Stephen Decatur, Isaac Hull, John Worden of the *Monitor*, Isaac Kidd and Captains Preble, Rogers, Bainbridge and J.P. Jones, Congratulations. From all of us.

Last night, in some sheep dip-village, in the province of 'somewhere-istan' in Pakistan, 25 Navy (I'm sorry, United States Navy) SEALs (SEa, Air, Land) dropped down and confronted the Babe Ruth of Islam, Osama Bin Laden. They killed him.

Let me repeat that for our friends on the west coast. They killed him. I haven't been this happy since I found out the bogey-man was make-believe.

For all the guys at Parris Island, slogging through the swamps; this one's for you. For all the guys strapped to their bunks in some storm in the North Atlantic; this one's for you. I can't forget the Army, the Air Force and the Coast Guard, nor can we forget all the good people getting up to go to work tomorrow.

But I can't seem to get rid of the nautical flavor of this good news. I suppose it's because it's my 'home team'. Thanks, fellas.

(Tony 'Buff', do you feel good?)

Let's end with a song:

'Anchor's aweigh my boys,
anchor's aweigh,
farewell to college joys
we sail at break of day, 'ay-'ay-'ay!
O'er our last night ashore,
drink to the foam,
until we meet once more,
here's wishing you a happy voyage home . . . !'

United States Navy. A Global Force for Good
James C. Mc Guire, GM3 5176234 USN

jcm
5/2/11

No More Unexplored Land

Strange it is, how satisfied I am at times.
          Calmness swells between my ears
                    at the prospect of no more monsters.
The only monsters now
are the ones I inflate,
add color and substance to,
or dream up.
          I never tire of charging windmills
          like the ancient Quixote
          but unaware that my horse grows old also.
The things I haven't seen,
I know about.
The problems I haven't faced,
I have solutions for.
I have personal histories
of people I haven't met yet.
          Finally, insight and excitement are enough.
          (. . . Lookin' for fun and feelin' groovy . . .)
          But each morning, when the haze lifts
          and the windmills come into view,
          I have to charge them.
The monsters are gone now.
Nothing scares me.
Not even death.

jcm
6/18/84

Dustin Hoffman, Boo-Boo Kitty and Me

Poor old Dominic, clanking down
the Saw Mill, apprehensive of the night.
Even he wasn't sure of the mood.
        The giggles we had at Giggles
        with Perry Mason, Jr.
The red Porsche that wasn't tradable.
        Trying to fend off the crush of people
        and drink socially and neatly.
Kissing on the corner of the 40th and Broadway.
        Mezzanine seats in the Broadhurst
        and watching you nod off with Act Two.
Trying not to get caught up in the fight
in survival with Willy Loman.
. . . and losing.
Trying to tell ourselves it was only a play,
but crying anyway.
A study in human frailties had found us
but had not beaten us.
We were better for it.
        Listening to Dustin as he waved
        from the limo: 'Thank you! Thank you
        all very much!'
And thank you, my darling.
It was another memorable night
to add to our already thousands.

jcm
6/15/84

'Introducing, the Duke and Duchess of Cambridge . . .'

Dear Louise,

I taped the wedding so the girls and I could watch it the following morning. Down in Ossining, the Hudson River Chapter of the Daughters of the British Empire enjoyed cucumber sandwiches, champagne and cake in Victoria Home. There was a picture in the paper the next day, showing the little old ladies all gathered around their TV set, wearing their big hats and sipping their champagne. It was a big event here, but then the Royal detractors came out. On talk radio the usual suspects had their fangs bared, pooh-poohing the expenditure of money in England. There were the usual derisive chants and gatherings here and in Great Britain. And (never start a sentence with 'and') as usual, the detractors, or, as I like to call them; mouthy non-combatants, haven't got one shred of logic or knowledge. They just whine for 'whining's sake'.

I prefer to be happy for my friends, the Brits. It was a wedding of two young people, televised to anyone who cared to watch. Everyone should've watched because it was more than a wedding. There was the kaleidoscope of color with the uniforms and the hats, every stitch, by the way, the English earned. There was the great stream of humanity coming down the mall, held back by one thin line of British bobbies. Not held back really, because the huge crowd was orderly and mannerly. When the line of bobbies stopped, the hundred thousand people stopped. No pushing and shoving but a quiet and steady movement of people. We here, can take a lesson from that.

The flyover of the Avro Lancaster, the Hawker Hurricane and the Supermarine Spitfire was a high point for me. The last two, the Hurricane and the Spitfire were instrumental in 1940, of making sure there would be a wedding for us to see. In World War II, 56,000 men in RAF Bomber Command, in planes like the Lancaster, didn't come home. When I see a Spitfire, I think of Paddy Finucayne in his shot-up Spit, too low for him to bail out, standing in the cockpit and telling his wingmen: 'This is it, chaps! Thanks!', just before his plane hit the Channel at 220 miles per hour. When I see a Hurricane, I think of my good friend, David Wilkie, recently hospitalized, who, as a Hurricane pilot, helped to fight the Axis to a standstill.

When the U.S. Army landed on Normandy on that gray, June day in 1944, they didn't land alone. To their left were the Canadians and the British, all sharing in the heartache and the victory. Together.

Then there was the 23rd of February, 1991. The land operation of the First Persian Gulf War was just hours from jump-off. The U.S. Fifth Cavalry's 3rd Tank Battalion was having its last briefing in the heat of the Kuwaiti desert. There was one British officer standing off to the side. His name was Colonel Anthony De Ritter of the Queen's Royal Irish Hussars, the 'Desert Rats'. The American briefing officer asked Colonel De Ritter if he would like to add anything. De Ritter stepped forward and said:

'I just want to tell you all, no matter how far you go tomorrow, no matter how fast you move, if you look to your left, you will see us.'

The next day, as the U.S. 3rd Tank Battalion moved, the 57 Chieftain tanks of the Hussars stayed right with them. On their left.

I see other things when I watch events like Charles and Diana, or the Coronation of Elizabeth, or Carnarvon Castle turning out another Prince of Wales. Yes, I see the pomp and ceremony which can only be properly done by the British. I see the reds, the blues, the feathers, the bearskins, the armour-plate and the fancy cutlery. It may seem silly to some, the non-combatants, but that not-so-big island has earned every stitch, every feather and every happily-spent Pound Sterling.

Louise, you wrote to me yesterday, (knowing full well that I'm Irish!) 'Jim, doesn't it feel good to be British at times like this?'

Yes, Louise. It does.

Jim

jcm
5/1/11

Doing It Right

I hold a friend's laughter in my hand,
watch the pulse in his neck jump.
I made him laugh
and I was better for it.
 I do a favor for a friend
 and feel the warmth in my heart
 even if he does not.
 I grow from the inside out.
I find myself close to a person,
closer than anyone before,
and yet, closer still.
I see it on her face;
lines and lines of words
reaching out to my understanding.
 Each and more is a personal monument,
 an obelisk in a city park
 with my name on it,
 my name on the lips of someone
 faraway that I don't know.
Best of all,
I see myself the way I should be,
and not the way I am.
 I could've had more monuments
 but the quarries ran dry
 before the idea did.

jcm
6/11/84

A joint return

Could I do anything else for you
better than I do now?
        And you;
        Could you do anything more for me?
        More than you do now?
Maybe.
Maybe we could do it jointly;
for instance, looking down
        at a round, little face-
        blonde hair-
        blue eyes-
        all seven pounds worth,
        kicking and screaming,
and, oh yes!
        A big head!

—Collectively.
That's the word,
collectively.
It's not really a new word
but an old word.
I can't remember or imagine
anything we've done
that didn't have
a 'collective' ring to it.

jcm
6/4/84

Marching To Guild Hall

Back in 1939 (the year I was born) England was all alone, just about. The war was a few months old and the Allies were being pushed around by Hitler. America was neutral, for another two years. The news wasn't good. No one had heard of Pearl Harbor yet. Americans didn't even know where it was. And England was losing. The French, in their own inimitable way, were already planning on bailing out of the war and the rest of the little countries were on the verge. German raiders were on the high seas, sinking British ships and the Royal Navy couldn't track them down. England needed something.

December, 1939. The German pocket battleship, SKS *Graf Spee* came upon three British cruisers just outside Montevideo harbor at the mouth of the River Plate, Uruguay. The German ship outgunned the three cruisers, but the incessant attacks by them somewhat crippled the German and it went into the neutral port of Montevideo. The HMS *Exeter*, HMS *Achilles* and HMNZS *Ajax* all took a beating, but the German, not wanting to face the three cruisers again, came out of Montevideo and scuttled herself.

The Royal Navy had won.

In February, 1940, the *Exeter* and *Achilles* both came back to London. They came up the Thames, docked and the two crews marched up the winding streets to Guild Hall where the King, the PM and all of Parliament met them. They said there must've been 1,000,000 people lining the streets for the sailors.

I would like to have been there. The next time I'm in London, I'm going to find the exact route of the march and walk it. My friend, Clementine, works for the BBC and she's a historian. I'm sure she'll be able to track it for me.

. . . I would like to have been in the crowd or, one of the sailors. If I had been one of the sailors, I'm sure there would've been a Molly.

Somewhere, in one of the numerous pubs by Guild Hall, we would've run into each other. I wouldn't have been able to pay for a pint that day and somewhere, there she would be. A little star tattoo in each ear lobe, more than a few extra pounds, lots of lipstick and loud. Very loud. She would've called me 'Dearie' a thousand times. I would end up giving her my cap which said: 'HMS *Exeter*' on the front band. I'd never see her again, but I would think of her often, and the million other Londoners who came out to see us that day . . .

jcm
2/11/09

Mental Labor

These are the hardest of days
made even harder by myself.
Cash flow has thinned to a trickle—
Old women are crying in the streets—
My ears pick up the snap, crackle and pop
of used-up bones.—
Muscled cats with worried faces
stalk me from overhead branches.—
Youth goes laughing by,
giggling and screaming at my slowness.
But I still have you
to pour oil on my stormy waters.
I still have you to bring the word 'real'
into inane daily conversation.
I still have you to sweep the day away,
and mend the dents in my armor.
If I didn't have you,
I'd hire my own chaplain,
buy my own body bag
and charter my own burial ship.
There wouldn't be a minute
worthy of my time.
If I didn't have you.

jcm
6/2/84

The Not-So—Mighty Pen

Words scrawled on blank tavern checks—
on paper napkins—
on buck slips
and even matchbook covers.
I'd like to have them all back.
    A girl in Brown University
    has a cigar box full of my words.
    Why she kept them I don't know.
I'd like to have them all back,
up to and including this page.
    Some I hammered out—
    some flowed like mercury
    and came easy—
    some were born out of sarcasm,
    and hate,
    and laughter,
    and lovc
    A little of myself went into each one.
    I'd like to have
    all those little pieces back,
    because, like now,
    I feel some of 'my children' are gone.
I'm diminished by pages lost.

jcm
5/28/84

'To April's Breeze Their Flag Unfurled . . .'

To my fellow Americans and other advocates of inalienable rights,

The unsung Joseph Dawes was only one hour behind Revere. Dawes, the back-up rider, would eventually be the one who roused the countryside with 'The British are coming!', as he passed the Boston silversmith outside of Lexington.

On and on he rode.

'Ready to ride and spread the alarm, to every middlesex, village and farm . . .'

It would be a harrowing April night, this one. The sky was clear and the moon shone down on the trudging militiamen from such places as Acton, Menotomy, Bedford. They were all heading for the tiny hamlet of Concord, toward destiny. But before Concord, there would have to be a Lexington. There would have to be blood spilled before the fledgling United States would come to be . . .

12 yr. old Tom and Me in Concord)

My son, Tom, and I travelled to Lexington that April day back in 1975 to see the 200th Anniversary Re-enactment of the Battle of Lexington. President Ford arrived by helicopter. In a town of 18,000, there were a quarter of a million souls. We saw the entire thing, starting at 3:00 A.M., the exact time the British arrived in Lexington.

Every April 19th, I think of that time in Lexington, in 1975 with my son and in 1775 with those stalwart minutemen. No matter what's going on, my eyes always seem to find the 19th and I think back to those hopes and dreams that were laid bare on that grassy Lexington Commons. There they stood, 32 of them with their Captain Parker. More than 700 British regulars were filing into the town, led by Major Pitcairn. It was an uneven match but none of the minutemen turned to run. Not one.

'Disperse, ye god-damned rebels! Disperse now!', screamed Pitcairn. Parker, standing in front of his ragged line, turned and yelled to his men:

'Stand your ground and don't fire! But if they mean to have a war, let it start here! . . .'

Many times I think of the trials and tribulations we all go through. I think of my friend, Eddie Rourke down in his bunker, trying not to listen to the blather coming from the White House. I think of my Son-in-Law, Richie, walking around in the nuclear plant, trying not to get contaminated. I think of my wife. My children. My friends. All of us, struggling at times, trying to make ends meet; trying to make sense out of Washington; wondering where our country is going. And then a calm comes. A tiny sense of well-being slides into the room. I look at the calendar and realize, we'll be all right. Everything will work itself out. The rough part is over. It's been over for a long time now. We'll get through. We always do.

And now, if you'll excuse me, I have some contemplation to do. My wrist chronometer tells me it's exactly 0312, April 19th. Major Pitcairn is coming into the Commons on his white horse and Captain Parker is motioning for me to hurry. I have to go. I have a birth to watch.

jcm
4/19/11

Memory Traps

Just for the sake of anti-thought
or to keep yourself honest,
try to think of the day
you would want to forget me.
Try, for the sake of argument.
First, you would move away
leaving everything material behind you-
everything;
letters-
empty white boxes-
empty green boxes-
everything resembling apples-
everything.
And just say, for honesty sake,
you wouldn't think of me.
At all.
You'd be able to conquer your own mind,
a plus in will power.
You'd have done it,
you'd have won.

But what about mirrors?
Would you give up
your own reflection?

No.
And that's when you would see me.
Every time.

jcm
5/26/84

Polished Diamonds

I'm susceptible on a beach,
any beach.
One might say that I'm 'beach crazy'.
Love comes easy on a beach,
I can spot it walking toward me
from a mile away.
        Love found me once.
        On a beach.
        We were in love
        long before we walked the sand
        but the salt water has a habit
        of cleaning the body and the mind
        to the point of naked reality.
The mines of Johannesburg
or the opal holes of Coober Peedy
can't hold a candle to Hatteras.
Polished stones and shells underfoot
and worn glass gleaming in the sand
make Hatteras one big jewelry store.
One has only to pick up a special shell,
hand it to a smiling face and say:
        'I love you.'
        You'll always get an
        'I love you' back.
I hope to find love again soon,
when the hot July winds blow.

jcm
5/26/84

Fort Sumter and That Dastardly Dog, Edmund Ruffin

Just about now, 0112 on Tuesday morning of April 12th, 150 years ago almost to the minute, the American Civil War started. The Confederacy opened fire on 138 members of the United States Army stationed in Fort Sumter, a three-tiered structure in the middle of Charleston Bay, South Carolina. Four years and 622,000 deaths later, the war ended. It had been and still is, the most costly war the United states ever participated in. Every person who died was an American.

On that fateful morning of April 12, 1861, there happened to be in the forefront of the Southern troops in Charleston, Edmund Ruffin. There were seven forts and gun emplacements surrounding Fort Sumter and Ruffin begged the Southern Commanding General, Pierre Gustave Toutant Beauregard, to fire the first shot. Beauregard gave him permission. So, Ruffin, in the early morning gray of April 12th, fired the first shot as he pulled the lanyard of a 32-pounder, the shot arching across the water from Fort Johnson to Fort Sumter. The war had begun.

I have a good friend, George Davis. He was a Master Chief in the Coast Guard. He always told me that the Civil War should have been named the 'War of Northern Aggression'. He always told me it was a war against the South for economic reasons, for States Rights, for any number of things, but never for the main reason: Slavery. As politically incorrect and untimely that reason is, for whomever you happened to side with during that conflict, that reason is why the Civil War was fought. Edmund Ruffin thought it was the reason also.

Edmund Ruffin, a Virginian, was a fire-breathing secessionist. He was 67 when the war started. He was 71 when it ended. When word reached Charleston in 1865, that R.E. Lee had surrendered the Army of Northern Virginia and the war was over, Edmund Ruffin, the fire-breather, killed himself. He put a short-barreled shotgun under his chin and pulled the trigger.

When I was standing on the parapets of Fort Sumter in 1974, I thought of Edmund Ruffin. When I was in Gettysburg on Little Round Top and tried to visualize the men of the 20th Maine rushing down the hill against great odds, I thought of Edmund Ruffin. When I walked through the Gettysburg graveyard with my grandson, Richard, I thought of Edmund Ruffin. I walked through the USS *Cairo* down in Vicksburg, Mississippi, trying to feel the heat and hear the noise her crew went through, but Edmund Ruffin kept clouding my thoughts. At the West Point graveyard there stands a marker simply reading: 'ANDERSON' (and underneath) 'SUMTER'. It's the grave of Major Robert Anderson, Commanding Officer at Sumter that day. I think of Ruffin whenever I see that.

I can only hope that somewhere, on this 150th Anniversary of Fort Sumter, the ghost of Edmund Ruffin is re-enacting his death. Shotguns back in the 1860's were almost always 12 gauge. It would've been nice if that round in Ruffin's gun was a buck-and-ball and not birdshot. The former would have made a fitting mess.

One more thing for my friend, George Davis: When you were a Master Chief in the Coast Guard, it was not the 'Coast Guard', rather, it was the U.S. Coast Guard. I don't have to remind you what the 'U.S.' stands for.

'He loosed his faithful lightning from his terrible swift sword . . .'
God bless this republic.

jcm
4/12/11

Uncharted Water

Someday I'd like to find an ocean.
        Well, maybe not an ocean
but a gulf, or a bay, or a small sea.
I'd even settle for a tiny inlet, a cove,
a weed-choked tributary, anything
that others haven't seen yet.
        Some unnamed, uncharted water
        that would be mine and mine alone.
We stopped along the ocean highway in Maine,
remember?
I wondered aloud whether or not
that little cove had a name.
Remember?
There was a sand bar across the mouth
as it led to the sea.
A wall of fog shut the gate on the cove
just as it entered the sea,
as if to say: KEEP OUT!
        Oceans are like that—
        majestic, pushy, authoritative.
        Oceans only hang with other oceans,
        they don't need the inlets or coves.
But I do.
        Even little known places have been found-
        the Weddell Sea, Gulf of Lions, Bay of Biscay,
all of them.
There's nothing left for me,
but I always look

wherever I go.
I always think, just beyond this hill,
just around that bend,
when this road ends, I'll find it.
In the mountains
I'm always aware of sea level signs.
That way I know exactly
how far I am away from where I live.
Each visit to sea level
is a new experience, a new love affair.
I keep going back, like I've always done.
If I trace my cells to the beginning
I find that I came from the sea.
We all did,
but unlike the rest,
I'll be going back someday for good.
No morbidity intended, or sorrow,
just one more journey,
back to where I came from.
Back to where I belong.

jcm
5/26/84

Looking On You

My eyes have seen newsworthy things,
beautiful things,
things that others haven't seen.
    I collect great joy from a so-so day,
    just to make it hard to pick out
    the good things.
I know, just from being with you,
everything seems to take on a richer tint,
another dimension.
I enjoy it.
I enjoy looking at you.
When you're not around me
the world goes flat into waves
of black and white.
Nothing is beautiful to me.
    If something ever happened to you,
    if one day you weren't here anymore
    and there was no chance on ever
    seeing you again,
I'd prefer to be blind.
I'd donate my eyes to somewhere or someone.
Seeing what was left without you,
would be like not seeing at all.

jcm
5/22/84

'Every Man Has His Agincourt . . .'

(A Parody for A.F.)

The firing had died down, finally. The men huddling behind the remains of BRG1 were quiet for the most part, still aware of the terrorist on the hill, waiting for them to come out from cover again. Lt. Formato listened to the high-pitched voices on his radio. He had known this would happen, everyone talking at once, clogging up the airwaves. They had all been told a thousand times but now that it had hit the fan, all radio protocol had gone out the window. Indian Point, after all these years had been attacked.

They heard Weibrecht moan again, inside the crumpled BRG. There was nothing they could do for him. If they went around to the front, the terrorist on the hill would nail them, the same as he had nailed Nicky. For some reason, thought Anthony, no help had come. What had seemed like an hour had only been twenty minutes. The radio had informed him of the two terrorists inside the Emergency Diesel Generator Building, 200 feet of open ground in front of them. Anthony knew they were trying their best to destroy the generators, a known vital area. If that happened, he thought . . . Something had to be done, and now.

He looked at the huddled officers around him. Brennan, obviously the slowest man on site. There was Kelly, with her NY Ranger headband and no helmet. Johnny Rock's teeth were chattering but he held his rifle tightly. Jason had been to Iraq. He looked the calmest of all. Frankenberry and Hinck were the last two. Seven of them. They knew what they had to do. They had to rush the EDG and put an end to the threat. As far as Anthony knew, the other intruders were dead, except for the one on the hill. He could be neutralized if they took back control of the EDG. There was no time to lose, he thought to himself, as he looked at his tiny force.

He checked the magazine in his 9mm. and faced his motley band.

'You know what we have to do. You know where we're going, right?', he said. They all nodded.

'If any of you come through this, I want one of you to get a hold of Jim Mc Guire and tell him what was said behind this BRG. It will give me the last word.' And with that, Lt. Anthony Formato spoke to his charges, slowly, but with a hint of urgency:

> '. . . This story shall the good man teach his son;
> and Crispin Crispian shall ne'er go by,
> from, this day to the ending of the world,
> but we in it shall be remembered,
> We few, we happy few, we Band of Brothers;
> for he today that sheds his blood with me
> shall be my brother; be ne'er so vile,
> this day shall gentle his condition:
> and gentlemen in England now a-bed
> shall think themselves accursed they were not here
> and hold their manhoods cheap whilst any speaks
> that fought with us upon St. Crispin's Day . . .'

Anthony stood, as did they all, and with one, short roar, rushed around the corner toward the Diesel Generator Building.

Down by the river, a breeze swept through the tops of the tall elms. Some said afterward, they heard a bugle on the other side of the river.

jcm
4/4/11

New Life

I filled my lungs with you
when there wasn't any room.
I flushed them out
and kept your oxygen deep inside.
All my old thoughts,
my old beliefs and my old religions
had to go.
They were plotting against me,
trying to make me like everyone else.
I flushed out my eyes
after they'd seen everything
and filled them with pictures of you.
Everything was new.
Everything was fresh.
I practiced new smiles.
I was going to make it,
then, in my dream, I took your hand.
        I woke up,
        sitting bolt upright in bed.
        I wondered, panic rising,
        if you were real.
Opening my hand slowly,
I noticed the charred and reddened skin
of my palm
as if I'd just grasped a lightning bolt.

jcm
5/21/84

When No One Waited For You

Just when you got it all together,
when it all seemed to make sense
and the numbers were straight,
no one was there.
You wanted to tell your story,
your wants and needs
but there were empty ears all around.
No one was there, waiting,
ready to see the new you.
No one—
but me.

It's true I have my warped philosophies
coupled with long-term listening demands,
and sprinkled with anxieties
but at least I waited
when others didn't.

They could've waited
instead of running ahead of you
trying to catch their own elusive vanity.
They could've waited,
but they didn't.
I did.
I'm all you have,
because, you're all I have.

jcm
5/21/84

'Twas The Night Before Christmas . . .'

Dear Kathleen,

Today is Friday the 17th. Eight days before Christmas. B. went to work and I'm doing my Christmas chores, wrapping presents for the boys in Virginia, hanging cards in the dining room and later on I'm wrapping B.'s presents. Kimmy is coming home and both of us are excited. So, I was in the kitchen wrapping stuff and I remembered what you told me the other day about Nanny and your car loan; how you went down to her house for Christmas and how she had 'one more' present for you and it was just a little note telling you that the money she lent you for your car was paid in full. How like Nanny that was! I don't think any of us will ever get through another Christmas without thinking of her and her fantastic holiday surprises. B. and I were saving for Paris one year and she gave us a big check in a little red box that said 'Paris'. I still have the box. It's almost impossible to remember everything about her and her Christmases because if you think of one thing, it makes you remember two other things.

I can still remember her car in the driveway on Sherwood Road and the many trips I had to make out there to carry all the presents in. You kids were floored as were Mommy and I.

Every Christmas, even going back to the 40's, when I wanted a Flexible Flyer sled in the worst way, but they were so expensive. I was 10 years old and we lived on the second floor at Simpson Place. All the presents had been opened by Aunt Eileen and I and Nanny said:

'There's one more thing . . . ', and with that she reached under the couch and she and your Grandpa pulled out this giant Flexible Flyer! I remember it being so long it took forever to clear the couch. My Dad and I immediately took it down to the cellar and scraped all the red paint from the bottom of the runners and he waxed the bare steel to make it fast on the snow. I can remember thinking back then, 'where did they get the money for all this stuff?' I guess the thing that made her happiest was making other people happy. Don't you think?

In 2007, B. and I lost our Moms. There was no way we were going to stay here for Christmas so we went to England to see the Mortelman's. On Christmas Eve we went to midnight mass at Westminster Cathedral in London. All they did was sing, and those English can sing! When I was in kindergarten in the Assumption, back when I was 4 years old, the nuns invited Nanny up to the school one Christmas week to hear me sing 'Adeste Fidelis'. Nanny said the nuns cried when I sang. What song did they play at Westminster Cathedral that Christmas midnight? That's right. We had tried to get away from home that Christmas, but 'home' followed us. We sang 'Adeste Fidelis' with the congregation and I could feel Josephine and Florence in the same pew with us. B. said she never cooks or bakes during the holidays without thinking her Mother is right there with her. And, thinking of Nanny at this time of year is easy too. I don't think she made all those Christmases lavish with surprises and more presents than we could count, just to show off.

I think she did it so we would remember.

Love,
Dad

jcm
12/17/10

Night At The Edge of The Ocean

Faded beach umbrellas
slanted, tattered edges
motioning to the breeze.
Hunched figures
heads down, walking slowly
looking for that special shell.
Short wooden chairs
legs deep in the sand,
tired from the day,
resting.
Far out to sea
toward Gibraltar
and the Azores,
the sky and ocean black
from the absence of sun.
Tanned bodies
dark now, with the end of day,
lips white, eyes shadowy.
After sunset
the crest of each wave
carries the moon.
They'll find us there,
walking, heads down,
fingers locked.
Looking for that special shell.

Barbara on Boiler Beach

jcm
6/13/78

Stickers

God! How that dog jars my memory!
He had more burrs and thorns
in his coat
than ten acres of underbrush.
It took a month to clean him up;
he seemed to grow
as each burr came out.
        He had a neat little tongue
        which you commented on,
        time and time again.
But he didn't behave,
and he chewed everything in sight,
and he discolored the rug,
and he was lovable and nasty
at the same time.
He always came back, though,
when you let him out;
and you loved him.
    He was a lot like me.

jcm
5/11/84

Pearl Harbor Day,
or,
'Why I Dislike The Japanese'

Dear Kathleen,

Today, December 7th, is Pearl Harbor Day again. This is the day I go out and stare at my Honda and try not to take pictures with my Nikon. This is the day that has always made me nervous. Pearl Harbor has always bothered me. I suppose it's because of all the history I read.

Nanny used to tell me that when the news came over the radio on that Sunday back in 1941, the nation went into shock. The Japanese had attacked Pearl Harbor. She and your Grandpa were listening to the radio in the kitchen and when she looked up, your Grandpa was gone. She found him in the doorway to my bedroom. I was only two years old and I was taking a nap. She said he just stood there and looked at me. I guess every parent must've gone in and checked their kids that afternoon.

The following morning, Monday, your Grandpa and his five buddies went down into town to enlist. Nanny said she bundled me up and went with them. She didn't want him to go in because of me, I guess, plus he only had one good eye. He'd been shot in the left eye when he was a kid down at the docks by his friend, Tommy Burkaiser. They were shooting 22's at bottles and your Grandpa was shot. He lost just about all the sight in his left eye.

So, the six of them went down to enlist; Leo Palmero, Leo 'Nookie' Mc Caffery, Joe Ravase, George Jones, Tommy Burkaiser and your Grandpa. Nanny said downtown Peekskill was a madhouse.

There were lines outside of the Post Office with scores of men trying to enlist, pushing and shoving. She was carrying me, watching your grandpa and his friends struggling to get into the building.

The Army took his five friends but not your Grandpa. The minute they found out he couldn't see out of his left eye, they didn't want him. He tried the Navy. Then he tried the Marines. Finally he tried the Coast Guard. Nobody wanted him. Nanny was happy, but he wasn't. Back then was different than it is now. Most people would've done anything to defend their country. He just wanted to go with his buddies but instead, they went without him.

During the war, he had a big National Geographic map on the kitchen wall with different colored pins for each of his friends and where they were. There was one for Charlie Martin too. He was your Grandpa's cousin and he was in the Navy. Every time one of them moved to a different place, he would move a certain pin. We spent a lot of time looking at that pin-covered map in the kitchen.

When the war ended, they all came home. Even Charlie. When he finally took the map down, I was 6 years old. I can still remember all the old pinholes in the wall. His buddies all came down to the house and had a giant party. It was a great time. Years later, I saw the Jimmy Stewart movie, 'It's A Wonderful Life', about poor George Bailey, cemented in his hometown. There was always something going on at the Bedford Falls Building & Loan. He spent the entire movie frustrated that he could never get out of the small town and have his Great Adventure somewhere. He reminded me of your Grandpa, watching his friends go off to fight a war.

I never blamed Tommy Burkaiser and his errant .22 bullet which kept your Grandpa from going with his friends. I blame the Japanese. Subsequently, I imagine it was sort of a redemption for him when I went into the Navy in 1957. I guess he figured part of him finally made it in. There was a man, who in 1934 was the Middleweight Sub-Novice Champion of the Diamond Gloves with one eye, yet he couldn't go with his friends to war.

It's December 7th again. The Mitsubishi Zeroes and Nakajima Kates are about to appear over Diamond Head and descend down on my unsuspecting and beloved Navy. My cousin Charlie is about to come home with his seabag full of Pacific island stuff, and your

Grandpa, Thomas Anthony Mc Guire, is down in the kitchen, moving his pins around on the wall map I can hear Leo Palmero coming up the wooden stairs, yelling your Grandpa's name . . .

I hope by nightfall, all of this will go away again.

Dad

jcm
12/7/10

Mountains of the Mind

I'd like to live long enough
to look back on the things
that bother me now
and laugh at them.
Time piled on time
has a way of softening sharpness,
like stones in a brook—
like eastern mountains
weathered and rounded off.
rocky crags no more
but sanded-down humps, more like hills.
    Linda's mother made her put a shirt on
    one hot, summer afternoon.
    I never thought I'd swallow that one,
    but time showed me that it was sexual,
    girls being different from boys.
    It bothered me until I was twelve.
Katie bothered me,
she still does.
We were a 'could have been'.
But now, she's a rounded mountain in the distance
complete with a carpet of oak trees.
        Friends grew old and died.
        Some didn't grow old, they just died.
        Today, they're a separate mountain range,
        rounded, tree-shrouded
        and able to be scaled with street shoes,
        though some of them are taller than others.

I have other mountains now,
just as personal, just as dominant as the old ones.
They're topped with soaring peaks
and wreathed in clouds.
I'd like to watch time wear them down,
be able to laugh at them,
watch them become lower and lower
until I can see over them.
I'd like to soar above them and smile,
before I go.
Just once.

jcm
5/11/84

Evolution to a Lower Degree

A period of evolution passed through me
without even stopping to say 'hello'.
It came and went,
like a cough in the night,
like a sliver of lightning
without the benefit of thunder.

    I won't be lied to anymore;
    not to say it won't be tried
    but to say that I won't allow it.
    To doubt, not disbelieve—
    to scrutinize, not analyze
    will hand the flag back to honesty again.

If the iguanas on Galapagos can do it,
I can too.
They took to the ocean
when the land became barren of nourishment.
The iguanas and I are out of our element now.
Time will tell if we're to survive.

        The Galapagos are teeming with iguana,
        all sizes, all ages,
        but there is only one of me.

jcm
5/11/84

Honeyboy

Dear Joseph,

I don't have to tell you that Sunday was a very moving day for everybody in New Rochelle and elsewhere. I never saw a crowd like that. For your Poppa. I was in the line outside for an hour and fifteen minutes before I got inside. I was in the line so long, I got to meet some new friends. I only remembered one name, Lou. Shorter than I, long black hair, about 60. He looked like Paulie Walnuts. He played golf with your Father and he knew him for dozens of years. He told me he would be in that line even if it was raining on him. There were two guys behind me arguing about leaf blowers, so loud that a little old lady told them to 'shut the hell up!', and she broke everybody up. Her name was Millie. We were standing in front of the driveway and a big Lincoln was trying to get out. The driver got out and said to us:

'You have to move! I can't get out!' I yelled back at him:

'We're not going to move. We're all Catholics!' Everybody laughed.

You should be very proud of your kids. Lexy is bee-yoo-tee-full! Mike is a young man now. No more the awkward kid. Marie almost fell down when she saw me. She didn't expect to see me. Ma was wonderful. I couldn't let go of her. I was glad to see Glen again. He hasn't changed at all.

Remember, keep Thanksgiving as small as you can. For Ma. When parents go, and go they will, the family always seems way, way smaller. It's not a good feeling. The more the person was loved, the bigger the space that's left. You've always been a good son to them. You're the patriarch now. Stay healthy.

The real reason I sat down tonight to write you a note was this: Today, while I was in the line outside, another little old lady and I were talking. I said to her:

'Have you ever seen so many people?' Do you want to know what she said to me?

She said: 'This is what happens when you've been nice to everybody.' What a nice thing to say about your Pop. I don't think I'll ever forget that.

The other thing I was thinking about on the way back up the Hutch, was this: I thought of all those people who came to see your dad off today. Then, I thought of something that Margaret Mitchell said once. Margaret Mitchell, the author of 'Gone With The Wind', was asked to give a eulogy when her father died. She said that she looked down at all the faces, all the faces of her father's friends, and said:

'. . . In my Father's garden, many flowers grow.'

La Famiglia,
Jimmy

jcm
11/22/10

Going back again

Memories are the garden of the mind;
a rose bush here—
a cluster of fragile pansies there—
a crocus parade,
dipping and bobbing their angled heads,
a garden where nothing dies.

For a long time
I had my work cut out for me.
All the while I loved you,
you didn't like me.
Just a few minutes in the afternoon
and just as much time
in the morning.
In the blank time in between
I had to remember your face,
so I wrote and wrote
while the garden grew around me.
Just a few minutes each day,
to look at you,
to talk.
For a long time it was all I had.
Apparently it was enough.

jcm
5/11/84

Goodbye, Sorrento

When I read about Sorrento's Hotel Dei Principe, I remember reading just 'continental breakfast 7-9'. There was no mention of the glass-enclosed dining room, perched on the lip of a 400-foot granite cliff overlooking the majestic Bay of Naples. There was no mention of Vesuvio's bulk looming in the distance or the gray-blueness of the water not unlike the blue of my Kimmy's eyes. It was only 0730 and I was squinting already. The day before we had been subjected to the horror and timelessness of Pompeii and the ragged grandeur of its battered skyline.

As I tried to hurry through my scrambled egg whites and espresso, I saw myself back in the Great Room of Gracchus, Senator of Rome, in his house in Pompeii . . .

. . . We were halfway through an earlier version of parchesi when the small game tiles moved imperceptibly on the board. Gracchus was reaching for his wine when he stopped midway and looked at me.

'What was that, Titus?'

'I fear, Senator, another quake.' I said, and with that we both looked past the raised interior fountain at Vesuvio in the distance as that ominous red-tinged black cloud started its upward journey . . .

'Is that real butter? You won't be happy until you clog all your arteries again!', Darling Barbara said, interrupting the Senator and me.

But, my mood was indestructible as I munched my roll, watching a two-masted modern day bark, slowly moving toward us from Napoli, rubber tires dangling from her streaky sides. I thought it was a bark but it wasn't. It was a three-tiered trireme with a lateen sail, long powerful sweeps protruding from her blue-and-white sides, hunching powerfully through the water. Up on the castle on the stern stood Senator Gracchus with his friend, Titus Romulo. It was three weeks before the eruption. God! We had great times back then! . . .

jcm
10/13/10

From The Rim Of The Glass

It was a way to kill some time
before the dialogue and dinner—
the typical walnut and chrome bar,
teeming with Beautiful People
who usually frequent those places.
You know the places;
the pristine and sanitary hotels
that nestle close
to big business beehives,
hoping for a piece of the pie.
　　Fortifying my flaccid scotch
　　with a supplemental splash,
　　I began my scan.
They were all there—
the two gays on the edges of their stools,
the stern group of executives
with paper napkins stuck to their glasses,
seated with stools between them,
afraid to mingle—
cautious with their trade secrets,
and the covey of quail.
　　There were three of them.
　　Two were still taking night courses
　　in makeup application.
　　Number three was on the dark side of thirty.
The Look came at me from across the serving bar,
across the lemons neatly sliced,
across the spigots of carbonation
and across the rim of my glass.
　　I looked back.
She was satin-wrapped in blue and black.

Hair like piles of chocolate custard
and brown eyes, still as death.
    (Years from now I'm sure they'll
    have changed to hazel eyes with
    amber flecks.)

Was this a bona fide scoping out?
If so, she left her contacts at home
and found me sinfully handsome.
    . . . Or was she just eyeballing
    this roundtable of human collection
    like I was?
But she looked again.—
Then a third time and I held her stare.
Being a gambling man no more,
I let her stare me down.
    My drink, a casualty of tampered measures,
    I turned to go,
    to listen to the dull dialogue
    and polite applause.
    Before I made my exit
    I turned to look once more—
    setting in motion
    a split-second scenario:
Satin Lady, you made my day,
for if that Look was real,
if it had teeth to bite with,
I thank you.
But no thanks.
    I'm jaded, spoiled,
    and heading north where the air is clear.
    Where the only sound is reality—
    like a ball peen striking an anvil,
    splitting and cracking the air—
    where I'm Admiral of the Ocean Sea.
        Where a white dove waits for me.

jcm
5/6/84

Sorrento Centerfold

I'm thinking about writing a short piece about our trip to Italy. I'm going to call it; 'Where Are All The Fat People?'

The Italians, especially the women are so, so trim. It's the best way I can universally and generally describe them. The men, of course, are for the most part, always in shape, dressed nice, stylish, but the women! The women were sculptures. All of them were, let's say, 'photogenic'. Even my darling wife said so.

We were a witness to a memorable Sorrento moment, but it could've been in any town in any province in Italia. It was late afternoon. We were in front of a church where a wedding was going to start. The streets were full of traffic and people, but . . . .

Across the street from the church, waiting for a break in the traffic so she could cross, was a tall blonde, with a yellow (like the sun) strapless gown and holding a bouquet of white flowers. A tall blonde, stopped for traffic, waiting to cross the street, could be seen anywhere. But this was Italy.

Her hair looked like a waterfall and she just stood there, like a statue. Here was the glaring difference:

I looked around and noticed every man, that was EVERY man, had stopped and was looking at her. Every man in front of the church, every man on the church steps, the men crossing the street, on the sidewalk, old men, you ng men . . . It didn't matter. They had all come to a halt and were staring at her. I have to admit also, my feet would not move. Even B. said; 'Look at that!', and she was talking about the men. I didn't see even one man give her a cursory look and move on. No one. They were all frozen, waiting for her next move, which of course, would've been ultra-fluid. She never did move. I wouldn't have either, probably.

That night, in a restaurant, I checked my pulse. Sure enough, it was just as I thought.

I had died and gone to Italy.

jcm
10/12/10

Day's End

Lying here next to you
in awe
of your instant sleep,
observing your face
from my propped elbow platform
I watch your lashes flicker,
like tiny paintbrushes
curving up and away
from the crest of your cheek.

Somewhere there are lovers
picking their way along cobbly banks
by blue glass rivers.
Silver maples with leaves
like pearl clusters in the night
dip down toward emerald frogs
with bulbous eyes.
Dragonflies with thread-lace wings
hover like doll house gliders
wary of the lovers . . .

My river is the hallway in the dark,
picking my way from memory,
careful not to brush the fragile pearls,
aware only of the clock's electric hum
not unlike the whirr of dragonfly wings.

jcm
5/1/84

Dog White Beach—1944

There is nothing nice about that body of water. It's always gray. Different shades of gray. On a sunny day, the turbulence doesn't stop because of the cross currents and the warmer water of the Spanish coast mixing with the colder water coming in from the Dutch coast. Even on a sunny day the English Channel is gray. Sometimes light gray, sometimes dark or mottled gray, but always gray. I've sailed the length and breadth of the Channel and I've found it no different than the Great North Atlantic maelstrom, just smaller.

Sixty-six years ago today, the Great Crusade started on the western side of the Channel, at Normandy. The Germans had four years to get ready. They had the Great Atlantic Wall which stretched from Norway to Spain. At Normandy, as in other places, they had the entire beach 'zeroed' in. Just after dawn the 116th Regiment of the 29th Division landed on a forlorn piece of beach, code-named Dog White. Up and down the beaches for 80 miles, the Allies were coming ashore, but there, at Dog White Beach it was the worst of times. Americans from Central Virginia, from places like Hadleyville, Roanoke and Belt Creek were struggling to get ashore while the German MG-42's and PAC-40's raked them to pieces.

Adolph Hitler had sent a written message to his soldiers on the Atlantic Wall which read in part:

'. . . This will be the first time you will face the American soldier. You will find him not so formidable. His country has just come through a terrible Depression. They will be scrawny and under-fed. They will not be the soldiers you are. There will be many of them but you will find them not to be very worthy opponents.'

The boys from rural central Virginia were almost decimated by the German guns on the high ground. Brigadier General Norman Cota, West Point Class of '17, saw the whole thing playing out in front of him. The Americans were hunched behind a gravel shingle, trying to keep low. He saw this as he walked the line, oblivious of the enemy fire, the soaked and shot up soldiers watching him. He said aloud:

'There are two kinds of men on this beach! Those who are dead and those who are going to die! We're gonna get off this beach!'

And come off the beach they did. First, by ones and twos, the men crept forward until the entire unit surged up the embankments, firing their weapons as they went. It took most of the day but they dislodged the enemy and took all the high ground on their part of Normandy.

Hitler had been right in some ways. The Americans were scrawny. Some of them. The Americans were also under-fed. Some of them. But ALL of them were 'survivors' of the Great Depression. They were the ones who had made it through. They were the ones who, surprisingly, came up that hill in the face of terrific fire and won the day. Fourteen months later, it was the German who lay prostrate in front of the Allies, all the fight in them gone . . .

Fifty years later, at the anniversary of D-Day in Normandy, President Bill Clinton addressed the gathered participants at the National Cemetery at Courville-Sur-Mer. He said:

'I look at these men, seated here in front of me and think: their gait is a little slower now. The stairs they used to climb so rapidly are a little steeper now. If we pass them in the street we probably wouldn't give them a second glance, but we must remember one thing; When they were young, they saved the world.'

jcm
6/6/10

A Promise Kept . . . Roundabout

Not many days,
just a few.
That's all we had.

(‘. . . We'll come back here in three years,
no matter who we're with, no matter where
we are. We'll come back.')

So easy it was
to promise under summer sun
gazing at a tanned face.
'I Know A Famous Poet' shirt-
The Plantation rednecks-
So easy it was
to promise, to tell you nice things.
'Are you two newlyweds?'
Boiler Beach, sand fly bodies . . .
So easy it was
to promise and watch you smile.
'We'll run the dunes, beat the tall grass
until we reach the sea . . .'
So easy it was to be imaginative
without a price tag,
just a photograph with words.
But now we will run those dunes,
we will beat that tall grass
and we will reach that unattainable sea-

jcm
4/30/84

That Time Before

Those million words are packed away,
big preparations hold the floor.
Our lives are not as simple now,
as in that time before.

We didn't have the urgent need
to wring perfection from the core.
I loved you and you loved me.
in that time before.

The dialogue of money talk—
will it make us rich or poor?
But we were wealthy in our days-
remember the time before?

Don't get me wrong, I want to live
my life with you, I'm sure-
We'll fill the bill and make it right-
we'll open every door.

Yet . . . how many years ago was that?
Two, three or more?
When every season was Autumn
in that time before.

jcm
4/30/84

'We Are Ready Now, Sir!'

It is 0315, 3:15 A.M. EST, the eve of one of the most cataclysmic votes in American history, the senate race between Brown the Republican and Coakley the Democrat in the great commonwealth of Massachusetts. The outcome will either stop President Obama's stampede into a welfare state or it will send us all into a much lower standard of living, one we're not used to. Everything hinges on the voters of Massachusetts, the bluest of the blue states. The odd thing at this late date is, it's coming to a neck and neck finish. The people are tired of being pushed around by the socialists and the Chicago mob. In about twelve hours we will all know whether or not it will be Morning in America or Mourning in America.

If this were April instead of January, the events in Massachusetts today would bear a striking resemblance to those events in the same state, 235 years ago . . .

Massachusetts, home of the greatest and oldest ivy of them all, Harvard University. Home to Massachusetts Institute of Technology where they're making human skin without the use of humans. Massachusetts, where the Pilgrims landed, but more importantly, it's our Cradle of Liberty.

'One if by land, two if by sea . . .' The British were marching on Lexington on that cold morning back in 1775. Would the farmers and the minutemen stop them? Could they? There were 26 adult males in the village of Bedford. They called themselves the 'Bedford Blues' and were led by one, Isaac Hayes. During the night, they marched from Bedford to Concord to head off the British column from Boston. They were joined by other militia groups from Acton, Lincoln, Menotomy and other towns.

Arriving at the Buttrick mansion overlooking the North Bridge on the Concord River, Hayes and the Bedford Blues saw the British redcoats massing on the other side. Adjutant Joseph Hosmer, knowing the militias were tired from marching through the night, asked Hayes:

'When can your men be ready?'

Hayes replied: 'We are ready now, Sir!', and with that, the Bedford Blues marched down to the western side of the North Bridge and lined up. They were told to disperse by the British commander. They didn't, and were fired upon. Isaac Hayes and his drummer fell dead. Then with their red flag emblazoned with 'Conquer or Die', the Blues blasted away, killing four British regulars! They rushed across the bridge and they did something we would never find in the history books. They scalped the King's four dead soldiers! The great War for Independence started right there in Lexington and Concord. The people of Massachusetts, after witnessing the Boston Massacre with Crispus Attucks, the surprise Tea Party and the silversmith Paul Revere, rose up to cast off the shackles. The Cradle of Liberty sits in only one place in this great and glorious land. Massachusetts.

Today, the Minutemen will have to rise up again. They will have to put down their plows and cell phones and pick up their flintlocks and ballots. They will have to come once again from places like Lowell, Wakefield Dorchester, and yes, Bedford. They will have to fire that shot, the one they will hear in Las Cruces, New Mexico and Pismo Beach, California and Medicine Hat, Wyoming. They will have to cock that hammer back, aim, and bring down this attempt at a socialized society if we're to survive at all. We're all depending on the 'new' Minutemen. Maybe tomorrow, a newspaper in some other American town will start their editorial with some poetic license from a borrowed stanza by R.W. Emerson:

> 'By the old North Bridge that arched the flood,
> to [January's] breeze their flag unfurled.
> There the embattled farmers stood,
> and fired the shot heard round the world . . .'

jcm
1/19/10

April 27th

Seventy-five and sunny—
that's what they said.
It wasn't until Jeremiah had galloped
away into the dining room
and the last baked onion
had been gobbled down
that we realized our time was near.
Did you feel it too?
Friday was the first day of the year,
our year.
Winter started last year,
but this year belonged to us.
Today we realized it,
through the dusty lime clouds
spread on the lawn like confectionery sugar,
and the wicker chairs looking breezy
and transparent by the window.
We crawled around on the warm grass
like puppies and got our first sunburn.
Winter's residue filled a plastic bag
and the smell of charcoal
came through the open screens.
The sudden explosion of a beautiful summer day
told us.
Today, I could feel the Hatteras sand under my feet.
Today, I could feel the 'you and me' of summer.

jcm
4/28/84

The Little Tug That Could . . .

About an hour ago, at 0230, I went out in the parking lot of Stew Leonard's and put the national ensign down to half-mast. I wonder how many people today will ask why the flag is at half-mast? All the news programs today will devote their usual 15 or 20 seconds worth of old Pearl Harbor film clips. I'm sure they'll show the crumpled *Arizona* burning and the capsized *Oklahoma*, and then they'll interview some old sailor and give him their usual 5 seconds. Then, it's back to the Christmas season and the Giant's win over Dallas and some knifing in Queens. Pearl Harbor will disappear for another year.

For the past decade or so, whenever December 7th rolls around I find myself thinking once more of the little yard tug, *Hoga* (YT-146) which happened to be at Pearl Harbor that Sunday morning also. The USS *Hoga* was moored at 1010 dock when the Japanese struck. Chief Boatswain's Mate, Joe Mc Manus was down below shaving when he heard a torpedo strike. He later found out it was the *Oklahoma*. All ten of the *Hoga*'s crew (the cook was ashore) quickly got the ship underway and then went across to Battleship Row to fight the numerous fires that were erupting from the ships.

It was about 0845 when the *Hoga*'s moment of glory arrived. The battleship, *Nevada* was the only capital ship to get underway during the battle. She came down Battleship Row with American flags flying from every mast and spar. Her idea was to get out to the open sea, but the Japanese had other ideas. They tried to sink her in the channel, thereby blocking the United States Pacific Fleet from coming out. Bombs rained down on the *Nevada* and she came to a stop, down by the bow. She was sinking. In the channel. From across the harbor rushed the little *Hoga*, and pitted her 350 tons against the huge battleship's bow. While she pushed the giant ship out of the channel, she hosed down the *Nevada*'s fires with her fire-fighting gear. The *Hoga* beached the stricken battleship onto Hospital Point, thus freeing the movement of ships in and out of the harbor afterward. For that, the USS *Hoga* received a Presidential Unit Citation. The little tug spent the next week fighting fires and retrieving bodies from the water. She spent the rest of the war at Pearl Harbor as one of the yard tugs.

There were 181 ships in the harbor that dreadful December 7th, 1941. One by one, they disappeared from the Naval Register. The last capital ship was the heavy cruiser, *Phoenix*. She was sold to Argentina, renamed the *General Belgrano*, and sunk in the Falkland Islands War in 1982 by the British submarine, HMS *Conqueror*. There was a Coast Guard cutter, USCGC *Taney*, at Pearl Harbor that day. She's part of the Baltimore Inner Harbor complex today, visitors welcome. All of the rest of the Navy ships, one after another, ran out their time and were either sunk or broken up for scrap. The *Nevada*, after being part of D-Day in Europe, was used as a target ship during one of the Bikini Atoll blasts. The *Arizona*, of course, is still at Pearl. Most of her crew is still on board, 1,177 of them. So, that takes care of all the ships which were at Pearl Harbor that day, but not quite. There is still the USS *Hoga*. She's still afloat.

After the war, she spent 40 years in Oakland, California as a fireboat, distinguishing herself again. When she was retired, inquiries went out to various cities to see if any of them wanted the old tug for a marine park or shore attraction. Finally, North Little Rock, Arkansas asked for her. They wanted to make her part of their Arkansas Inland Maritime Museum. That was in 2005. As of now, the *Hoga* is tied up, slumbering away in the Suisin Bay Reserve Fleet in California. Apparently, transferring the tug all the way to Arkansas is very expensive. As time goes by, maintenance becomes a problem for the *Hoga*. There is no one to care for her. Perhaps the good folks in Arkansas, with other problems day by day, figure it's just too much for them. After all, it's just a tugboat.

No, it's not.

The *Hoga* represents a cataclysmic day in our history. The *Hoga* represents bravery under fire, assisting others, saving ships, fighting the fight the best way she could, and after all these years, she remains intact. I think of Chief Mc Manus, feeling the concussion of the torpedo hitting the *Oklahoma*. I think of the Captain of the *Nevada*, feeling his ship sinking and then watching as that little tug came barrelling across the harbor toward him. I think of Jason Robards, Jr., the actor, but also a 17 year-old radioman aboard the light cruiser,

Honolulu, over at 1010 dock. I think of my Mother's neighbor, a Seaman 1/C named John James. He's still on duty, at his battle station, on board the *Arizona*.

Later on this morning, I'm going to make a call to the Arkansas Inland Maritime Museum. I'm going to ask them when they plan on bringing the *Hoga* in from California. I think it's an appropriate day to make that call.

I don't think anyone in our current administration knows the difference between a 100-foot Navy tug and a fire hydrant. They can't be bothered. I hope someone else makes a call to Arkansas today. If they do, I'm sure that somewhere, back there in the fog of time, Chief Mc Manus and his mates will raise a glass to them for remembering their little tugboat.

The number is 501-371-8320.

'Thanks', to all my Shipmates.

jcm
12/7/09

Opal Earrings and Less

It was just like all the Christmases past;
the flawless tree,
glittering and shimmering—
the bird in her winter-white gown—
you—
me—

Only two Christmases ago
and just two memories remain . . .

I remember the opal earrings,
how they looked when you put them on.
I remember also, the cold, bare-faced doom
marching across my mind,
leaving no future footprints to follow.
It was a night to forget.
If I could.
Three decks below me, deep in the engine room,
both boilers were getting up steam . . .
The hull thrummed with activity . . .
Mooring lines were being cast off,
making sickening splashing noises . . .
Blurred figures stood watching from the pier,
out of focus . . .
No bands played . . .

I was outward bound,
and I knew it.

jcm
4/19/84

USS New York (LCS-21)

This past Wednesday I went down to 48th St. in Manhattan and went on a tour of our latest man-o-war, USS *New York* (LCS-21). As I walked around the ship, looking at all it's equipment, I thought back to the Lebanon crises, a few of them. This is the perfect ship for the next blow-up. It literally bristles with 30 mm. rapid fire cannon, Rolling Airframe anti-missile launchers, chaff launchers and more M-2's than I could count. But it was the cargo deck and flight deck that surprised me. There were AAV's, ACMV's and a great deal of other amphibs I can't remember. There were weapons to look at and weapon systems; an M1A1 tank, a 155 towed howitzer, an Osprey, an Apache and some LCAC's. It was a 28,000 ton ship and almost yearned for trouble. There were 700 Marines and 350 Navy crew aboard. The Marines were aboard to be deployed anywhere, anytime, for any emergency.

The biggest crowd however, was down on the pier, with their cameras. Thery were taking pictures of the stem, or bow of the ship. The 'cutwater' as it is officially called. The very first part of the bow to go through the water. There, the 7.5 tons of World Trade Center steel resides, in the form of the existing bow. One can see the different welds as the *New York* sat at her berth. Given its head, I can imagine the ship heading toward trouble all by itself, without the help of a helmsman. I imagine that WTC steel will find trouble without any help at all.

The shooting at Fort Hood in Texas yesterday, should remind us all of the Moslem fanaticism which is slithering around the world. The Moslems may have the oil and the wealth and the myth of 72 virgins in heaven, but we have the USS *New York*.

Just two more things: The motto of the ship is 'Never Forget'. The jack, the small flag on the bullnose, the bow, will read 'Don't Tread On Me'.

We can all be proud of this ship and the men and women who sail on her. For all intent and purpose, they are us.

jcm
11/6/09

World Trade Steel visible on the cutwater of the USS New York

Thank You For The Flowers

I was halfway down the highway today
when I remembered what it was that I forgot.
I forgot to thank you for the flowers.
    Oh, I know I gave them to you
    and that I bought them in Mahopac.
    I also know it was my idea,
    not yours.
    I also know you were surprised
    but I don't know why.

You should know that flowers grow
not from organic miracles,
not from sunshine alone,
not just from specially nurtured seeds,
and not from healthy rainfall.
Flowers grow because of people.
Like you.
  They're grown to be picked and presented;
  to make faces like yours smile,
  to return all that color, fragrance
  and symmetry to their rightful owner.
  That's why flowers grow.

So you see, they were yours from the start.
I'm sorry I forgot to thank you this morning—
for the flowers.

jcm
4/19/84

The King of Hounds

Dear Clan Mortelman,

We received your note last night about Herge. We are all saddened here in Brewster. B. told me and the first thing I thought of was the one thing I always thought of when I heard his name; 'Himself', rushing down the circular stairs in your house as a big puppy, losing his footing and watching his gangly form tumble to the bottom!

He never learned NOT to take food from the table. He thought it was his right. But he was a family member and I'm sure the 'Herge stories' will be reverberating from the dining room walls in the years to come. I read a story once and if I can remember it correctly it went like this:

A man once found himself walking down a wooded path on a bright, sunny morning. He didn't know what he was doing there, but it was a nice morning so he kept walking. It was then that he noticed the dog walking alongside him. It was a mottled brown, black and gray dog. It was the man's old friend, his hound who had passed away years and years before. Suddenly, the man knew where he was.

The two of them walked along the path for a short distance more until they came to a high, white wrought-iron fence. They walked down the length of the fence and came to a big white and gold-colored gate. Another man, in a suit, was standing inside the gate.

'Hello, neighbor!', the man in the suit said.

The man and his dog came up to the gate. 'Is this Heaven?', he asked.

'Why, yes it is! Come right in.', the proprietor said, moving toward the gate.

'Can I bring my dog in too?', the first man said.

'I'm afraid not, friend,' the second man said, shaking his head. 'No dogs allowed in Heaven.'

The first man looked down at his dog and said; 'That's all right. I think we'll keep walking.', and with that, they continued down the path.

After another hour, the sun grew hotter and the path started to rise at an uphill angle. The man and the dog were both thirsty. He figured they would come upon something soon. Just a few minutes later, they came upon a split-rail fence with fields and farmhouses in the distance. They continued on a little further and came upon a big opening in the fence. An old man was sitting on a stump inside, whittling a piece of wood.

'Howdy!', the old man said. 'Have you been walking long?'

'Yes, we have.' answered the man. It was then that he noticed a water pump inside the fence with a metal bowl in front of it.

'Do you suppose I could have a drink of water?', he asked.

'Of course. Come on in.', said the old man.

The man looked at the old-timer. 'Would you mind if my dog came in for a drink too?'

'Come ahead, everyone's welcome.' said the old man. Thery came in and had a long drink of the cool water.

'What place is this?', asked the man.

'Why son, I thought you knew. This is Heaven.'

'That's strange,' said the man, 'the place back down the path said that IT was Heaven.'

The old man laughed. 'Now son,' he said, 'how could that have been Heaven, if they wouldn't let you bring your best friend in.'

Jim

jcm
10/8/11

Short Journey

I don't have to stand on the rim
of the Grand Canyon
to find beauty and grandeur,
nor do I have to float down the Nile
and walk through the Valley of the Kings
to involve myself in mystery,
and I don't have to walk
down Paris streets
to comprehend my own civilization.

Sometimes,
all the beauty, mystery and understanding
I need is in the nerxt room,
humming a tune
and folding laundry.

jcm
4/19/84

Remembering Tony Judt

To: Justin Ferate
http://www.justinsnewyork.com

Thanks, Justin,

I still like the line; 'I'm an American by chance but a New Yorker by choice.'

Jim Mc Guire

To: Jim Mc Guire

Dear Jim,

It's a great line. Thank you!
Do you know to whom it's attributed? I love it!

Justin Ferate

To: Justin Ferate

Justin,

You sent it to me once. It was 'A New York Paean', by Tony Judt, the former Director of the Remarque Institute. His book, 'The Memory Chalet' will be out soon. Unfortunately, Judt died about a year ago.

It was a great piece on New York being the only 'world city' in this country. That was his last line in the piece. I have some friends in England who used to live here in New York, and I like to rub it in now and then. That line comes in handy. When all the smoke is gone and the air is cleared again, the line stands out, sort of like E.B. White's little tree in Oyster Bay. No, I don't want to buy a cabin in Maine to 'get away from it all.' Nor do I want to move to central Pennsylvana to escape the threat of terrorism. I don't want to retire to Florida and have dinner at 5:00 P.M. and load up on fried food.

I want to stay right here, where I can point out the building which used to be Aeolian Hall where Gershwin first played 'Rhapsody in Blue' to a New York crowd. I want to walk down 5th Avenue and remember 18 straight St. Patrick Day parades when I marched with the Westchester A.O.H., carrying the biggest Irish tri-color in the parade. I want to stand across from 150 Liberty Street and think of the firefighters streaming out of their house and looking straight up at the smoke coming out of the World Trade.

I've been to Paris and London and Rome. They were wonderful. But they don't have Columbia Presbyterian. They don't have Yankee Stadium. They don't have the Plaza. They don't have the pulse of New York. They don't have the sound and the fury and the quietude and the ideas all in one place.

I wouldn't trade it for anyplace on earth. Neither would you. We are, Mr. Ferate, like Tony Judt said; 'Americans by chance and new Yorkers by choice.'

Jim Mc Guire

jcm
10/4/11

The Long Sigh of Autumn

Concern for leaves in Autumn
is food for small talk
in elevators,
        every street corner
        and usual November conversation
        over backyard fences—
The great concern for something dying,
something ending,
something coming to a close
cancels out the little rebirth
Autumn holds.
        Hard it is, to keep our minds on growth
        when colors disappear from our eyes
        and images of dying things
        carpet our thoughts
        as shriveled leaves
        carpet a forest floor.

jcm
4/19/84

Memorial Day—2012

Memorial Day will be here in a couple of days and it will be time for another holiday story. I hadn't given it much thought because I usually do it at work, in the wee hours of the morning. It's usually a good time to think about things and that's when I come up with it. But today, the Friday before Memorial Day, it came walking up to me.

I told my wife, Barbara, I would go shopping for her for Memorial Day over in Shoprite in Carmel. I had the usual list with an addition of something called 'Jicama', another 'salad thing'. I got my*R.F. Keller* baseball hat out and put it on. I figured, it's Memorial Day weekend. All the old sailors will be out, wearing their hats. I may meet some. Famous last words . . .

Over in Carmel, I had just picked up the mysterious Jicama, when I heard:

'There's one, Marie!', and in front of me appeared this giant of a man, about 6'5", probably in his 80's. He pointed at my hat and asked:

'Is that your ship?' I told him it was. He reached out and hugged me! His wife had appeared alongside also. When he put me back on the floor, he said: 'I told my wife, this weekend, if I run into a tin can sailor, I'm going to give him a hug!'

'I was on a DE. That's kind of a poor man's version of a destroyer.', I told him. He shook his head.

'That's the type of ship I'm talking about. Besides, they're all tin cans.', and then he told me his story:

It seems that he was on the USS *Comet* (AP-166), a lumbering troop carrier, which had just arrived at Leyte Gulf in the Philippines in 1944 to debark more than 1,000 soldiers into landing craft. This was always the hairy part of the job, he said. They had to just sit there, loaded with troops and try to get them off before a Japanese submarine happened by. The troops had just started climbing off when they received notice of a sub contact! The loudspeaker started blaring out a sub contact signal.

'We all froze and looked at each other.', he said. 'That's when I wondered if I was ever going to get home, to say nothing of all the soldiers on board. I was just a kid, but I was scared as hell!'

He said, they all looked out, away from the land, expecting a torpedo wake or somethng. People were running in every direction. It was then, he said, he saw the two tin cans. One of them came from forward of the bow at an angle, the same time one came around their stern, their klaxons were 'Whoop-Whoop-Whooping!' (his words.)

'Those guys were angry! None of them looked over at us. They were all looking forward, toward wherever the Japs were. I never saw anything like it. They were making turns, some big knots. Their fantails were buried in the wakes.' Just about then, his wife, Marie, gave a heavy sigh. She probably heard all this before.

'They were almost out of sight when we heard all the depth charges going off. We could feel the bangs on our hull.', he continued. 'Later on we found out, they both sank the sub. But that day, those two little guys were like the cavalry. I never saw anything like that again.'

'Were they destroyers or destroyer escorts, like this?' I motioned to my hat.

'They were like that.', he said, pointing. We had a short discussion about APA's and the difference between a convoy DE and a fleet DE, like mine, and then it was time to continue shopping. We shook hands and then I said to him:

'I hope I don't disappoint you, but I wasn't in the war. In 1944 I was only 5.'

He laughed and pointed to my hat again. 'Was that your ship?'

'That it was.', I answered.

'Then, that's all I have to know. Whenever we carried troops anywhere else, I always looked for those little guys. It always made me feel good. It made me feel safe.', he said, and shaking my hand once more, he walked away.

'Have a good Memorial Day, Buddy!', he called over his shoulder.

'You too!', I said. Then, as an afterthought, I called after him; 'So long, Shipmate!'

So that's it. A few days early, but important enough for me to put it down. I hope it was important for you too. So here's to the veterans, the ones who live in Watertown, New York, in Maplewood, New Jersey and every other place in this free country. And also to the ones who lie beneath the lilacs, on a hill outside of town. Let's remember them, all of them. And on Memorial Day, as we turn the rack of lamb on the grill and push a shoppng cart in a grocery store in Carmel, New York, let's not forget how we're still able to do those things and who the ones were who made it possible.

God Bless America
J.C. Mc Guire GM# USN
5176234

jcm
5/25/12

Bumper Crop

Back in the raw and uncertain days
we went outside
and together we tore the paper envelope
to spread the seeds,
hoping something would grow.
So many barricades to climb over—
so many problems to beat down.
It wasn't all easy.
Or happy.
At times it must've seemed
like climbing sand dunes—
two steps forward, one step back.
It wasn't enough to defend
ourselves against all elements,
we had to batter each other also.
Sometimes the tops of dunes
seemed so far away.
Sometimes, we stared at the barren ground
wondering if the seeds would take hold . . .
Today we can look out any window,
in any direction and see the fruits
of our labor—
thousands of acres; soybeans, alfalfa,
corn, apple trees, avocados and golden wheat.
. . . Abundance.

jcm
4/17/84

The Great Marseille— Barcelona Road and Sea Race between the Uss Yellowstone And Elsa's Simca

Six hundred of us had just left the partly damaged city of Naples, Italy on the good ship USS *Yellowstone* and were headed for some northern climes just west of the French Riviera. Now you're talking, we said! When Naples was rebuilt, it would be the home port of the U.S. Sixth Fleet, but for right now, it was trying to clean up from the ravages of WWII and making a slow progress of it. We looked forward to where we were headed, Marseille, France.

Marseille, from seaward, had this long, sloping mole leading into the protected harbor. It was a low profile city with slightly higher hills to the north. Again, I had no camera and I paid for it. The houses and the buildings were multi-colored and everyone within sight was waving. The U.S. Navy was coming! With money.

We tied up at the regular piers which was a treat. We usually had to anchor out. Our division officer told us about the communists who ran the city. There were certain sections we were banned from, maybe, one-third of the city. We had to wear our uniforms ashore. No civvies were allowed. This was long before the terrrorists scares and the Navy wanted to 'show the flag'.

My first night on the beach, in France (I couldn't believe I was in France!) I followed my usual custom of getting as far away from the waterfront dives and waterfront creatures as I could. I went into the town itself and looked for a little bistro in the tangle of windy streets until I found one. I wish it had a better name, but for what it was worth, the American Bar seemed just about right. It was a quiet place, a long hall-like room with tables and chairs; two of the chairs occupied by two sailors off the USS *Aristede*, a reefer ship which made the trip north with us. Oh well, I figured, now there were three of us. I sat at the bar and looked around. It didn't take me long to notice the center of attention.

A girl was sitting by herself at a table almost in the center of the room. The men in the bar were all looking at her, but no one had made a move yet, so it seemed. Even the other two sailors were deep in conversation about her but had not moved. She was in her early 20's, I think, short blonde hair, swept back on the side. She had a big black-and-white fur coat on, swept open with one arm, while her other hand held a reddish-colored drink . . . legs crossed, white high-necked sleeveless dress, the entire picture. She glanced at me for a second, but she knew every eye was on her.

'Well, Charlie,' I said to myself, getting off the stool, 'This isn't Peekskill.'

I sat down at her table, plopping my white hat on another chair and looked at her. Up close, I knew I had my hands full. I would probably be 'dismissed' in a second or two, but it would have been worth it.

'What are you drinking?' I asked.

'Pastes Tomatose', she said instantly, not looking at me. She had gray eyes, like channel fog. I ordered one of those red, foppish drinks.

'Would you like another one?', I asked. By now, a smile had forced itself onto my face.

'What made you come over and sit down?', her question coming out of nowhere. Now, she was looking at me! I wondered whether or not I had a decent shave. I decided to play all my cards at once.

'I had to.', I answered. 'I came over to tell you you're beautiful.'

That's when she smiled her perfect teeth smile. That was also the instant everyone else in the room seemed to disappear.

We talked and talked the rest of the night. Her name was Elsa. Elsa Groneau. She said she was a teacher. Teacher? The more we talked the more mesmerized I became. There was a jukebox in the place that had only one song on it. It had about 50 45's but it only played one song. Edith Piaf's 'Milord' was the big hit in France at the time, autumn of 1960. It was such a big hit, some places refused to play anything else. (51 years later, I still have a 45 at home of 'Milord'. I never tired of it.)

She noticed my skepticism of her being a teacher and invited me to her school the next day. I went. She taught the equivalent of second grade. I forget what they call it in France, but she asked me to tell the children what I did in the Navy, on the ship. I did, while she translated for them. They clapped when I was done.

My ship was in Marseille for three weeks and for three weeks we were together. Once, in her little convertible, a white Simca Aronde, we went to see Brigitte Bardot's house. I wanted desperately to see her but she wasn't home. We watched the house all day. No Brigitte. On the way back to the city, she asked me if I would like to meet some of her friends. Of course, I said.

Driving down the beach road, she suddenly stopped the car and blew the horn. About 15 or 20 people down by the water waved and started running up toward the road. As they got closer I realized something wasn't quite right. It wasn't long before I realized that I had never been to a nude beach before! Let's say, it was an interesting hour.

Elsa called me 'Char-lee', or 'Shar-lee'. She gave me the tour of Marseille and the towns around it. We even drove through the forbidden communist section with the top up.

The time eventually came when the *Yellowstone* and I had to leave.

It was my last night in Marseille and we were exchanging addresses, when she said to me, 'Char-lee, where are you going next?' I told her we were going down to Barcelona for two weeks. She announced;

'I will meet you there.'

'Sure!', I laughed.

'No,' she said, 'I will meet you there.'

Later on, at the dock, we embraced. 'Goodbye, Elsa. Write to me.'

She looked me full in the face. 'I will meet you in Barcelona in four days.'

To make a long story even longer . . . she did.

Four days later, around 1000, we pulled into Darsena Del Morrot in Barcelona where we Med-moored, stern first. As we pulled into the protected dock area, I saw the white Simca! 'I don't believe it!', I said to myself, adjusting my binoculars. But, there she was, the only one on the pier except for the line handlers. She was wearing her big fur coat, spreading it open and leaning on her car. As our stern drew closer to the pier, the catcalls started from everyone on deck. She was hard to miss! I waved but she couldn't pick me out, we all looked alike.

When we secured from Sea Detail and the bridge was secured, I rushed down and changed into my liberty uniform. I had to get into a long line at the stern brow and by the time I got onto the pier, about 30 of my shipmates surrounded Elsa and her car. I could see her blonde hair in the middle of the throng. There were officers in the forefront, trying to see if they could hit a home run, but she wasn't speaking. Yes, she was scanning the crowd for a 3rd Class Gunner's Mate with no money!

Andy Warhol said once: 'Everyone has their fifteen minutes of fame.' Well, my fifteen minutes was about to arrive.

I elbowed my way through the crowd . . . 'Coming through! Hot stuff! Move!'

'Char-lee!', she cried. I waved. Every head turned to see who it was.

Yes, guys. It was me. She ran up and hugged me, kissed me between the eyes and squeezed my cheeks. I remember Mr. Lanchantin, our Navigator, standing there with his mouth open and his tonsils showing! I threw my white hat in the back seat of the Simca and got in. She got behind the wheel and started the car. Just before we left, I turned and waved to them. If I live to be 100, I'll never forget their faces at that instant. They're frozen in time and the memory is worth a wheelbarrow full of Rolex's.

We drove off into the sunset, on a white horse named Simca.

The rest would be anti-climactic. We toured around Barcelona, saw the bullfights and rooted for the bull. We climbed the hills west of the city to see where those beautiful bells were. I bought her a Spanish mantilla. When she turned, wearing the mantilla, my description wouldn't do it justice. Not even now. That's another picture branded on my brain. It was a memorable two weeks. I loved Spain.

We were going to Naples after Barcelona. Again, she said she would meet me there. And . . . she didn't.

It had been 220 miles from Marseille to Barcelona. It would have been over 1,000 miles to drive back to Naples. She wrote to me for almost a year. I wrote to her. I hinted at the possibility of Ollie Thompson and I moving to the Costa Del Sol when I got out of the Navy. We probably would've and Elsa most likely would've arrived in her Simca. With a friend. But, life changed. I never saw her again.

Last Autumn, my Darling Barbara and I had to make an emergency landing on Sardinia because of a sick passenger. We were flying from Rome to Madrid. On the tarmac, I suddenly remembered Elsa and gazed north. Somewhere up there, I thought, past Corsica and on the Riviera somewhere, there must be a little white Simca convertible with a short-haired blonde driving. She's probably the same age now as she was then, I thought.

People like Elsa never get old.

jcm
9/25/11

Counting Headstones

Any old graveyard,
any hint of battlefield
or ruined fort
is mine to tell about.

If you grow weary of it all
I have an apology ready.

I flood you with facts and stories
of other times.
I hope you don't mind,
for if we're to be anythng at all in the future,
we have to know what we were like in the past.
I think it gives us an edge.

Anyway, if I don't do it,
who will?

jcm
4/11/84

The 1961 Bay Of Pigs Invasion Or How I Learned To Hate Fidel And Love The Browning M-2

'The Skipper told me to get two .50's onto the bridge wings, now!', Brown said, the sweat running down his face from under his sunglasses. 'Doggie' Brown was the Chief Gunner's Mate on board the USS *Yellowstone(*AD-27). He was my boss. Our ship, all 16,000 tons of her was down for Fleet Training Group exercises based in Guantanamo Bay Naval Base, Cuba. It was April, 1961.

Things were happening fast and the rumors were flying. Early in the morning we were hearing things like; The Cubans are coming! We're invading Havana! They're going to bomb Gitmo! Are you kidding me, I thought? This was peacetime. I get out in September. This can't be happening.

'Chief,' I started, 'Those guns are four decks down! They weigh 85 pounds each. How do we do this?'

'WE? WE?', he blurted. 'WE aren't doing anything. YOU are! Get Mc Coy to help you but get those guns up here, pronto!' He pointed at the swivel bases on the port wing where we were standing. 'You know where they go. I want one gun on each wing. They'll be bringing the ammo up too.'

'Who's bringing the ammo boxes?', I asked. Brown started swinging his arms over his head, spitting as he screamed:

'Get those guns, NOW! The ammo's coming! It's coming!' And with that, he clambered down the wing ladder. I remember thinking; his stock is dropping. Brown's usual happy-go-lucky demeanor was rapidly leaving him. So this is what he was like under pressure . . . His stock was definitely dropping.

By the time I got to the armory, mess cooks and clerks were carrying the .50 caliber ammunition boxes out, on their way to the bridge. Mc Coy and Joe Mc Gorry were down there also, monitoring the move. They knew why I was there.

'That .50 is waiting for you, Mack!', said the smiling Mc Gorry, pointing at the big M-2 in it's cradle. I outranked both he and Mc Coy and they knew it. They were about the only guys in the 600-man crew that I DID outrank.

'Joe, get one of the cooks to help you take that other .50 up to the starboard wing, okay?', I said to Mc Gorry. His face dropped but he nodded. Mc Coy, whose name was also 'Joe', was still looking at me.

'You and I will take this one up to the port side. Okay, Joe?' As I said that to Mc Coy, I went over to the cradled .50 to lift it from the bulkhead. Now, the reader has to understand: This was an 85-pound machine gun with a canvas parts and tool bag slung underneath. It was chest-high. I was definitely showing off. I weighed a sun-baked 160 then, not the svelte 220 pounds I weigh now. I took it by the barrel and by the breech and lifted. I felt my aorta explode, my ribs disengage from my spine and then the gun was free from the bulkhead! As nonchalantly as I could, I turned and set it down on the air vent outside the armory hatch. My pulse was clanging against my temple. Mc Coy was facially impressed. It was usually a two-man job, lifting and hanging those machine guns. It was to be my isolated high point for the day.

We locked the armory and carried the guns topside, four decks. The first deck wasn't bad, then they became progressively worse. By the time we got it to the port side wing and locked into the mount, we had had it. Mc Coy promptly disappeared and I loaded the machine gun. It had a WWII side loader, '1945' seemingly stamped on everything aboard the *Yellowstone*, even the long, olive-drab cans of Spam. We had another name for it. Also, another name for the chipped beef on toast for breakfast every morning. But, I digress . . .

As I pulled the long belts of .50 caliber ammunition from their cans, a yeoman (whose name I forget) walked onto the bridge wing. He told me about the invasion at a place called Isola De Pinos, down the coast. It was to be formally named the Bay of Pigs Invasion later on. They were fighting on the beaches and some of the attacking Cuban rebels had a ship sunk. Castro's planes were lambasting the beaches down the coast, the yeoman said. Would they come up here to get us? The yeoman looked at me expectantly. Did he think that I knew? I was a 3rd Class Gunner. No one told me anything.

No.', I answered. 'Want to do me a fave?'

'What?', asked the yeoman.

'Could you get me a cup of coffee? I can't leave this gun.', I said. The yeoman nodded and left. I noticed he had pressed whites on and his hands were very pink. If I remember correctly, his fingernails were perfect. I say this now because he never came back with my coffee.

The gun was ready, not even a safety to fiddle with. It was an ominous gun, the M-2. It was called the 'Ma Deuce', but mostly just a '.50'. If I remember correctly, it's rate of fire, rounds per minute, was 750. It had a range of 2200 or 3000 yards. Maximum effective was around 2200-2300. (I hope I'm right.) If an aircraft came straight at a .50, the aircraft could probably be brought down. If the aircraft was a jet, well . . . Hail Mary, anyone? Castro had a number of T-28 jet trainers which had been outfitted with machine guns and rocket pods. He also had B-26 light bombers, some Argentine prop fighters and a collection of Corsairs, Spitfires and Hurricanes. There was a Cuban air base just over the mountains to the west, Santiago de Cuba. They could send their planes directly over the mountains and right onto our base. To me. *(Uh-Oh! Where's my rosary?)*

It didn't take me long to realize the conspicuous prominence of my ship and subsequently, of me. There were eight destroyers in port, all bristling with guns. Two fleet tugs were on the other side of the pier from my ship. They also had .50's at the ready, but they were much smaller, about 1,000 tons. The destroyers were about 2250 tons and we were eight times bigger. If a hostile plane ever came over those mountains to the west, there would be one prominent target in Guantanamo. Me. My big, vulnerable repair ship would be the obvious target, but once I opened up with the M-2, I would become the star attraction.

I should interject here . . . I speak as if I fired guns at people before, instead of targets. Not true. Actually, in 1958, I DID fire at another person. Oddly enough it was in Havana, just up the road. But, that story is for another time . . .

Until something concrete happened, that hot, hot Guantanamo day was held in abeyance. I turned to look at what should have been our main battery, the 5" 38 on the bow. The gun, when it worked, hurled a 55-pound projectile 10 miles. It hadn't been fired since

1946; the gears and gauges having been painted over numerous times. It was just a hood ornament, useless. It was then I noticed through the open bridge hatch, the starboard .50 caliber standing there, across the way, unmanned! I had no sound-powered phones and no regular ship's phone either. I was the only one up here. Where was everybody?

Then, as if on cue, Doggie Brown's scrawny, little pinched face appeared at the top of the ladder.

'Chief! Nobody is on that gun!', I said, motioning toward the starboard side. 'Where's Mc Coy?'

'Never mind about Mc Coy. He's busy.', said Brown. I began a slow, methodical distrust of my Chief.

'We're not even at GQ (Battle Condition)!', I said.

'Nobody is.', Brown mumbled, still not coming all the way up the ladder. I told him I didn't have a helmet or phones.

'What good would a helmet do you?', he laughed.

In desperation I said to him: 'Why don't you take over the other .50? Two is better than one.'

Chief Brown started back down the ladder. 'I don't know anything about a .50. I never fired one.', he said. My blood boiled! I ran to the top of the ladder, just in time to see him reach the next deck.

'How did you ever make Chief?', I yelled, but he was out of sight.

'Goddamit!', I yelled down, sure he could hear me. Then, in desperation, I yelled:

'Coffee . . . ?'

Now the sweat was dripping from me. I wasn't even in my 'battle duds'. I was wearing cut-off dungarees and a blue San Juan Royale Hotel shirt. There was no one else in sight. They had all scurried off the weather decks and were holed up inside, like rats. The M-2 was hot from the sun. The deck was cooking and the thin sheet steel I stood behind was oven temperature. I walked through the empty bridge over to the starboard side and looked down at all those beautiful destroyers. All their guns were manned; the 5's, the 3 50's, the 20 and 40 mm's, their own .50's. I yelled down at all of them. Most looked up. When they did, I blessed myself. All of them laughed.

Things began to heat up around noon. An armed yacht came up from seaward, loaded down with Cuban rebels, flying the American flag. I could make out their crossed bandoliers, like in a John Wayne movie. A destroyer, the USS *Monaghan* challenged them with a light but they kept going. They got to the narrow end of the bay, crossing into Cuban territory and disappeared. Later on I heard gunfire and a heavy machine gun. We saw smoke and then nothing. The town of Caiminera was around the bend. That was probably their objective. We never saw them again.

I saw planes along the crest of the mountains to the west but they were our carrier Sky Rays. Smoke was rising from Santiago. I didn't know what it was but I knew it wouldn't be long now. The *Monaghan*'s Morse light was blinking like crazy, but I didn't know to who.

Was this how it was going to end? Some big flash of light and then, nothing?

'God?', I said aloud.

'What?'

'Is this you, God?', I asked.

'No, it's Jackie Kennedy. What is it?'

'Is this all I get, God? Twenty-two years? I don't even have a family yet! I don't have anything.', I said aloud again.

'Is that what you want? Things? What happened to your imagination?'

'I'd like this day to end, God, with no perforations in my hide.', I said.

'You got it. But now I have to go. They need me down the coast at Isola de Pinos.'

. . . Later that afternoon, we began to get news of the invasion. It had failed. Castro's forces won the day. It was just a case of mopping up. Finally, my vaunted crew reappeared; Mc Coy, Mc Gorry and the Dog himself, Chief Brown. They took the guns and the ammunition back to the armory. I didn't touch a thing and they didn't say a word.

We found out the next day the reason for the smoke over Santiago. It seems that two B-26's, bombed up, were told to bomb the beach down the coast. They took off, unloaded their bombs on Santiago airport, flew to Miami and defected.

Right around 1900 that night, the temperature was still in the high 90's. I was by the fantail, having a cigarette when it dawned on me. I didn't have any coffee that day! I started down to the mess decks.

On the way down below, I thought about the messed up day. I felt bad for the good Cubans. Their intentions were good. I also thought about dying. My picture would've been in the Peekskill Evening Star back home. There would've been interviews with my parents and neighbors and Janie would've been shattered, but just for a little while. If those planes came in and hit my ship, they would've gotten me too. What would've been missing from the Evening Star's story of my demise would have been this:

'. . . Before a Castro T-28 managed to come in on the big ship from amidships, Gunner's Mate Mc Guire had shot the canopy from a Cuban Corsair and the aileron from an ancient British-made Spitfire. with his machine-gun. The T-28 however, fired two rockets into the bridge wing, silencing the Browning, and sadly, Florence and Tommy's boy.'

Most of the things in this world we don't know. But, there are some things we do know. I know, for a fact, without a doubt, an enemy of this country would had to have gone through me and something like Mr. Browning's machine-gun to reach his objective. I never doubted that for an instant. I felt good as I reached the empty mess decks. I was Admiral of the Ocean Sea.

Richie Giannamore was in the scullery, steam coming out of the window.

'Richie! Any coffee?' I asked. He saw me through the steam.

'I just cleaned the urns. No coffee.'

'Richie! I didn't get any all day! I'm dying!', I whined.

Giannamore leaned on the scullery combing and yelled:

'What do you want, everything? Get outa here . . . !'

jcm
5/25/11

'. . . And I'll Be In Scotland Afore Ye . . .'

My ship, the *Yellowstone*, visited Greenock, Scotland one Autumn. Greenock lies up the Firth of Clyde near Glasgow. We were too big to pull in to the docks at Prince Albert Piers so we miked out. That's a mooring procedure using the ship's anchor chain attached to a big buoy so the ship swings on the chain. The first day we were there, I had the duty so I couldn't leave the ship. Civilians were coming out to visit the ship. It's something we always provided when visiting a foreign country. Our liberty boat, which seats 100, would go in to shore and bring out anyone who wanted to see the 'big American ship'. I was on the starboard side in undress blues when the liberty boat came huffing up to the brow down below.

I looked down into the boat full of civilians just as she looked up.

All I saw was jet-black hair and red, smiling lips. I motioned for her to come up where I was when she came aboard. I met her halfway. She was bundled up in a gray coat, pulled tightly around her neck to keep warm. Her name was Jeanne. (For the life of me, I can't remember her last name!) I remember she told me she worked in a refrigerator factory in Greenock.

We spent the rest of the afternoon touring the ship. My friend, Tony Bufarele had a motion picture camera and took shots of us as we walked around. He sent it to me only just now, a few months ago, on a DVD. The next day, she invited me up to her house above Greenock for dinner. I arrived by cab and met her entire family. She had some friends there also. I imagine it was to show them what she found down in the harbor!

After dinner, Jeanne's father and I went out on the porch with a few pints and he told me about the German air raids during the war and how the Germans wanted to flatten the Clyde Ship Building areas up toward Glasgow. Those works were turning out British destroyers and the Germans wanted to destroy them. The upper Firth was beautiful. Bishopton was across the way with the famous Loch Lomond right behind the town. The meadows, flecked with cows, came right down to the water's edge. I told him this was the way my river, the Hudson, must've looked in the old days.

It was a good day with Jeanne and her family. Her mother served fresh ham. I remember that. For the next month, Jeanne and I were together every day but one. That one day I had the duty and couldn't get out of it. She came down to the piers with a sheet and waved it toward the ship. She called me before she came down and I saw her from about a quarter mile away, waving it. I sent her some dots and dashes with the Morse light, and her father managed to see it also, all the way up in the hills.

When I was ashore, we managed to go up to Glasgow and walk around the city. We had a picnic once, high up in the hills where the Scottish Games were held in the summer. We hit every little hotel for lunch, where she would show me the proper way to drink tea and how to make it, etc. Most of the time we would poke fun at the way the other spoke. I could listen to her all day, with that brogue scraping along in the air, every fifth word unintelligible. She took my hat once, and ran with it, until the Shore Patrol stopped her. I told the SP's I didn't know her, but only for a moment! I think our favorite was feeding the sea gulls potato chips through the windows of the hotels.

Like all good things, this one too, had to come to an end. On my last night ashore, we walked down toward the piers. Both of her arms were locked on my right arm. Every few feet I would hear her say; 'Oh!' . . . , under her breath. I didn't know how I was going to do this. I was only 21and not that well-versed in goodbyes. Jeanne was 20. We were nearing the Prince Albert gates and she started slowing up, trying to make the last few minutes last, when the whole scene changed.

Three Scottish toughs, across the street, began taunting us, saying things like; 'Yank, leave our women alone!', and things like that. 'Yank?' Did they think it was 1944? I made some comment about their birth legitimacy and the chase started! They came after us but we only had a block to go. Jeanne and I ran, laughing the rest of the way down the street. I could see ahead of us, the two RN's behind the gates to the pier. It didn't look like they were going to open it.

Surrounding the entire pier area was an 8-foot brick wall with embedded pieces of broken bottles lining the top. I had to get over that wall. I let go of her hand and leaped onto the hood of a car next to the wall. I climbed to the roof, put my hands on the top of the wall between the broken bottles and vaulted over, as if I had done it a hundred times. I landed between two jeeps.

'Charlie?', I heard her voice from the opposite side.

'Yes, Jeanne. Everything's fine.'

'Charlie? Will you come back sometime?', I heard her say. We both knew the ship wasn't coming back. She knew we were going to Plymouth and then home.

'I'll try, Jeanne.', I said.

'Please write?', she asked.

'I will. Goodbye, Jeanne.'

There was a pause, then: 'Goodbye. Goodbye.'

The next morning when we left, I scanned the pier with my binoculars. I searched the hills for her house. I didn't see her . . .

I think of her now and then, whenever I have a bottle of Glenlivet on the table, or there's a Sean Connery movie on the tube, or when I see an exceptionally beautiful Scottish woman. Times like that. She was more than a Scottish accent and more than just a girl who worked in a refrigerator factory. She was a northern beauty who graced my arm for a whole month, back when I had no money in my pocket and the world was young.

jcm
6/6/11

Lovers

Lovers don't have it easy.
One can never say; 'Lovers have it made.'
Everything and everyone
is against them, berating them.
It must be jealousy.
    I think society can be verbal
    against lovers
    but mentally side with them.
    The little places,
    quiet places
    and warm places are saved for lovers.
    The average people never go there,
    they wouldn't fit in.
'Music for lovers only',
'All the world loves a lover.'
    Down deep, lovers are special people
    with special interests,
    set apart from the world.
Haphazard lovers and one-night lovers
don't get to join this nucleus,
only the real lovers, the serious ones—
like you and me.
As lovers go,
men are the worst.
They have to deal with practicalities
which blunt the arrow
and dull the shine,
but only a little.

The best of us (men)
aren't very pretty in the dark.
The worst of us in a dark room
can make you rich
or very poor.
We all, as one,
have to listen endlessley to—
'Do you really care about me?'
'Why are you nice to me?'
'What will happen to us?'
We all find ourselves less articulate
the closer we get to you,
and the more knowledgeable
whenever we're away.
Only one thing is very certain—
To a man,
we all need you
more than you will ever need us.

jcm
11/1/85

The Peekskill Indian

My Uncle Jimmy passed away recently. James J. Jacoby of Montrose, N.Y. He lived in Florida the latter part of his life, but no one really 'lives' in Florida, they move there to escape the robber-baron taxes of New York. Jimmy and my Aunt Irene lived in Florida but they will always be New Yorkers to me.

I didn't sit down at the keyboard today to extol the virtues of my Uncle, though there were many. Those who knew him will probably read this and nod. Those who never had the chance to meet him will have to ask those who did. I couldn't relate any stories anyway, for fear of forgetting some. I will say this, however, there was my Father, Tommy Mc Guire, my main person. My Grandfather, Charlie Borecky, a 'poster-boy' grandfather if there ever was one, and then there was my Uncle Jimmy. He was my own personal hero. He could've been my own father.

When he passed away recently, I remembered an incident way back when . . . back when the Washington Senators were a team in the American League and Yankee Stadium hadn't undergone its first modernization yet. It was 1952 and it was summer . . .

Jimmy called the house, looking for my Father. He wanted us to go to the Yankee game with him. He was bringing my cousin, Jay. My Dad hadn't gotten home from work yet so my Mom told him the two of us would meet them down at the Stadium. Later on, my Father came home and we drove down to the game. The Yanks were playing the Senators that night but the chances of finding Jimmy and Jay in that crowd was impossible. We managed to get seats along the right field line, up in the mezzanine.

I can't remember whether or not the Yanks won but the incident which followed, I had wondered about until now.

When the game ended and the crowd started filling up the field (the fans were allowed on the field after the game, back then.) we started looking for them. There had to be 15-20,000 people at the game and most of them were on the field. Then, I saw them.

They were coming out of the left field stands, by the foul pole. I pointed to them but my Father couldn't pick them out.

'Where?', he asked.

I pointed again, toward left field. 'Right there, coming toward the infield!' Sure enough, right there in the middle of the crowd was my tall Uncle Jimmy with little Jay.

'I still don't see them.', my Father said. I told him they were between short and third, about to walk onto the infield dirt.

'Yes! There they are!', he said. 'How did you ever spot them?' I just shrugged and we started waving to them, but of course, they didn't see us.

For years afterward, whenever the family got together for holiday dinners or birthdays, that story always came up. How it was that I managed to pick them out of that big crowd. In the course of the story, my Father would always look at me quizzically and ask the same question: 'How did you ever do that? How could you pick them out?' I never had a good answer. Until now.

I thought about it the day I listened to 'Taps' at the cemetery while the Army personnel slowly folded the flag to present to my Aunt, while my Brother-in-Law, John, and I held our salute. I thought about it for days afterward, whenever I remembered a myriad of things about Jimmy. And then it finally struck me.

It was easy to find him that night in the Bronx, looking down at that crowd. He was the tallest man in the Stadium that night. That's how. He would've been the tallest man in the Stadium on any night.

He was the tallest man I ever knew.

jcm
7/20/10

December 8th

The clock was calling me
and I had taken no precaution
for the lateness of the hour.
    I was lost again,
    mired down
    in the wilderness,
    woods, thickets, brambles
    and forest
    of you.
It happens every time.
When you're not in sight
I can think clearly.
When I'm with you again,
hours are just a series of gray lumps
to be shunned and forgotten.
I haven't the time to think about going,
leaving you.
Time means nothing.
It's only when I leave you
I become aware of it.
    When I left, you were sad.
    If only I could make you understand;
    I cared about you then as when I first saw you . . .

jcm
12/8/84

Heloise And Abelard, Suzanne and Neal

Dear Anna,

I have 26 books by R.M. This one, 'Fields of Wonder' is not the first one with an inscription or even with flower petals. But, it is the most poignant. I feel there were other forces at work here. I can almost see Suzanne and Neal, deep within the bowels of London, in 1975, just two faces in the crowd.

I'll write again what Suzanne wrote on the inside:

> 'Feb. 14, 1976
> Dearest Neal,
>
> We made the fourteenth of February and I never thought we would do it. I love you more each day, and I know that we will have a happy life together.
>
> Love always,
> Suzanne'

She also put red petals in two places in the book. Neal, obviously never took them out. The little spots made by the fresh end of the petal had slightly stained their place on their respective pages. They had undoubtedly met one year before, on Valentine's Day, 1975. Suzanne remembered the date and wrote her message to him on the inside. She picked Rod McKuen to 'deliver' her pronouncement to Neal. They could've had a problem or two the first year, but after the smoke had cleared and the road became level, they realized they were meant for one another. Suzanne, the more vocal of the two, I would believe, hung it all out by announcing her love for him and for the hope of a happy life together. She was ready to take on the rigors of life. With him.

The book was sold exclusively in the United Kingdom, for one pound sterling. It found it's way to my mailbox by way of the Read America Bookshop in Nashville, Tennessee. I would like to think it went this way; 35 years ago . . .

Neal, we'll give him a last name of, let's say . . . Mc Gruder, worked in Victoria Station in London on the main level in a hot sandwich shop on the right side of the ramp leading up to Victoria Street. He was an average-looking chap, in his 30's, say . . . 36. It was Valentine's Day of 1975 and it was the day that flowers outnumbered the hot sandwich carriers at Victoria Station. Men were hurrying home with their fragrant bouquets of roses, carnations, asters. A girl walked up to Neal's counter, looking at the signs overhead. Neal smiled automatically. The girl smiled back. Suzanne had come into the picture.

She was a very pretty brown-haired girl with wide-set brown eyes. Neal just stood there, watching her. She ordered a half-sub of Swiss and fresh ham with no mustard. Neal made the sandwich in seconds and handed it to her, wrapped in red-and-white paper. The girl was looking at him the whole time.

'Are you going to give your girl flowers today? It's Valentine's Day.', she said, taking the sandwich.

'I don't have a girlfriend.', he said matter-of-factly. 'What's your favorite flower?'

'I've always been partial to Lilies of the Valley.', she said, still holding her sandwich.

'Bruno?', called Neal to his partner, 'Take over for a minute!', then to the girl, he said:

'Wait here a moment, please.', and with that he bolted out of the side door of the shop and walked the few feet to the florist booth next door.

A minute later he appeared beside the girl, Suzanne, with a sprig of Lilies of the Valley for her.

Her name was Suzanne Buckley and she was 32. She worked at Brown's Hotel over in Berkeley Square and she took the train home each day to Edenbridge in Kent. After a few dates with Suzanne, Neal took her to his flat in Walworth. They walked down Belgrave Road to

Pimlico and took the underground to Walworth. He made her dinner which was at its best, semi-edible. It was something they would laugh about in the years to come.

Neal was in love. It was something, he realized, that had never happened to him before. Time went on and seasons changed. They talked of things they would like to do, together of course. She would read Rod Mc Kuen to him and they would discuss the poems over glasses of wine

There were arguments of course, with a one month stretch of petulance on both sides before they ended whatever it was that started the argument.

Then, on the following February 14th, Suzanne gave Neal the Mc Kuen book. She had wrapped it in Sunday comic papers which made him smile. When he unwrapped it, the dust jacket tore slightly, on the binding front. (The tear is still there today.) He read the inscription and that night they talked in terms of 'forever and ever' and Neal would tell his friends later on, it was the best night of his life.

Suzanne had written; 'I love you more each day, and I know that we will have a happy life together.' And they did. For 33 more years.

In 2009, February 21st, to be exact, Neal Mc Gruder, age 69, passed away suddenly from insulin shock. There were no children. Suzanne Buckley Mc Gruder moved from London to Nashville, Tennessee in the USA to be near her only sister, Gretchen. Two years after that, she inherited her parent's house in Kent and moved back to the United Kingdom, leaving most of her belongings in Tennessee. The book, 'Fields of Wonder' with the flower petals sat on a shelf in a bookstore for eleven months before a recording artist who shall remain nameless, from Brewster, N.Y. purchased it on Amazon Books.

. . . And there it sat, in a mailbox, on a rainy June afternoon, until I retrieved it and opened it once again to the light.

jcm
6/23/11

February 7, 1983

(Monday Morning)

My left ear burned—
further in, my mind was scorched
from our conversation minutes ago.
I raced northward through
the February slush
like a subchaser in the Chesapeake.
Everything I held dear
weighed on my mind like separate anvils,
my life changing by the second.
No time left for contemplation
and even less for complacency.
Everything blurred,
blended in the whiteness ahead of me
but each piece had its proper place.
Klaxon bells hammered at my brain.
It was time to save the ship.
You weren't a luxury or a need
but a necessity. You always were.
You were ethereal, a dream, a slice of fiction
but also reality.
Time would test us and not find us spent
like a tired bullet.
Ahead of me, I could feel the heat
from the open door—
through the fire and smoke ahead
we would find each other.

jcm
4/13/84

Poem By Helen Young

Helen Young, from a previous story in this book ('Je Pense, Donc Je Suis'), a former college classmate, wrote this poem in 1982. She was 92 at the time.

WHAT IS TIME?

I looked down from my kitchen window
on a little hill,
where traffic passes in an easy stream,
it was a
misty,
Japanese print morning.
Only the sound of cars,
splashing themselves with water,
could be heard.
Out of the haze
a small man appeared,
bent over
as if watching where his feet would take him.
He carried his faded green umbrella,
drawn closely to his head
as he shifted along in the water.
For all the world,
he looked like a toadstool.
Could this be Time
passing me by?

Some time ago,
while taking a shower,
I reached up to turn on the spray,
the warm soothing water
ran
between my fingers,
down
my arms
over
my body,
legs
and
feet.
I had the same feeling
and asked myself
the same question.
Is this what Time is?
Warm,
pleasant
and soft.
Is it
passing me by?

H.Y.

Jcm
11/15/12

Mist-Covered Mountain

Barbara and I were living in Danbury. It was the summer of 1985. Through subterfuge and master-planning, she somehow got me to talk about bagpipes now and then. She wanted to get me a nice set because I always talked about them and how I wanted to play them.

The best bagpipes made were Clark and Dykeshead. They had two big shops, one in Greenock and the other in Inverness. I'd been to the one in Greenock. I watched them construct bagpipes. I think the youngest pipe-maker was 150 years old.

Barbara had this great friend named Barbara Johnson. She lived in northern Vermont, about 5 miles from the Canadian border by St. Albans. She was getting married that summer. She and her husband-to-be were spending their honeymoon in Scotland. B. gave her a job to do. Buy a set of bagpipes, Clark and Dykeshead. Barbara Johnson would be near Inverness so B. thought it was a good idea. B. told her friend to send a postcard from Scotland. If she managed to get the pipes, send a card showing a piper. If she couldn't, send a card with just scenery.

Months later, I was out getting the mail and in the bundle was a postcard from Barbara Johnson. I yelled into the dining room window to Barbara, telling her she had mail from her friend. She came barreling out of the house and grabbed the card out of my hand. We still have it. It was a close-up shot of a pipe major, holding his bagpipes.

Move ahead to Christmas morning . . . I came out of the shower naked, which is the way, of course, we all get out of the shower. I had to go to work at IBM Armonk on the holiday. On the bed was a long, wrapped present. B. was standing on the other side of the bed, with a camera. (Uh-Oh! What's going on?)

'Open it, Jimmy!', she said. Dutifully, I opened it . . . I was going to be a piper! Oh, my God! They felt so good and looked so good; the chanter, the three horns, all carved from gemsbok or impala or something, the heavy tassels . . . I almost cried.

Since I was a child, I always stood at attention when a pipe band marched by. I remember waiting and waiting for the bagpipes to come by. No parade was complete unless I heard those great, shrieking military tunes.

She went to take a picture but I stopped her until I had a pair of BVD's on, and that's the way the picture sits in the album. I called Barbara Johnson that day and she invited us up to her house after the holidays.

Barbara's house sat on a low hill on seventy-five acres. What a house! They had a dumbwaiter to bring firewood up to the master bedroom. Off the master bedroom was a dressing room and off the dressing room was a sitting room where she sat in the mornings, having her coffee. The sitting room window faced south onto Mount Mansfield, the highest mountain in Vermont. Her husband had all the trees trimmed discreetly into a big, natural 'V' so the mountain was in full view. At night, her husband, Eric, would go outside, come back with snow cones covered with maple syrup which was tapped from his sugar maples and we would slurp away with glasses of scotch. They had birds on their feeders I never saw before. Black and red squirrels ran back and forth and the temperature was below zero. It was a paradise. She also had a dog who looked like me. I had a great beard then, and the dog and I, looked like father and son. She even named the dog after me. She called him 'Trapper John'. That's how she addressed me too.

The following year we brought the baby up for Christmas. Priceless pictures with Kimberly and 'Trapper John'! She said she wanted me to play 'Amazing Grace' under her bedroom window after my lessons were done. I told her, not only would I play 'Amazing

Grace' under her window, I would play it naked! We drove home that year, a fresh Johnson Christmas tree tied to the roof of the car, a new baby, hands sticky from maple syrup and a promise to play the pipes under Barbara Johnson's window . . .

I started taking lessons from a fireman who played in the FDNY Emerald Society pipe band. He lived in Shenarock, over by Yorktown. I would go over three days a week, just before I went to work. His house was on the way to Armonk. The bottle of Bushmill's was always on the table and his three red-haired little girls always stood in the kitchen doorway. We played away, filling the house with his tunes and my chords and scale. That was as far as I got.

Then . . . Barbara Johnson died. Cancer. She went so fast, we couldn't get up there in time. She didn't want anyone to know. Barbara and I were devastated. Her husband had her ashes spread atop Mount Mansfield, the mountain she had looked at every morning. I told B., when I learned 'Amazing Grace', we were going to the top of Mount Mansfield and I was going to play it. For her. I told my wife I wouldn't care who was there, I was going to play it naked.

By the time I reached tune-level with the fireman/instructor, he told me that he had a spot in the 9th Regiment Bagpipe Band in Manhattan waiting for me! I had marched in over 20 St. Patrick's Day Parades with the Westchester A.O.H., carrying a huge Irish tri-color, but this was different! Then, the Irish Gods struck. I started losing the feel of the chanter. I couldn't feel the little flat holes anymore, throwing my notes all over the place! I kept trying to look down at the chanter, but it was down by my waist. That's not the way the pipes are played. The fireman started his frowns which turned into pursed lips which turned into halting play. It was a mystery. I just couldn't feel the holes anymore. I went to a doctor and found out I had Carpal Tunnel Syndrome. There was an operation but it wasn't quite the fix-all. The healing percentage was low, so I never had it done. There's been no improvement yet, for CTS. So, back in the mid-80's, my dream of marching past the bishops standng on the steps of St. Patrick's, with me wearing the black and green kilts of the 9th Regiment Band, playing 'Mist Covered Mountain' on a cold, cold March 17th, were over. Sorry, B. Sorry, Dad. Sorry, Jimmy, Maggie, Charlie, Patsy and Bridget. Sorry, Barbara Johnson . . .

Barbara got me an antique bagpipe case. I take them out now and then to show people. I clean them once a year, making sure the reed and pipes are set and tuned. Then, I put them away. It wasn't much to ask, to play 'Amazing Grace', naked, under a bedroom window in the cold forest of northern Vermont, for a very nice lady, was it?

Long ago there was an Irish poet named (what else!) Patrick Shea. He ended a poem once, with these words:

> *'The skirl of the pipes has ended*
> *and too, the incessant drum.*
> *The banners will wave on another day*
> *but for him, the parade is done.'*

Author's note—In 2012, a CTS procedure was attempted on my right hand at Putnam County Hospital. It was a failure.

jcm
5/23/11

Searching Out

How I like to curl
armadillo style
into myself,
and scan
the horizon
for poems
scattered like crazy,
white clouds
across the blue
eternity
of
my
mind.

jcm
6/13/78

Open Letter to 'Charlie' Mc Guire

Dear Charlie,

Today was the day when all good things and bad things were remembered. And Charlie, I have to say, most of the things weren't so good. All you ever wanted was to be the boss. For eleven years you tried. You were the most independent dog ever to walk on four legs. For that reason we'll miss you.

We thought you would live for 20 years. That's what we used to say every time you did something wrong. Like the time you bit Joanne Gair, all the times you growled at the judges in the dog shows and were disqualified, and everytime you made a deposit on Sampogna's driveway. Remember the day you almost took that German Shepherd's face off? We couldn't take you anywhere. You hated everything, vacuum cleaners, packing boxes, cats and people. Especially people.

There were other things of course, that we all remembered. Especially today. That time you came out of the surf at Newport Beach with the ten-dollar bill in your mouth. Those times you went up against the Newfoundlands, St. Bernard's, Shepherds and all the rest and came away with the blue ribbon. All the houses that were robbed on our street, but never ours. You protected 'your' home and we won't forget you for that.

I thought of all those things and more today as I carried you deep into the woods to your final resting place. I'm sorry that you became sick so fast. We'll never remember you as being crippled with arthritis or losing your sight so quickly. Rather, we'll remember those short, little legs sending you around the yard like a battering ram. Those legs that were so muscular and strong, the same ones that dug a thousand holes in the lawn.

Charlie, I hope as I write this, you're somewhere with other dogs, running together in some faraway field. I'd like to think that your ears are up like they used to be and your ripping bark can be heard over all the others. On top of everything, Charlie, I'm happy that all the pain is gone forever. You didn't deserve that.

If we could afford it, we'd have a big stone marker for you. On it we would inscribe:

CHARLIE
Welsh Corgi-Pembroke
Taconic Hills Kennel Club
First Place
Best in Class-Working
Our Dog

And if you could write your own epitaph, I know you'd write: *'I was Charles of Hollowbrook Highwater. I wasn't the best dog in the world, but I wasn't the worst either.'*

Goodbye, 'Saba'. Sleep well.

jcm
9/22/83

A Slice Of Time

How kind she was, that sweet eastern girl,
sending me big wedges of the moon to eat,
glasses of sparkling raindrops to ease my thirst,
downy clouds to lay my head upon,
nymphs to sing me love songs till I slept.

. . . But then there came the nail in my shoe,
the muggy days, cloudy and damp,
sour milk and fatty meat on my plate,
stubbed toes, headaches and razor nicks.
The unhappy side of living is here,
for she's not here anymore.

jcm
6/9/78

Abigail of Kenosia Trail

I had to do something today that now and then, husbands and daddies have to do but hate doing it. I had to take our dog, a 16 year-old Pembroke Welsh Corgi to the vet to have her put down. Her name was Abby. She was just about totally blind and deaf. She had internal problems and her body was failing her rapidly. It's the absolute worst part of having a pet; days like this. I held her like I held all my babies when they were small, in my arms, as the doctor administered the shot. She simply went to sleep. All her anxiety and fear were gone. The darkness and the silence she had been experiencing were gone. And, as always happens, the sadness and the pain for our family had just started.

Corgis are shepherds. They are the smallest of shepherds, but shepherds none the less. At dog shows, they will always be last in line, in back of dogs like German Shepherds and the great Newfoundlands. They were bred in Wales over one thousand years ago to tend cattle in those small fields the Welsh have. They had great heart and a great bark as they darted in between the legs of the ponderous cattle. To a cattle farmer, they were worth their weight in gold. We sent away to the A.K.C. once, to get her lineage. We found eight champions among her ancestors. A champion is always denoted by a 'CH.' before their name, meaning they had won a major show at one time. Abby was never entered in any show. She was a family pet and a better watch dog than a $10,000 alarm system. When it came time to fill out the papers for the veterinarian, I came to the line where they wanted to know the name of the dog. Her full name was Kempio's Windflower Abby. On that line I wrote: 'CH. Kempio's Windflower Abby'. In our home, she was always a champion.

When my children were small and a pet died, I always told them they had 'gone to Wyoming'. It sort of softened the blow, helped them to get over the obstacle of the pet not being there anymore. Or, I may have said that for my own benefit. This morning in the vet's back office, as I held our little Corgi I had this Honest-to-God vision of a young and vibrant Abby, back in Wales. She was in a small field with a surrounding stone fence, eighteen cows, tall grass and gnarly oak trees beyond the stone fence. Her farm was high up in the Penscelly Hills of South Pembroke and she was queen of the field. Her keen eyesight picked up the far off movement of a gray owl in one of the old oaks. Her big ears perked up as she heard the farmer from far across the field call:

'Go on, girl! Pick 'em up!', as he motioned with his stick toward the cows. She was off in a shot, knifing through the grass like a red-brown bullet, heading toward the cows. The farmer watched the Corgi run and smiled to himself. He knew the dog would bring the cows in before dinner. 'That's a good dog!', he murmured.

That's a good dog.

jcm
10/16/99

Rag Bag

You may scribble for hours
while an idea 'flowers'

    if you have one on the way.

You may struggle and strain
to evoke from your brain

    some truly great words for today.

When they're all written down
you may read with a frown

    and discover in utter dismay,

after all that spent time—
though your efforts may rhyme—

    you really had nothing to say.

jcm
6/13/78

Joltin' Joe Has Left And Gone Away, Hey! Hey! Hey!

If you walk east from the Stadium, starting on the corner from Stan's Sports Bar, and turn left when you reach two blocks, you'll come to a little Italian joint DiMaggio used to frequent after some of the home games back in the old days.

'Joe said they had the best pasta e fagioli in the city!', Rizzuto, whom DiMaggio used to take with him to the eatery, said. '. . . and if Joe said it was the best, then it was the best.'

The other day when the news came that Joe DiMaggio had passed away in Florida, all the accolades started; . . . was the 'greatest living ballplayer', 'a great American icon', etc. But I had this picture of the tall DiMaggio and the diminutive Rizzuto, hunched over plates of pasta and beans, late at night in a little joint in the Bronx.

My mother and father used to take me to the Stadium when I was small. I was ten years old in 1949, the very first baseball season I can remember clearly. Whenever DiMaggio came up to bat, my father used to pick me up and stand me on my seat so I could see over the heads of the people in front. Whenever there was a shot to center and Joe started after it, I can still feel my father's hands under my armpits lifting me high over the heads in front so I could see DiMaggio make the play. He used to tell me:

'Watch everything that man does. Watch him at bat and out in the field. Someday people are going to ask you what he was like and you'll be able to tell them.' You were right, Dad.

My father ran into him one day, long after he had retired from baseball. My father was in contract negotiations for his union at the Picadilly Hotel in Manhattan. He was waiting for an elevator in the lobby when the door slid open and there stood the Great DiMaggio. My father was dumbfounded. All he could blurt out was, 'Hi, Joe.' DiMaggio went by him and said: 'Hi, kid.' That bothered my father for years afterward. He and my mother were the same age as DiMaggio, yet he called my father 'kid'.

Most people remember him as the bent over, white-haired and well-dressed fellow who used to throw out the first ball on Opening Day. But he was much more than that. He was the inner workings of the Yankees. There was lovable Yogi and the blur of Rizzuto. There was the angry Raschi and the steady Allie Reynolds. Mantle, the head-ducking country strongboy, Gene Woodling and King Kong Keller and 'Old Reliable' Tommy Henrich. There were all sorts of names but there was always the Great DiMaggio, the heart and soul of the Yankees. It's been 48 years since he retired but it seems like his presence was always out there in center field. Up until two days ago.

I'm sending my son, Tom, some clippings and newspaper specials about Joe DiMaggio. He usually puts them away to maybe give his own son someday. It's the best I can do. I can't impart that special feeling back when I was ten and the greenest grass was down there in front of me and the loudest people were all around me. I can't pass down exactly what it was like, watching the fellow with the number '5' on his shirt, striding to the plate. I would like to because my son is a great baseball fan, but I can't.

My Uncle Jimmy resembled Joe DiMaggio back in those days. People told him so. He even had a tryout with the Yankees, my mother told me. If I can remember correctly, his favorite player back then was Yogi. Jimmy was the best ballplayer in our family. My mother was in love with Johnny Lindell, the left fielder. My favorite player was Lindell too. My father raved about Tommy Henrich. Tommy Henrich could do no wrong. Years later, I remember asking my father how come DiMaggio wasn't his favorite player.

'Well,' he said, 'You couldn't have DiMaggio. You had to pick someone else.'

'Why?', I asked. My father thought for a moment then said:

'You couldn't pick DiMaggio. You had to pick someone else on the team, because DiMaggio belonged to everybody.'

'His number's in the Hall of Fame,
he got there blow by blow.
Your kids will tell their kids his name—
Joltin' Joe DiMaggio.'

jcm
3/10/99

Last Will and Testament

When dark clouds begin to hover
over this measured time I live,
when for me this life is over
these things I'd like to give:

My footprints on the sands of time,
daydreams I used to weave,
happy days with faith sublime,
this I'd make my last bequeath.

I'd like someone to covet these
and cherish them to the core.
I trust it would bring them inner peace
as it gave to the one before.

jcm
6/13/78

Did You See Time?

Did you see Time tonight?
He is tired
and has a weary face.
He never rests
you see,
and when I saw him
this morning
staring at me
from behind the mirror,
he looked even older
than he had the night before.

jcm
6/13/78

Baseball Haiku

The coral cast of dawn-
rising clouds of gnats
on the empty diamond.

The heat, the noise-
the runners lead; mirrored
in a drop of sweat.

Seventh inning stretch-
if they don't win it's a shame.
Goodbye, Harry.

Motionless cotton-clad bronzed men-
tensed, poised-
waiting for the last strike.

Tired players leave-
the warming sun recedes-
A rabbit plays left field.

Tiny water bursts,
drumming dugout roofs-
changing base paths to canals.

Vacant wet green seats,
green reflected puddles.
No game today.

jcm
6/18/98

'. . . *The Footless Halls of Air*'

Dear Louise and Family,

I saw your note on my e-mail yesterday. It read simply 'Dad', and I knew what it was. The inevitability of yesterday kind of softened the blow, as if a blow like that could be softened, but my thoughts went out to you and the rest of your family, but maybe more to you. You know me, and what I like to read about. Your Dad and I had some great conversations about the War, the Hurricane fighter and a lot of other things. Every time I would bring it up, you would always tell me of how he was most proud of his scientific accomplishments, and rightly so. But, in the back of my mind, I could never see him as what he was after the War, which in itself was wonderful, rather, I saw him back in the 40's as the champion he was. And always will be. One of my favorite writers always asked the question when it came to the face-to-face of war; 'Where do we get such men?' David Wilkie was one of those.

In World War 1, the French had an ace, Georges Guynemer. He was one of three great French aces. Guynemer, however, was the hands-down favorite. He would visit schools and speak in front of classes. He would walk the streets of the cities of France, greeting passers-by. He was a friendly man and he loved visiting school children the best. In 1917, Georges Guynemer, with 53 Germans to his credit, was shot down himself, and killed. The President of France, Georges Clemenceau, didn't know how to announce it to all the French schoolchildren. Finally, he announced the demise of Guynemer this way:

'He flew so high, that God kept him.'

Yesterday, my friend, David Wilkie, arrived at Croyden where his Hawker Hurricane stood on the runway. He climbed into his plane, taxied down the runway, '. . . slipped the surly bonds of Earth' and took off. He climbed and climbed, pushing his great Hurricane higher and higher.

John Gillespie McGee finished your Dad's story:

> '. . . Up, up the long delirious burning blue
> I've topped the wind-swept heights with easy grace,
> Where never lark, or even eagle flew;
> And, while with silent, lifting mind I've trod
> The high untrespassed sanctity of space,
> Put out my hand, and touched the face of God.'

David Wilkie flew so, so high. He flew so high, that God kept him.

jcm
3/5/13

Goodbye, 50 Coachlight

Dear Tom, Brie, Kathleen and Kim,

Saturday, Barbara (Mom) and I drove down to 50 Coachlight to wrap things up before the closing. It was to be the last time we would go there.

The woman buying the condo wanted us to replace a burned out light bulb in the garage door opener and we wanted to collect anything we'd left there. There were two new doors on the bathrooms that we wanted to check out also.

Right off the bat, Barbara started remembering those elaborate dinners Nanny used to put out for us and how no one could finish them. She used to make something euphemistically called, 'Southern Dinner'. Remember that? It was like a giant pork stew with tomatoes and sliced potatoes and God-knows-what, but it was good. Remember the halooshkie and the peroigies? My favorite was the fried sweet potatoes, blackened with sugar which of course, I couldn't eat.

I found my little vacuum in the hall closet and we filled half a bag with some other junk, trying to empty the condo out. It looks good, the old place. For those of you who haven't seen it in a while, all the rooms have been repainted again. The doors on the bathrooms have been fixed and the rugs have been steam-cleaned. It's ready for the new occupant, whoever that may be.

Five years plus have gone by since Nanny boarded that 'train' at St. Patrick's. There've been two little families in the condo since then. Both families have been great tenants and we'll probably remain friends with them. The last family, the Morris', moved into a rented house in Montrose but their daughter keeps asking her mother, 'When are we going home?' Nanny would've liked all of them.

Barbara and I did all we were going to do, but we still lingered for a few minutes. It was very, very tough to leave the place. We were coming up from the garage, about to put the garage door opener back in the kitchen, when I told Barbara that I wanted to go back in myself and that I would meet her in the car. She's so cool. No 'why's' or, 'How come's', she just turned and walked to the car.

I went in and deposited the opener in the kitchen cabinet. I was very aware of the silence. That's a word we never used at Nanny's house, right? I walked around the rooms, now all freshly painted and empty. Her sewing room which only had pathways through all the quilting material, now was empty and huge. Her bedroom where the dozen rosaries used to hang on the drawer handles was just squared-off white walls. I found myself talking out loud, sort of to myself and sort of, to her.

'We had a lot of fun here, Mom.', I said aloud. I was in the hallway, just outside the kitchen, remembering Nanny saying on those Christmas days:

'Bridget, your presents are on the couch.' The couch itself, of course, couldn't be seen. The presents completely enveloped it. Tom's presents were over in the corner because he would make an orderly pile no one could get near. Kathleen's presents were scattered all over the living room floor. When Kim came along, her presents took over the couch and once again, the couch disappeared.

They were good days; Christmas, Thanksgiving, Easter, St. Patrick's Day, it didn't matter. There was always warmth in that house that didn't come from the baseboard heat.

My sister Eileen, Momma Lion and a minor American author

I was looking through the kitchen door at the chip on the end of the stove top, ready to leave., when I heard her say:

'You'd better get going, Barbara's waiting for you!'

I looked around the corner to the left. Sure enough, past the console TV and the pictures, there she was. In her favorite flip-up leg rest naugahyde Lazy Boy.

'I love this chair!', she said, smiling.

'Kathleen has it now, up in Hopewell.', I said aloud.

'She has so much of the furniture at her house.', she said again. 'Isn't she funny?'. She laughed.

'What smells good? What are you making?', I said out loud again.

'I'm making halooshkie. Irene and Jimmy are coming over later. Maybe I'll give them some to take home to Coby.', she said. 'Would you like to take some home?'

'I don't think so, the refrigerator's stuffed.', I said.

The silence was deafening.

'Well,' she said, 'Better get going.'

I half-waved with one hand, turned and left.

I got behind the wheel, looking at Barbara's beautiful and sad face.

'I hate this.', she said.

As I backed out of the space, I looked over at the kitchen window of 50 Coachlight. She would always be in the window as I pulled away and we would both wave. The last time I saw her in that window was March 9th, 2007. I waved toward the window then, as I waved that day. I don't think the blinds moved, but I can't be sure. I didn't have my glasses on.

Dad

jcm
12/12/12

Bibliographical Note

So, there it is. I started out with hopes of being David Mc Cullough and ended as a modern-day Jack Kirouac, hung over from punctuation problems, double entendres and colloquialisms. So much for effort and packing one's own chute. I've encompassed sixty or more years with 'Wind . . . ', including the work of 'Is The Beer Cold Yet?' I'm not sure of the accomplishment, but it was a fun ride.

As Shelby Foote paraphrased Chaucer, I'll paraphrase Foote with '. . . Farwell my book and my devocion.' (sic) All through this last of decades, the drawn-out time it took to write this last of books; my debt to those who went before me, dead and living, continued to mount, even as I hit 'save' on 'Goodbye, 50 Coachlight'.

This last of entries for 'Wind . . . ', 'A Death In The Family Of Man', is, for want of a better description, an epic. It was written 34 years ago during a dark time. It's never been seen which makes me think it should have stayed in the bottom of the drawer. But, for what it's worth, I'll solidify my spot in this 'Kirouac-ian Span' with the inclusion of it.

So, anyhow, 'Farwell my book and my devocion . . . 'I'm indebted to you also, the reader. Not for the reading, but for the finishing of it. You must be a good friend.

jcm
2/25/13

A Death In The Family Of Man

Epic

. . . I begin this last of poems as I began the first,
with sometimes bombastic, sometimes whining
statements of myself—
that only a few, if any, will read and ponder over.

I am.

What I was remains enigmatic.
What I wanted to be, is still conjecture,
but, I am.
I am a card-carrying member of the Family of Man,
no more or less important than my fellows.
No less than the stamina of the long distance runner,
no more than the diabetic black man selling peaches
by the side of a Delaware highway.
I was told that I was different from other men—
but I wasn't.
It was just a spot check of a bugle call,
a high note at a precise second.
No one listens to the instrument when tucked away
in a carrying case.
I wanted to be different but I didn't let myself.
(. . . he has great potential!) Still a spot check.
I loved to watch those gray geese against the gray sky,
loved the mournful honk, not unlike that midnight
train whistle filtering through the screened window
of my childhood bedroom.
But we all loved the 'V' of the geese in Autumn—

we <u>all</u> loved the pristine and sad sound of the
nightly train.
I was no different than you,
nor you different from me.
I was not the first one to find the red leaf in the raked
pile nor will I be the last.
Original thought like original sin was not mine to claim—
we live our lives as copies of the ones before us,
never alone
never apart
never unique.
We all know when the time comes to shut one eye,
to close down that third dimension.
When depth is needed no longer, we fall back on
length and width, which is sufficient.
Depth, having given its all, all it will give,
can be shut down, the plug pulled.
Depth becomes an obsolete tool,
no material to work with.
So, I shut one eye, saving my other to see my way
off the curb to join the procession of the others.
It was fun while it lasted, riding the tail of
that comet earthward, watching the white tail spew
out behind me like swirling sheets of white paper.
Coming face to face with myself, I let go and landed
lightly on the curb, minus my imagination, my depth.
The road was filled with the tramping feet
of one-eyed people.
They beckoned.
Stepping from the curb and falling into step
was the easiest of all.
I would think about it later.
My typewriter and pen were left far behind me,
around the dark corner the procession just passed.
I wouldn't need them.
All my trigger albums have turned back into plastic,
and all my razored lines (. . . he writes like he talks,)

the one with the double edges and the needle points
have all turned back into a day-old bowl of alphabet soup

*

I marveled at the configurations of earth,
the crystal-blues, the forests with their foggy tops.
I marveled at a face, priceless and peerless.
I am curious no more.
We all have our limitations.

*

Mine came quite unexpectedly but not without warning.
Fending it off needed bigger weapons, ones I didn't have.
So now it's gone, tucked away in a room full of memory
banks and musty old trunks and worn photo albums.
But it <u>was</u> there. That much is true.

> Imagination must soar—without sound.
> It must have wings, many wings, inverted
> gull wings.
> It must be paper-thin, enabling it to pass
> through tightly packed trees or crowds of people.
> It must be narrow for safety and wide when it composes.
> It must generate its own power relying on
> no other source, not another person, or
> another person's words.

When our imagination, our drive begins to falter,
to appear sluggish on the turns, we must look for a quiet
meadow, an empty field to lightly put it down.
With me, when my craft became powerless
it was too late to find that happy place,
that corner of solitude.
So the sidewalk found me, the one-eyed people beckoned.
I closed my one eye and joined their march to nowhere.
The tramping of many feet,
the controlled unison,
the absence of depth,
the empty, wet streets,
the buildings without windows.
It was a parade, a measured shuffle,

a sea of backs, ranked by fours.
My shirt turned gray, my trousers baggy,
I fell into step—bare feet on wet
pavement.

We pass buildings, broken buildings, buildings without
fronts, just stark panoramas of what the rooms looked
like when people lived in them.
There, a sheet dangling lifeless from a second story
open room. Plumbing and light fixtures stand out
like bones, like innards of a house that once lived.
Wallpaper shards lean tiredly from the wall, bending downward.
The buildings sag, the rooms, naked and uninviting.
These were the Tears of Man.

*

What went on in those rooms before the Death came?
Children's parties and joyous dinners?
Lovers locked in an embrace, down to their
entwining toes, oblivious to all?
Were there whispered promises and nods of
assent in the dark?
Were there loud, festive dinners where everyone
gorged themselves?
Was there a woman in that room crying to herself
quietly?
Was there a man, hunched over an empty table
with fingers drumming?

*

Do we all miss the things we took for granted?
Do we think of the December smoke of our breath, or the
cool, pungent aroma of apples in a country warehouse?
Did we ever pick a pine cone from the forest floor only
to toss it from the car window on the way home?
Do we remember lasting embraces, where muscle played to
muscle, and the familiar texture of cheek on cheek,
the one hand gripping harder than the other through
the wide sleeve of the coat?
Why were the waving goodbyes and the waving
hellos always the same?

Autumn was my favorite time of year, but it was
the same for the multitudes.
No one hated Autumn, we all loved it.
I was no different.
It was a joining of minds that brought on that melancholia,
not just my mind.
We all thrived on strengthening, getting ready
for Winter, watching the trees twist and creak.
I was not the only one to see that.
You did too. And so did they.
I made the mistake of calling it my own.

My beach, my sea, my sunrise, my pine and fir
symmetry, my green mountains with cloudy shawls,
my morning mist caught unawares by the sun. They were
never mine to have, to write about, to think about.
They belonged to the Mc Kuens, the Noyes', the Byrons,
the Frosts and the rest.
I merely rented them for a page or two,
like we all did.
We were no different from one another.
No matter how we tried.
Just pulsing carbons, hastily-built prototypes
trying to scrape a little of the gold from their crowns.
There was talk of imagination and structure
but it had already been imagined and structured
by far better minds than ours.
We shared the credit that was not ours to share.
I was one, one who shared.
Now the debt is here to be paid.

I'll pay it.

Once realization set in, I had to look inward
for my own imagination, my own soul.
There was nothing to be found, just bits and pieces,
shards, wood splinters, a partially-colored drawing.
That's all.
There should have been something profound,
something ungarnished, untainted, fingerprint-free,

but there wasn't.
Unanswered questions abounded like sheep on a hillside.

*

It's good that you never took anything from my eyes,
for once they saw, or so they seemed to see,
They saw lines of age,
they saw youth and strength.
They saw people, but not as they really were.
They saw that endless beach, stretching into infinity.
. . . If only I hadn't stopped,
if only I hadn't turned on my heel
to go back,
I could've walked that beach,
day in and day out
until I caught up with Him.
I could've walked all the way
down to Brazil, down to
Tierra del Fuego,
and on a rocky slope I could've
built a stone house and would've
come face to face
with the end of the world.

*

But I didn't.
I turned around and went back.
Back to the other years where I competed with braggarts,
wise men and pretenders to the throne.
They were just like me, and I, like them.
They too are in this long line of march, somewhere.
I'll miss the length and breadth of danger,
the anxious moments when victory is fleeting.
I'll miss the back of the bus driver's collar
and the sticky handrail.
I'll miss the waitress that dropped my change
just short of my outstretched hand.
The pelting of a snowball or the fury of the mob.

I'll miss the mystery of giving birth
and the guilt of taking it away.
Missing other people's words won't be anguish enough for me,
for they've all been said before,
at different times,
to different loves.
I've said and written them too, with meaning and
strength, but I forgive myself.
Not in the saying or the writing, but in the doing.
The doing reshaped other lives without authority
or permission.
The fact that it worked leaves me empty with hands tied,
and there are no words of atonement,
no back-tracking.
I came, and I went.

. . . I clambered inside the great Belgian the day he
broke his leg. His great eyes and flaring nostrils
bore fear and the unknown. I went inside of him,
that powerful, taut-skinned animal. I soothed
him, talked softly, rubbed his massive neck.
He looked at me once, just once, with those
delft-blue eyes, talking. They killed him,
turned him into a ton of dog food. From the
strongest, to pet fodder. A part of me went
with him into the ceramic bowl by the side
of a thousand kitchen sinks. I had no right to
feel for him. Nor he for me.

I wrote of oceans and sunrises and the wave's
regimentation. With just a flickering of know-
ledge, I wrote and wrote. Then I went home,
where there was no ocean. If I had loved it,
If had called the ocean all, I should've stayed
and become part of it. But I went home.

A travesty of imagination.

All the Italian orphans are now in the Red
Brigade. I unwrapped a frostick for a lad
that later, I'm sure, put the bullet into Moro.

Tunes of God flowing out to me every day,
never heeding,
never alert.
Leading my charges out of the church, out of peace.
Bombastically proclaiming iconoclastic mush,
a spokesman for the deaf, dumb and blind.
I had no right to wear that self-made crown,
hand-wrought by toothless beggars and old hags.
. . . All in the name of imagination.

I claim nothing from darkened, soundless rooms,
and the bare backs that were turned to me at morning-time.
It was just a place I happened to be at the time.
That's all.
There was no romance or feeling in those hot, dreary
hallways, fishing for that last peseta, drachma,
or handful of cold shillings.
And lastly, the only savior was thought,
there were no moments of peace.

Scraping some cell, some drop, some precious
sight and throwing it away.
The musty corridors of wet elbows from the bar.
The soiled clothes that reached into the soul,
all stood for future imagination.
Someday. Someday, I'll write about the world's
greatest cathouse.
It's been done before, by better minds than mine.
So I lost.
I left my usable self back there somewhere.

The lost loves were the ones that counted.
The love I could've given to a
parent,
a wife,
a child,
a person who needed and still needs.
could've pushed my energy to a free side
instead of my narrow, ego-tainted imagination.
I could've saved it all for that priceless
and peerless face, but no.
Who gets two chances at stardom?
One was a long time ago
and one was now.
I sent in regiments when I should have employed divisions.
I was diversionary, only to arrive here, in the line of march
with the one-eyed people.
What would it take to go back?
Therein the answer lies,
to go back.
Keep on going . . . I should have said.
But no.
I should have gone home, pulled my blanket up to my chin,
the blanket with the airplanes on it
and looked out toward Tuller's house.
I should have been happy with words like 'Sand Bank',
'Snake Hill', and 'Peckerhead'.
Instead, I ventured into adulthood and took what was mine.
And I took what wasn't mine.
But, that's neither here nor there. It's over. Done.
Never to be rectified.
Never to be forgotten.
So, I march, trying to keep in step.

*

We, all of us, think of heaven as white sheets,
green fields and for some strange reason, harp players. Wrong.
Hell, we say, is constant fire, stoking of blackened furnaces,
overseen by hellish demons, probing with red tridents.
Wrong.
Hell is here. There is no other, no smoky, forbidding black hole.

Hell is here.
Hell is knowing. Hell is frustration and futility.
Hell is being immobile to the point where you hurt
other people better than yourself.
Hell is uncaring, waiting for tomorrow to fix things.
Hell is lying to one's self and waiting.
Hell is laziness, diverting attention to irreparable things.
We all have our own Hell, right here, right now.
Sometimes our own Hell comes covered with nectar,
like loving.
Hell can be imagination, and most surely is.
Imagination prolongs it, makes it into something
that really isn't there.
It's there, but only temporary.
To love a tree temporarily is all right, or a rose bush,
or a black-eyed goose.
When another person is loved, then it becomes a penance.
Not to follow it through makes it a Hell for you and for them.
Maybe they didn't want that type of Hell, but too bad,
you were the captain, the leader, the innovator.
Suffering is two-fold.
That's what I think about as I trudge in this endless sea
of one-eyed people, the only view I have is
the backs of gray shirts.

*

To behold the daybreak?
Never in countless milleniums will that be
more of a shock to the human soul!
I reveled in it, fell to my knees in it,
felt it's infant warmth on my face.
I felt the cold sand beneath my feet.
My God was there, talking to me.
He said; 'Here comes another one of my days. Do good in it,
treat it well and bask in its goodness.'
I did sometimes, but sometimes I didn't.
I kissed it off as a daily thing. I shouldn't have.
I should have taken each day and held it within me.
Being sad to see the day go was no indication
of my sincerity.

I mocked the sunrises, countless times.
I'd like to have them back now.
I'd treat them differently.
I'd say; 'God, here I am again. I made it through another night.
I'm ready for this new day.
I can't stretch my arms any further.
I'll be good to it.'
The day would be the same, hot, humid, windless,
but I'd know that inside of me was peace,
solitude, a knowing.
The Sun would say to the Earth; 'I'm sending down another one,
one filled with some pretty good things. Is there anyone, anyone
at all down there to listen?'
And I'd like the Earth to answer;
'Yes, there's one, one fellow. So come ahead, send it down.'
And I'd catch it. I'd catch it all,
with my feet anchored in the sand
and my arms strong enough to grab it.
I'd take all that heat and all that goodness
and hold it to me.
And then, after I knew that I had it all, I'd give it out.
I'd give it to the fellow with the sandals and black socks.
I'd give it to the kid trying to build a sandcastle with a spoon.
I'd give it to the old matron sitting under the umbrella,
to the pesty sand flies, to the perennial sea oats and the
half-empty beer cans.
I'd give it to anyone walking along,
the sunburned fellow who just arrived from Philadelphia,
the tan and bronzed beach honey who lived there all year long.
I'd give it to the young married couple lying on their motel towels
because they forgot to bring the big blanket.
I'd give part of that day to the woman in the supermarket
who didn't have enough money for stew meat.
I'd give part of that day to the not-so-pretty girl
on the street who never, ever, once in her life had a date.
I'd give some of that day to the silver-haired woman
with decades of sight behind her eyes and thought

that it was all over.
I'd give some of that day to the birds in the lower branches
afraid to drift down to the bread on the lawn because of the cats.
I'd give some to the old fellows sitting with their pipes
with the smoke of yesteryear, drifting up through
the brims of their hats.
I'd give some to the kid on the corner,
hopping and jumping to an unheard tune,
knowing he can't get a paycheck.
I'd give some to the girl who wasn't asked to the prom.
I'd give some to the nun about to wonder about her commitment.
I'd give some to the check-out girl in Waldbaum's
whose husband beats her.
I'd spread some on the tops of pilings for sea gulls,
just for making the day more beautiful.
I'd give some to those faceless people in the windows
of upper Manhattan, unable to buy air conditioners.
Some of the happiness of the day,
I'd give to people who think they're alone,
just so they wouldn't be.
I'd give some to the people I should have loved but didn't.
I'd give some to the people who thought the worst of me
and still do.
I'd take a piece of that beautiful day
and give it to the people of Greenock, Scotland
for filling my heart one September day.
I'd take some of that concentrated sunlight
and shine it on some stones in a nondescript graveyard,
not far from here,
for all the people I knew and loved.
I'd take the remnants of that day
and throw it in a circle,
as far as I could throw it,
hoping it would hit someone I hadn't thought about.

*

But most of all, I'd save the tenderloin of that day, the best part,
the part that was most important. It could be the blood-red of the sun,

minus it's heat at the end of the day, just sitting on the mountains like a red #6 ball, or the soft heat of 4:00 in the afternoon, when your skin can't take anymore and your eyes are raw from the earlier part of the day,
the time when the sun is gentle, like saying 'goodbye'.
I'd take that special part, hold it, so it's all together,
and give it to you.

*

Because, I know you'll argue but you deserve it. I know you'll keep it and watch over it, that special day.
Every 1st, every number one day of each month, you'll take it out and look at it.
You'll know . . .
And for myself, I'll keep nothing.
Not a ray, not a sweat bead, not a glare.
I've seen it all,
all there was to see,
the misspent imagination,
the long and arduous lines of type,
the spending of idle time.
I'll just keep the memory.
It's enough for me, for any season.

It's all I can give you, the best part of the day.
I wish there were more, like I promised, but there isn't.
I know the quantity and the quality,
but it's not mine to give.

We'll keep in touch, humanity, you and I.
Just look for me out in the street, marching,
forever marching with those gray-colored people,
one eye covered,
for block after block, mile after mile.
The door we entered is the same we exit from.
Death doesn't have to be cold, hard, dirt heaped upon dirt.
It could be the steady tramping of feet,

the incessant thought of knowing
nothing else is going to happen.
And it won't.
I can take it, not through strength but through style.

*

Watch me, I'll be the one they remember,
I'll be the last one in march.
(Who's that fellow in the funny hat?')

Watch me from the tops of buildings, the tops
of mountains, the platforms of reviewing stands.
I'll be the last of the few, the last in line.
Call it penance, call it punishment, call it a reward,
it's what imagination brings.
Imagination that had a good start but had no end.

When I march by, wave your flag, maybe clap a little.
I'd like that.
And I promise, I'll glance your way,
if only, just only,
you glance mine . . .

. . . and wave to me a small 'hello',
and I'll wave to you, a small 'goodbye' . . .

*

-30-

jcm
5/12/79